Moll of Goose Fair

Moll of Goose Fair

Elise Sibbering Kellett

The Pentland Press Limited
Edinburgh • Cambridge • Durham • USA

First published in 1995 by
The Pentland Press Ltd.
1 Hutton Close
South Church
Bishop Auckland
Durham

British Library Cataloguing in Publication Data.
A Catalogue record for this book is available
from the British Library.

ISBN 1 85821 337 1

Typeset by CBS, Felixstowe, Suffolk
Printed and bound by Antony Rowe Ltd., Chippenham

For Cliff, my husband,
and lovely family

With a special dedication to
Mrs Patti Squires
of Atlanta, GA

Contents

Chapter 1

New Beginnings

Moll gazed up at the low beams of the cottage she had lived in for all of her eighteen years, and thought longingly of the morrow. The very next day was Goose Fair and she had hidden away from the prying eyes of her sisters the red ribbon, the very first she had ever owned, and wondered if her mother would miss the dozen eggs she had so willingly given the travelling man in exchange for this wonderful piece of frippery. 'Some day,' she thought, 'I shall marry a rich man and wear velvet and spangles for the rest of my life.'

Her eyes swept scathingly around the tiny room she shared with her three sisters – the walls dank and green with mould. Jinny Greenteeth, the witch of the water, could place her mark forever more on this hovel – she, Moll Wakefield, would leave it on the morrow.

Spring, in all its softness, had arrived at last after a fearful winter. 'Spring,' breathed Moll. 'A time for new beginnings.'

Quietly, so as not to disturb her sisters, she turned away from the dark shadows creeping across the room. A ribbon of moonlight shone through the small window and she felt the magic of tomorrow already creeping into her bones. With a sweet sigh of contentment and anticipation, she drifted quietly into sleep.

Morning dawned bright and sunny in the year of Our Lord 1662, as Moll leapt out of bed and slipped the brown homespun dress over her head. Even though she had washed it several times in the stream yesterday, the smell of cow's milk still tainted her nostrils. She ran into the herb garden and picked sprigs of rosemary and 'lad's love' to tuck inside her bodice. Tugging the long wooden comb through her thick black curls, and with the red ribbon safely hidden beneath her lacings, she walked down the rickety staircase to join the rest of the family.

Her young brothers and sisters were running and screaming down in the yard. 'Filthy urchins,' she thought. With a sigh she reluctantly walked down to join them, picking up the heavy wooden pail of milk which her sister Bess had left by the barn. She wended her way carefully through the mire into the low mud and wattle dwelling. Her mother was thirty-six years old, but she looked old enough to be Moll's grandmother, thanks to having borne ten children and having to exist on what the family could produce. Her once lustrous hair was lank and streaked with gray, her slight shapeless figure was garbed in dark homespun, and her wooden shoes worn over thick knitted stockings added little femininity to the picture.

Life was hard for wives and mothers, especially in the winter months when meat to serve a hungry family was simply what they had managed to salt down during pig-killing in the late Autumn. The constant struggle against poverty, children born in quick succession, dark, dank homes and the like, took its toll all too soon.

Moll saw the trials and tribulations her mother had endured, and was terrified that no door would be opened for her to escape from such drudgery. Well, she knew the implications of an early marriage, and also that parents felt a certain relief when their daughters married. At least it was one less mouth to feed, which meant more for the little ones. On the other hand, her mother looked to her for help with the smaller children, since she was the oldest. Looming all too close on the horizon was the distinct possibility that her betrothal might be imminent, for whispers had been buzzing around the village all week that Jem, the big raw-boned cowman's son, was in need of a wife, and that Moll was his first choice.

Entering the room where the family lived, Moll felt sickened, as usual, for the smell of unwashed bodies was stifling. She knew without a doubt that the time had come for her to leave, as she looked at her poor dear mother, who appeared even more faded and unhappy than she could ever remember.

Moll swore an oath to herself that today she would get a hiring at Goose Fair, for if she didn't, the image of her mother was a foretaste of how she would look in eighteen years' time. God's teeth, she would have a better life than that, and perhaps even be able to do something to help the family! This was the one ambition in Moll Wakefield's mind as the morning of the fair dawned. She bade her family goodbye and walked up the winding lane which led to the village. Moll, her thick black hair bound in the red ribbon, bent over the mill pond and laughed delightedly at the glowing face reflected in the water; seconds later she wriggled her hands quickly in the water. Old Jinny Greenteeth would drag her in if she left her reflection whole, but now she had broken the witch's power.

As the village came into view, her excitement mounted; even the trees told her this would be her lucky day. A fool banged her playfully over her head with a pig bladder full of air, and shouted gaily. 'A merry day, my beauty.' Moll laughed delightedly, and soon in the distance she could see the market place. Quickening her steps, she opened the lacings of her bodice and breathed deeply in the soft balmy summer air. The aroma of strange foods filled her nostrils – Marchpane, gilded gingerbread, hot pippin pies filled with cinnamon, venison pasties – oh, the smells were heavenly. Never had she seen or smelled such wonderful delicacies.

Quietly she joined the other maids and young men awaiting hiring, but hours passed and no one even approached her. The disappointment was dreadful, and just as Moll had decided that she would have to return home a failure, a middle-aged woman tapped her on the shoulder and asked her name.

'Moll,' she stammered, 'Moll Wakefield, ma'am.'

'Would ye be willing to be employed in London, wench? There's a job there for a young, strong, hard-working housemaid.'

'Aye,' gasped Moll, 'I can be ready to go whenever ye wish – the sooner the better.'

'Well, don't stand there gawking, get your things and be at the Tabard Inn by sunset,' Mrs Wilson said.

Moll's heart quickened, and back through the thronging crowd she sped to tell her family the wonderful news.

Her mother listened tearfully as Moll told her the exciting happenings, and that she would be leaving in the morning on the coach for London. This was the first time Moll could ever remember seeing her mother show any emotion. It was unfortunate that this should happen on the eve of her departure, for many times in the past she had wished them closer, but her mother was always too busy with the daily round of chores and taking care of the little ones to spend time with Moll, or even to realize that her daughter needed her companionship so badly. She sadly whispered. 'We shall miss thee, child. God guide and protect you, always.'

At last Moll's few belongings lay at her feet. All that remained now was to say goodbye to her family.

'I shall always remember you and think of you, and I will send money home to you if I can,' said Moll. 'As least my leaving will make for one less mouth to feed.'

Her father roughly hugged her to him. She turned and waved a last goodbye to her family, and walked quickly across the field to the lane leading to the village.

With little ceremony, Moll was bustled into the coach and soon it trundled slowly down the country road, to begin the long journey to London. A starry-eyed girl, she eagerly awaited a new tomorrow, not realizing that her home was almost a two-day ride from the great city. Almost eight hours later, with every bone in her body aching, the jolting coach finally came to a stop. She fell gratefully out of the cheerless, lumbering conveyance, and stretching her stiffening limbs, learned that they would spend the rest of the night at the inn and could get something to eat at the coachhouse before bedding down. Moll followed closely behind Mrs Wilson, the lady who had hired her, and seating themselves gratefully, they waited patiently at the long wooden table for the serving maid to come to them. The maid, however, was too busy with the young lads in the corner, twisting and twirling away from the groping hands, which tried to undo her laces and lift her skirts. Moll saw one gallant spin the wench deftly into a corner, kiss her passionately on the mouth, his hands caressing her breasts; then, quickly undoing her laces, he turned her to face his companions with her breasts exposed. To the sound of loud cheers he carried her across to his companions and each of them attempted to fondle her amongst raucous laughter and confusion. Horrified, Moll watched the girl, who was laughing gaily as she extricated herself from the men and, retying her laces, cheekily held out her hands to the gallants. The clink of coins fell resoundingly on Moll's ears, and for the first time the young wench seemed to be aware of her two lady customers, and quickly straightened her dress. With an exaggerated wiggle of her hips, she slowly came over to where Moll and Mrs Wilson sat.

'What do ye lack, luv?' she asked.

Mrs Wilson ordered cold meats, capon and wild boar, with salad, followed by strawberries and cream. Moll had not feasted so well in her life. As they ate, she wondered why Mrs Wilson had spoken so little throughout the journey. She also wondered why the serving wench had received money. Perhaps Moll had a lot to learn in this new world. With this thought in mind, she followed Mrs Wilson up to a bedroom on the third floor, which had a very large bed in the middle, and a pallet in a corner. The housekeeper, with a curt word to Moll, undressed and clambered laboriously into bed. Moll slipped out of her dress and threw herself gratefully on the straw pallet until morning.

The new day was overcast and miserable. Moll, huddled in a wrap of Mrs Wilson's, followed her silently to the coach. On and on through the dank misty day the coach rattled and jangled until they came to the outskirts of the City of London. The wonder of it took Moll's breath away. There was a bridge, the largest bridge she had ever seen, with houses and shops built across it, even a church! Moll blinked in disbelief – people were being carried across in chairs.

'Sedan chairs,' Mrs Wilson explained.

Over the bridge they clattered and Moll pinched herself to see if she was awake. Fish sellers, cherry sellers, merchants selling cloth, peddlers with ribbons and laces, a dancing ape tumbling and dancing over the cobbles, not to mention ladies in wide dresses and velvet cloaks chattering together. Oh, the sheer wonder of it took her breath away. Moll had seen nothing like this ever before, or even imagined it!

On and on the coach rattled until they came to Cheswell Street. Mrs Wilson explained they were heading for Great Swordbearer's Court, her mistress's house. Moll's questions were answered with a 'Hush, child, you will see for yourself later'. She looked in wonder at the yellow and white timbered houses, the upper storeys almost touching across the narrow alley ways. Garbage and even worse trash flowed on each side of the thoroughfare, through open sewers. Ladies lifted their full skirts to protect the rich velvets from trailing in the filth, and Moll blinked as she saw the high pattens, or wooden shoes, which not only gave the ladies added height, but kept the hems of their expensive gowns clear of the wet streets.

Some time later the coach trundled to a halt outside a rather large, imposing residence. Moll was ushered into the presence of the lady of the house, Miss Roxanne, who was to be her new mistress, was only some five years older than herself. Upon being introduced, Mrs Wilson was dismissed with a wave of a lacy 'kerchief. Moll gazed with awe at this lovely creature, small with blonde hair rippling down to her waist, seagreen eyes and skin as white as milk. Moll walked humbly towards her. Milady's voice, however, belied her looks.

'Lud, wench, what a stench; we must tend to this first.'

'It's milk, ma'am,' said Moll.

'Zounds, art thou here as a wet nurse then, child?'

Moll explained that, after milking cows each morning for years, the smell was impossible to wash out of her homespun dress, and this was the only dress she possessed. This amused Miss Roxanne greatly as she remembered herself, not too many years ago, having just one dress, living in a tumbledown shack on the waterfront by the river and cutting silver buttons from coats of the unfortunate drunks who had imbibed too much catepument and malmsey wine, so ending their riotous living in the arms of Old Father Thames. Quickly returning to the present, for Roxanne's memories gave her little pleasure, she lifted her lemon yellow satin skirt, over which she wore a beautiful surcoat of dark green, and walked some short distance away from Moll.

'My eyes, wench, we'll dig thee out from under that coating of farm manure and see what the kernel is like – sweet, I warrant.' Quickly she reached out for a bell and two ruddy-cheeked serving wenches answered her call. 'Draw hot water and sweet herbs for a bath, quickly.'

Giggling, the two girls hurried away, and some time later a large upright tub made of wood and caulked with pitch was dragged into the room by two stalwart youths. The maids, one after the other, poured hot water into this huge tub, until it was full. Moll recoiled in horror! Did they intend to drown her? With this awful thought foremost in her mind, she kicked off her wooden shoes and ran quickly to the door. The mistress threw back her head and roared with laughter, at the same time signalling the two lads to lay hands on Moll and hold her fast. Moll was obviously not going to bathe quietly, and Roxanne ordered the two young men to undress her. Moll fought like a wildcat, but to no avail. Within seconds she stood naked, her high pointed breasts heaving. The two men looked at this nymph in wonder. Her face was ruddy as an English apple, soft red lips drawn back in fear, showing small white teeth, her black hair tumbling down to her waist. In adoration, they gazed speechlessly at the lovely white blue-veined breasts, slim waist flaring into wide hips, hands trying desperately to shield her nakedness from the onlookers. Her eyes lifted in silent plea to her mistress. Roxanne dismissed the two young men curtly and looked searchingly into Moll's frightened face. 'Moll, you have the body of a princess; keep it for a king. Let the peasants see thee, thou hast no reason for shame. Come, bathe thyself.' With a flourish, Roxanne kicked the old offensive clothing out of the room as Moll immersed herself in the hot, sweet-smelling water. It was as if her old life was slowly being washed away. She scrubbed her body, and then relaxed and enjoyed the warm water. Carefully, she stepped out of the tub and dried herself on the linen which Mistress Roxanne held, then a plain blue linsey-woolsey was handed to her. She dressed quickly, enjoying the luxury of a clean sweet-smelling dress, and pushed her long hair back from her face. She felt like a new person, and was thankful.

'Zounds, wench, I'll give thee a chance.' Moll looked up in wonder. 'Aye, you shall be my personal maid. Can you keep a still tongue?' Moll nodded. 'Are ye honest?' Yet another nod. 'Well, in the next room you will find a truckle bed, go and sleep and call me at cock's crow.'

Moll curtseyed to her new mistress and quietly slipped into the small annex, groped her way to the bed, slipped out of her new dress and spread it lovingly out on the rush-strewn floor. Gratefully she slipped between the coarse covers and pulled a coverlet over herself, which felt luxuriously warm and soft to the touch.

No further thoughts troubled her until the street cries of London, mixed with the sounds of bells that appeared to be ringing out Moll's arrival to the whole of Christendom, brought her swiftly back to Sunday morning in this great city. Hurriedly, she scrambled into her dress. Seeing a pitcher of water on the heavy oak table, she remembered her new position – she was a lady's maid. The blue dress dropped in folds around her ankles, and for the first time in her life Moll rubbed the hard yellow soap between her hands and washed herself thoroughly. After tying back her long hair, she knocked quietly on her mistress' door.

'Enter,' the voice answered, and Moll walked demurely into the adjoining bedroom. The beautiful tousled head raised itself from the lacy pillow. 'Summon the maids to bring warm water and lavender flowers.'

Moll called, and a young, blowsy, slatternly servant answered the call. 'Bring warm water and lavender flowers.' ordered Moll. Some minutes later the same bathtub was dragged into the room by the same two young men who had stripped Moll the previous evening. A word, obviously licentious, passed between them and searching glances did the rest.

'Begone, knaves,' roared her mistress, 'or by God's teeth, I'll have you clapped in Newgate.' The two lads scurried from the room as this threat fell upon their ears. Newgate Prison was no place to be threatened with in these times.

With a foul oath, quite belying her looks, Roxanne slipped out of bed and stood shivering in the cold morning air. Feeling she ought not to look at her mistress unclothed, Moll turned her face away. A hearty laugh was the only answer to this gesture and Roxanne handed Moll the soap. Fresh lavender flowers were strewn in the water and their heady fragrance filled the room as Roxanne stepped daintily from her toilet and stood naked in front of Moll. Her figure was slight – slim hips, small waist, high pointed breasts – and to Moll's consternation, she showed no shame at her nakedness. Moll said nothing and helped her mistress to dress. Roxanne donned a plain gown and velvet cloak and, as this was Sunday morning, no breakfast was allowed before church. The two women, mistress and maid, walked down the broad staircase to the street and, helping her mistress into the sedan chair, Moll carefully lifted the hem of her cloak from the dirty pavement as the coachman closed the door, and off the horses trotted to church.

Chapter 2

Moll Meets The King

Moll took stock of her surroundings. The house was large for a town house, consisting of a long gallery with small chambers leading from the main hall which appeared to be kitchens and grooms' quarters. To the rear of the house was a garden, quite small, but very lovely and full of flowers - lavenders, pinks, roses and gilly flowers. Moll admired the furnishings in the ground floor long room, one wall of which consisted mainly of large tapestries. One was a lady with auburn hair, picking what appeared to be a golden apple. Another was of a strolling player, holding a lute and gazing wistfully into a castle window. Small stools embroidered with 'stump work' stood by the long wooden settle, and a long oak table filled with apples and plums was in the centre of the room. A court cupboard ready laid with trenchers and white napery stood against the other wall, and peering underneath the table, Moll saw long forms on which to sit whilst eating - luxury indeed!

Ah, these last few days of Moll's life had indeed been strange and wonderful. Now she would polish up her mistress's bedroom until it shone, and give full freedom to the 'jolly robins' which fluttered about in her head. After diligently straightening up the room, Moll decided that she, too, must go to church. She slipped on a cloak with a hood to cover her head, and without a word to anyone in the house, crept quietly into the street.

She hurriedly pushed her way past the beggars and street urchins who called after her for money, and wrapping the cloak even more tightly around her, quickly headed in the direction of the pealing bells. Down St Martin's Lane she saw the great spire of St Martins-in-the-Fields, and entering the church, was amazed to see the hundreds of people awaiting the arrival of the vicar. But of course, she then remembered, if a person did not attend church on Sundays and Feast days, a heavy fine was imposed. The congregation suddenly surged to its feet and, as Moll was standing very close to the aisle, she felt a wave of commotion echo through the church. She turned her head sharply and as she did so, her hood fell on to her shoulders, accidentally exposing her raven black hair to the tall dark man walking up the aisle.

King Charles! The name echoed around the nave, and Moll found herself gazing up into two twinkling eyes. A wealth of black curls fell to his shoulders, red sensuous lips smiled, revealing white teeth, and a small moustache neatly covered his long upper lip. Spellbound, she stared, and slowly, deliberately, the King winked at her with a half smile on his handsome face! Moll was completely taken aback and felt herself about to faint! After the King was seated, the service of hell and damnation began, which was completely lost on Moll, who sat dazed throughout the service. She eventually found her way back to Great Swordbearer's Court, to the home of her mistress.

Events later in Moll's life made her remember this day. Charles remembered this day, too – perhaps it was her poignantly beautiful face that left a lingering impression upon him, but remember her he did.

Moll awaited the arrival of her mistress from Sunday worship, and ran quickly to the door on hearing the lackey's knock. Roxanne entered, and, behind her, followed one of the most handsome men Moll had ever seen. Little talk passed between maid and mistress, for Roxanne and her gallant swept quickly upstairs. Moll followed discreetly, wondering if she was doing the right thing. Hesitating in the shadows on the stairs she saw the gentleman kiss Roxanne on the lips, then on her neck, his hands fumbling with her dress. A tearing sound, and Roxanne's dress fell around her feet. The gallant picked up the beautiful girl, bent his head to her breast and carried her into the bedroom. Moll could hear the sound of the gallant's buskins being hurriedly pulled off and oaths sworn at the length of time taken to discard his clothes. Tiptoeing quietly to the door, Moll peeked in. Roxanne was lying on her back, the gallant, whom she eventually knew as Sir Richard Warringer, was running his hands all over her body and murmuring caressing words. Suddenly Moll saw him stand, naked, tall and erect; then, groping for Roxanne, he clumsily fell upon her. Moll quietly shut the door and pressed herself against the wall, barely breathing. God's teeth, what was happening? Better she leave now than play servant to this doxy, a whore, a London whore! She thought about returning home and marrying some fumbling red-faced yeoman who would expect sons from her every year. Would she grow fat like a milch cow, and, in order to feed the children, would she have to hire herself as a wet nurse to suckle the sickly children of the gentry? These thoughts horrified her. She thought of her friends, three of whom had married country lads and already grew big with child. The children in all probability, were fathered by the Squire, for each girl who married in the village was deflowered first by the Lord of the Manor. Better to have luxury as well, thought Moll, and Roxanne's words came back to her – 'Can you keep a still tongue?' With these words echoing in her ears, Moll waited patiently for her mistress's summons.

'Moll, show Sir Edward out the back way.'

Moll silently opened the door for his Lordship and led the way down the back staircase. Suddenly she gasped as his warm hand fumbled inside her bodice, and she felt something cold pressed against her breast. With a merry laugh the handsome gallant left. Moll struggled to calm herself, and retrieved a yellow coin from her bodice. 'God's oath,' she swore aloud, 'a golden Guinea.' Never had she held so much money in all her life!

After a light meal, Roxanne dismissed Moll, much to her relief, as it had been a strange, exciting and suddenly very tiring day. Taking some rushlights from the main hall, she placed them in the holder beside her bed, and by their sputtering light she bowed her head and whispered her prayers: 'From lightning and tempest, from plague, pestilence and famine, Good Lord, deliver me. Amen.' Stepping out of her dress, she climbed into bed, and this time, even the jolly robins fluttering around in her brain did not deter her from sleeping.

Morning dawned and Moll rose bright and early, deftly attended her mistress's toilet, cleaned the bedrooms and tripped gaily down to the servants' quarters for breakfast. The great open fire was blazing, even with the promise of a hot day, for meat had to be roasted and dishes prepared well in advance. Soup boiled in the cauldron and a great pan of fat sizzled on a long log in the inglenook corner. Moll joined the other servants at the table. Veiled chit-chat flowed from Will and Dickon, the two lackeys. The stout blowsy girl who brought up water in the mornings was Jesse, and a large buxom woman, simply called Dame Alice, tended the pot which by now filled the kitchen with steam. Questions were flung at Moll, who realized very quickly that a still tongue kept a wise head. Her quick wit kept the searching questions well at bay, and after the meal she quietly rejoined her mistress who informed her that a visitor, a gentleman, was expected within the hour.

This time a soft tap on the back door heralded the gentleman caller. A cultured voice greeted Moll, and he was shown up to Roxanne's bedroom. Moll kept watch quietly at the back stairs and was rewarded with yet another golden guinea for her trouble, this time pressed reverently into her hand, and with a sweeping bow the gallant's white plumed hat swished against the rushes of the floor, and the visitor was gone.

Chapter 3

Sir Richard's Dilemma

Later that evening, Roxanne called for Moll, and calmly presented her with a beautiful velvet gown trimmed with a colour known as dead Spaniard. Moll was delighted with this unexpected gift, and was already making plans to wear it to church on Sunday.

At long last Sunday dawned, and decked in her finery, Moll sallied forth into the street. Without warning, a coach churned mud from a puddle at her feet into a morass and her beautiful dress, one minute dazzlingly clean in the morning light, was a sorry sight. Tears welled up in her eyes, and a tall elderly gentleman alighted from his coach and very ineffectively dabbed at the mud-bespattered gown with his lace handkerchief. Too overcome to speak, Moll fled back into the house and fell on her bed in tears, heartbroken.

Sir Richard Howard was quite overcome at the distress he had unwittingly caused such a lovely young woman. Obviously, empty words of apology would not do. Odds fish, what could he do now to remedy this embarrassing situation? He clambered back into his coach and ordered the coachman to drive on. He would consult his dear friend, Dr Swainton, a capital idea! He would surely know the correct thing to do in such matters. The coach rattled on down the Chepe when suddenly Sir Richard spotted the doctor crossing the street. He tapped with his cane for the coach to halt. Quickly the coachman dismounted and spoke to Dr Swainton, who smilingly nodded, removed his hat, and swept a stiff, if not ungallant, bow to his friends and walked slowly over to Sir Richard's coach. The two men chatted amiably, and since they were directly in front of the good doctor's house, went in for a visit and some refreshments as they chatted over the hot steaming coffee and discussed the problem of the lady's dilemma.

'Well, to buy a gown for a lady of quality is quite out of the question. Perhaps a cloak? Yes, a velvet cloak trimmed with fur,' suggested Dr Swainson.

'Then 'tis settled,' said Sir Richard. 'My housekeeper will buy the cloak and it will be delivered by messenger tomorrow.'

Once this business was resolved, the two men were joined by some friends, who happened to come by for an unexpected chat. Mr Samuel Pepys passed the time of day with them, and talked of the great merchant ships due to anchor in the Pool of London the next day. One which interested the assembly was the talk of a great spice ship, *Queen of the Indies*, for most of the fellows had money invested in the great merchant fleet. And so the business of the day continued.

Meantime, Moll, still distressed, did her best to clean the evil-smelling mud from her dress, but it was quite spoiled. Wearily she folded it and placed it carefully in the large wooden chest. She really must be off to church, and throwing her cloak about her to cover her blue everyday dress, raced off to St. Martin's. The church was cold and cheerless and the vicar preached a sermon on vanity and strutting peacocks, but Moll's whole being was screaming like a mortally wounded bird for her lost finery, and she heeded not.

Life with Roxanne was pleasant enough for Moll. Robin was always kind and considerate towards her, acting as a buffer between Moll and the servants who resented Moll's position of trust with their mistress. London was still full of excitement for the country lass, as she roamed the great capital at will.

In the two years Moll spent with Roxanne she matured immensely, accepting without question the life her mistress had chosen for herself, and quietly reassuring Roxanne on her 'black days' that she was by far the handsomest lady in London.

'You mean the prettiest doxy, I'll warrant. Zounds, I must get some more marigold ointment from Boone, the apothecary, before my laughter lines turn into wrinkles as deep as cart tracks,' laughed Roxanne.

'Come Moll, do my hair. 'Tis too long and as thick as wild mint. Take out the tangles, me beauty, and we'll parade as fine feathered birds up East Chepe within the hour.'

The day proved sunny and warm as the two strikingly pretty girls stepped carefully over the ruts and filth of the road leading to the market. Gallants bowed low as they passed, and one or two brushed intimately close, as if by accident which caused Moll to give way to a fit of giggling as they turned the corner where the apothecary's shop stood.

Moll loved the smell of his shop, recognizing the herbs she had once picked, which grew in great profusion around the cottage. She recognized eyebright, wild parsley, heartsease. Memories of her family flooded over her, as the old familiar tangy smells stirred old forgotten moments of her past. Rosewater, marigold cream and lily of the valley perfume were ordered; a few coppers would ensure their speedy delivery, for ladies of quality did not deem it correct to carry purchases.

Moll's mouth watered as she smelled the hot pies and Roxanne, sensing her craving, called the pieman, who stopped to cut a pie into dainty portions and patiently waited whilst his two customers ate from his tray. Then they walked to 'Speeds', the bookseller, where the day's broadsheets could be purchased. The King's doings were fair news for the populace of London, and the coffee shops would be humming with news of his latest fashion fad or paramour. Roxanne purchased the sheet, and together they took a turn around the garden where, to Roxanne's amusement, a very handsome man made very explicit advances to Moll and, encouraged by her mistress, an assignation was arranged for the following Sunday.

Moll was excited and flattered by this attention, and spent the next few minutes wondering what on earth she would wear and what they would talk about. Roxanne gave her some advice about how to act the coquette, and to only order the most expensive delicate food and drink only the best wine, preferably imported; to be a good listener and to laugh, not indelicately, at any amusing remarks her escort might choose to make.

They chatted and giggled all the way back to the house, and, exhausted, fell into chairs. Moll rose quietly to undo her mistress's high wooden pattens, and rubbed her feet to obliterate the strap marks.

'Oh,' breathed Roxanne, 'You're such a comfort, Moll. You really are.'

Moll served her a cool glass of buttermilk, and then went up to her mistress's bedroom to tidy up the room, knowing that as soon as night fell the gentlemen callers would tap gently on the door.

Roxanne came up to change her dress, and by the glow of the rush lights, opened her box of jewellery. Lovingly touching each sparkling piece, she found a pair of dangling, beautifully set garnet earrings.

'Here, Moll. These are for you.'

'For me!' gasped Moll. 'But, madam, my ears are not pierced.'

'No problem,' said Roxanne. 'I'll pierce them myself with a silver bodkin right this minute.'

Moll hardly felt the needle go through the lobes as Roxanne immediately slipped the gold earrings straight into Moll's ear lobes.

Tears of gratitude welled up in her eyes, as she caught sight of herself in the mirror. Resplendent in the beautiful baubles so sweetly given. She turned, smiling, and dropped a low curtsey to her mistress, Roxanne.

Chapter 4

Attempted Rape

Moll kissed her mistress's hand and Roxanne, gratified by such a show of genuine friendship, lay back and smiled at her servant, who seemed more like a sister to her than paid help.

Sunday passed very quickly. The servants served cold meats and pasties, for no real work was done on the Sabbath. All household chores were completed by midnight Saturday.

Moll rested as the church bells rang out, and after the service she waked over to the garden where the incredibly handsome young man waited. He wore a plumed hat which he immediately took off, and with a graceful bow, introduced himself yet again as Todd Newsham, 'gentleman'.

'Come, let's walk, Moll. I know a beautiful spot by the river.'

He took her by the arm and they walked easily and amiably along the old tow path. Moll was absorbed in their conversation and listened with great interest on his discourse about ships and the city. Twilight came quickly, and a pale moon barely lit the way back. Suddenly, Moll felt her escort tighten his grip on her arm and, without warning, he pulled her roughly to him. He pulled at her dress until a tearing sound told her the dalliance had come to an end. He ripped open her bodice. The sight of her breasts inflamed his passion beyond endurance. She fought him off but he was far too excited even to notice. He forced her to the ground, lifting her skirts and fumbling with his own clothes, forcing his hardness against her until a stifled scream escaped from her strangled throat. He struck her hard across the face. She fell back, hurt and terrified as this monster of a man forced himself between her legs. There was little she could do. She knew her face was bruised, and she could feel a chip out of her back tooth. She daren't risk another blow, but was terrified just to lay back and let him rape her. A silent scream rose inside her as she felt him violating her body, trying to force himself, harder and harder, to gain entry.

With a superhuman effort she pushed him away, and pulling herself from underneath him, she took off her heavy shoe, and with all her strength hit out at his shadowy form. All she felt was the sound and feel of wood on flesh, as she heard him groan audibly as the blow struck. Sobbing uncontrollably, she took to her heels and ran through the trees as fast as she could, ignoring the scratches and heeding not whether she was heading in the right direction. Sobbing hysterically, she hammered on the first door she came to which showed a light, and was relieved to see the kindly face of a woman holding a lantern.

She gasped as she caught sight of Moll swooning on the doorstep, and hurriedly helped her inside the small wattle and daub dwelling.

'Zounds, girl, did your horse throw you then?' asked the woman.

Moll nodded, not wishing to tell anyone about her ordeal, not yet anyway. Gratefully she sipped a mug of warm milk, and slowly her mind calmed enough to utter a word of thanks.

'Could we get a message to my friend in Great Sword Bearers Alley?' Moll asked. ''Tis off Sword Bearers Court!'

The woman arranged to send her small son with a message to Roxanne, as it was only a mile away. Moll fumbled in her pockets and, thankfully, her hand closed on a small silver coin, which she gave to the boy. Too much, she knew, but she needed Roxanne desperately and this was the only way she could enlist help.

The young ragamuffin's eyes sparkled as he pocketed the coin, and ran to Roxanne with the message, for Moll knew Roxanne would be terribly worried about her by now.

In just over an hour, Roxanne arrived at the tiny hovel, thanked the woman profusely and pressed a handful of silver into her palm. She helped Moll into the sedan carriage, comforting her and wiping her tear-stained face.

'Hush, Moll, we'll soon be home. Time enough for tale telling then.'

After some hot soup, a bath, and being tucked into a warm featherbed, Moll told her sad story. She said she hadn't been raped, but had managed to get away in the nick of time.

'Marry,' said Roxanne, 'don't lose your virginity like that to a rapist, Moll. There're better things afoot, I'll be bound. Hush, now, and sleep; don't get up until ten o'clock. I'll warrant we can manage without you for once.'

She carefully snuffed out the candle and left Moll, sorely bruised yet comforted, to sleep fitfully through the long night.

Chapter 5

The Demise Of Roxanne

The following day, Moll, sore and still very shocked, rose slowly from her bed and gazed into the mirror with horror. Her face was all black and blue and she checked her front teeth, but thank God, she found them all sound. Her back one was chipped which she knew would cause her problems. Maybe she could file it down with a pumice stone before it went bad, she mused; perhaps when it felt a little less sore.

Roxanne was very concerned about Moll's near rape, and thought how easily one could be fooled by fine feathers. 'That popinjay will get his just desserts, I'll warrant,' she decided. 'I shall recognize him and some of my friends will relish a dual to protect a lady's honour, once word gets around.'

The morning was crisp and cool as Moll and Roxanne went over the horror of the previous evening, and Moll swore that she would never accept a casual encounter ever again. Meantime, she must cosset herself until both her mind and body healed.

Roxanne made few requests of Moll the following week, and Moll turned out the clothes press and ironed out the pretty ribbons on Roxanne's gowns. Her bruises healed quickly, but the experience played heavily on her mind. Roxanne knew that she was sorely troubled and tried her best to allay her fears, but Moll could not shake off the awful experience. Roxanne called to her to go to the seamstress and pick up a cloak that she had ordered.

Pleased to be out once more in the London air, Moll walked happily down Cheswell Street, and watched the cheeky London sparrows hop and flit about looking for crumbs, enjoying the warm sunshine. The pieman recognized her and waved a greeting. The children playing hopscotch smiled at her, and a tiny cat rubbed itself against her skirts. Smiling, she carried on to the dressmakers. The shop was empty, save for an old lady purchasing a petticoat, and Moll sank gratefully into a chair, realizing that perhaps her injuries were not fully healed, and that she must take the journey back more slowly.

Down Bakery Row she stopped to buy some gilded gingerbread, which she knew Roxanne adored, and watched a small monkey dancing to a man making music with a flute. Smiling, she turned, only to see her former assailant out of the corner of her eye. He was speaking earnestly to a young serving wench, who was obviously flattered by his intentions.

Moll was appalled that he was so soon trying to charm another victim with his wiles. She felt her body shake as with the ague, and feared she would faint with tension at the thought of confronting this monster. Her courage finally failed her, and with a heavy heart, she turned away, only to bump into one of Roxanne's gentlemen callers.

'Sir Ffoukes!' she stammered.

'Your servant, ma'am,' he said. 'Why, Moll, you look a bit wan. Is anything wrong? Perhaps after your unfortunate encounter you are unwell?'

Thank God he knew. Roxanne must have told him about her assailant. She turned to face him and stammered. 'Sir Ffoukes, over by the chandler's is a man dressed in dark blue, speaking to a serving wench. That man is the man who attacked me!'

Without a second glance, he strode over to the man who had assaulted Moll, and catching him swiftly in an arm lock, dragged him over to where Moll stood.

'Is this your assailant, ma'am?' asked Sir Ffoukes.

When Moll confirmed that he was the man, Sir Ffoukes spun the offender into the gutter, just as a horse and cart rumbled by, covering him with mud which smelled abominably. To add to his humiliation, the gallant gave him a hefty kick up the rear, which made the offender take to his heels and disappear around the corner.

Moll felt relieved that this kind man avenged her honour, and thanked him most profusely.

He smiled disarmingly, and pointing to his cheek, said, 'Plant a kiss right there, me beauty. 'Tis thanks enough.'

The rest of the day proved uneventful. Roxanne complained of a headache and kept to her bed and Moll, remembering the kindness of her mistress, tiptoed in to minister to her wants. Roxanne was very pale, damp tendrils of hair clung to her temples, and she slept uneasily most of the day. Moll was not worried by this illness at first, for vapours were common amongst ladies and Moll saw no reason to be unduly concerned. Next morning, however, she received no answer to her knock at the door, and upon entering Roxanne's bedroom, was shocked to see the deathly pallor on her mistress's face and the bed soaked with perspiration. Moll rang for a servant, and Bess Parker answered her call. She brazenly stood by the door, for she was not pleased at this lady's maid giving orders to the household staff.

'Fetch a surgeon quickly,' shouted Moll. In spite of her dislike for Moll, when Bess saw how terribly ill her mistress appeared she changed her attitude, and quickly went in search of the doctor. Bess soon returned with the Surgeon barber from Bells Yard. Moll recoiled in horror, for the man was filthy, and the stench of him was appalling. He followed Moll into the sick room and examined Roxanne.

'Tis the ague; she will recover quickly after she had been bled,' said the surgeon. Moll did not know the London fashion of bleeding patients for all kinds of ills, but the thought of it made her recoil in horror. The old villain pulled a knife from his bag and deftly cut a vein in Roxanne's arm. Blood flowed freely into the cup he held, and a moan came from Roxanne's lips. He left quickly with no further advice, demanding a crown for his visit.

The next day Roxanne steadily worsened, but in her moments of consciousness she smiled at the anxious young face always by her side. The hours dragged on, Moll bathing her mistress's forehead and praying desperately for her to recover. The next day, after a dreadfully painful night, Moll removed the filthy rag with which the surgeon had bound Roxanne's arm and saw to her horror a large pustule forming. An ominous red line ran up her mistress' arm and the wound was festering angrily. Some eighteen hours later, Roxanne was completely delirious and Moll was desperately afraid for her life. Quickly she summoned Bess again.

'Look after your mistress, and if you leave her before I return, God help me I'll cut out your tongue.' Bess guessed by the tone of Moll's voice that this was no idle threat, and she sat sullenly by Roxanne's bed, for she was no ministering angel and had left the two scullion boys vying for her favours in the kitchen. Just sitting by a sick bed for no obvious reason was a waste of time, for anyone could see that her mistress would require nothing this day.

Moll searched the city for wild herbs but to no avail and, much against her own wishes, was forced to purchase them from the apothecary's shop. Hurrying back to the court, she quickly placed the dried herbs in a mortar and blended them with oil to make a poultice. Racing upstairs, she opened the door to the sick room and with an awful sense of foreboding found Roxanne even worse than before. She dismissed Bess with a curt nod and gently unbound the arm. Gangrene - she recoiled in horror, and she lost hope that the herbs would do any good now. Her beloved mistress was beyond help. She cursed the surgeon barber and his filthy charlatan methods, and sobbed quietly by Roxanne's bed. The pale figure stirred and winced with pain.

'Moll,' she whispered, 'bring pen and parchment.'

'But, ma'am I cannot write,' cried Moll.

'Then send for Mr Drew, quickly,' was her faintly whispered instruction.

A servant was hurriedly dispatched on this errand and returned shortly with Mr George Drew, Roxanne's attorney, who was brought quickly to the dying woman's sickbed. Moll and the other servants waited outside the bedroom door, for Roxanne had requested privacy.

He seated himself quietly next to the bed, and began to write at Roxanne's faltering and weak dictation.

'I, Roxanne Sanders, having no kith or kin, do leave all I possess to Moll Wakefield, my faithful servant, to do with as she pleases.' With the help of the attorney, Roxanne managed to scrawl her signature at the bottom, and he affixed his red seal to attest the authenticity of the will.

Moll saw Mr Drew to the door, trying to hold back her tears. He put his hands on her shoulders and beseeched her to be brave for Roxanne's sake.

As he was leaving a messenger was arriving, and left a parcel addressed to Moll. Silently, Moll opened it and saw a beautiful deep purple velvet cloak trimmed with white fur, but her mind could not dwell on this finery, as her only thoughts were for her dying mistress. There was a note enclosed, which Moll could not read, so she set the note and cloak aside and ran back to her mistress.

The heat was oppressive, no air came through the thick tapestries and Roxanne was now unconscious and very still. Moll threw open the casement window; cries of London poured in from below and Moll quietly bent over her mistress, hoping the familiar sounds would rouse her one last time, but alas, her beloved lady would hear mortal sounds no more.

Horrified, she realized that her beloved Roxanne was dead! No farewell words, no sound, nothing. Moll wept bitterly at the futility of it all. She lovingly washed the lady with sweet herbs, combed her fair, beautiful hair and laid her small hands across her breasts. As she placed a spray of rosemary in Roxanne's beautiful hands she heard herself whisper, 'for remembrance'.

The burial was to be at St Martin's-in-the-Fields three days hence, and all the arrangements had to be made. Moll knew not who would attend the funeral, for the custom was for people to call and see the dead, so that all who wished would then follow in procession behind the family. Roxanne's body, dressed in white, was laid on an open bier; children scattered rose petals down the court. Since there were no relatives, the sad procession, headed by Moll, wended its way slowly to the church. On reaching St Martin's-in-the-Fields, a magnificent sight met Moll's eyes. Many sad-eyed gentlemen stood quietly waiting to pay homage to Roxanne, and some carried nosegays of sweet herbs which they placed at the foot of the bier. The funeral service proceeded solemnly, and Moll shuddered as the winding sheet was placed over the beautiful form of her mistress. Roxanne Sanders was laid to rest in the burial ground of St Martin's, loved and sadly mourned by half the young bloods of London.

Chapter 6

Moll's New Plans

After the funeral of her beloved mistress, Moll knew she must take stock of her possessions and form some sort of plan for the future. London was no place to be destitute, and although she had a few small pieces of jewellery and gold which Roxanne had given her, she was by no means able to keep herself without some form of employment to subsidise her meagre store of money. Apart from Kate, the young chambermaid, the other servants were still extremely hostile. This she knew she deserved, because of the many beratings she had given them, and considering all these facts. she decided to quietly leave the house after the servants were abed. She placed her possessions carefully in a large bag. But because of the threat of cut-purses and other rogues, she decided to wait until dawn. By then, she surmised, there should be a sedan chair for hire. Without being noticed, she slipped quietly out of the house at sunrise, with a last look back at the pretty mullioned windows before she lifted her hand to summon the sedan chair carriers and directed them to take her to St Martin's Lane where she hoped to find news of employment.

The streets of London were wet and muddy, and as they passed the Fleet Ditch, Moll was horrified to see the body of a small child, dead and bloated. She held her lavender-smothered handkerchief to her nose, and stifled a tear as best she could. A tear for the baby, a tear for Roxanne, and tears for all the misfortunes that had been heaped upon her so swiftly could have turned into a river of tears had she succumbed to this feeling of depression which threatened to engulf her.

'Odds fish, Moll, you're made of sterner stuff than this, girl. Life isn't always a bed of roses. There's always stinkweed growing nearby.' With this not very consoling thought, she gazed out at London's early morning scene and saw that St Martin's Lane was in sight. She rapped on the window and said, 'Stop here, please, and carry my bags into the Mermaid Inn,' which she noticed was close by. The inn was busy; ostlers were changing horses and the servants were still cleaning the debris left over from the previous evening. Moll wended her way between the girls who gazed wonderingly at this lady travelling alone so early in the morning. 'Maybe she's the new serving wench,' laughed one; 'Or maybe she's an actress,' screamed the other, a sorry-looking girl, very angular with a scrawny neck and broken teeth. 'Silence' said Moll quietly. 'Bring your master, or I'll have you both whipped.' The tone of her voice warned the two skittish maids that this was no idle threat, and the younger made a poor attempt at a curtsey and sped off to find Mr Blackstone, the landlord.

Down the rickety stairs he came, puffing and panting, his rotund belly bouncing in his haste to reach the bottom. Moll noticed the stained, smelly jerkin and hose, and wondered why he had bothered to wrap an even dirtier apron around his obviously filthy clothes in the first place.

'Please order your man to bring in my bags. I would like a room for the night – your best, and see that the bed is free from bugs,' said Moll, the distaste showing in her very demeanour, which was not completely lost on the landlord.

'Your servant, ma'am,' he replied, noting the quality of Moll's clothes, and in particular the fine pair of garnet earrings as they glittered in the early morning light, the ones which Roxanne had given her.

'Show me the room, please,' said Moll, and followed the landlord up the rickety stairs to a small room containing only a bed and a chest. Moll laid back the coverlet and was appalled at the dirty bed linen. 'Have these sheets removed and send up the maid. I'll give her money and she can go to the market and buy new ones. Odds fish, this bed isn't fit for pigs,' she exclaimed.

The landlord watched carefully as she opened her bag. Sensing him, she turned and said, 'That will be all, I shall go abroad for vittles.'

He smiled, and left his guest, calling the serving wench to wait upon her, as he trundled back down the stairs.

'What to do?' thought Moll, as she sat on the edge of the wooden chest. 'Well, first of all, I shall have to find work as a lady's maid or a sewing girl. Then, maybe I shall find a small shop and sell ribbons and laces until my luck changes, which I pray to the Holy Mother may be soon.'

The girl came sullenly to Moll's room, and as Moll opened her purse the flash of gold shone brightly in the morning sun, too brightly, for Suky's face lit up almost as brightly as the yellow metal itself.

'Now, me fine lady,' she thought to herself, 'oh, I'll buy ye clean white sheets, alright, and maybe "Will-the-Cutpurse" may be interested in your fine feathers and such. We'll see,' she chuckled to herself, 'oh yes, we'll certainly see.' She pocketed the coin, and left, repeatedly mimicking to herself Moll's voice, 'Fine lawn, oh yes, m'lady, fine lawn, so as not to scratch m'lady's fine skin.'

With this Suky left the Mermaid, turned left down the Fleishings Market, into Milk Street, and went into a wine shop. She asked the man serving porter for Will Swethrist. 'Oh, he's in the back,' said the vintner, 'go in, my dear.'

Pulling back the curtain, she went over to a swarthy-looking character, who was oblivious of her bad teeth and body smells, possibly because his own appearance wasn't much better. 'Why, it's Suky,' he cried, 'come, darlin',' and with a bound he caught her, giggling in his arms, buried his face between her almost non-existent breasts, and kissed her passionately, to the great amusement of his fellows. 'Now, what do ye have for me today, darlin', besides your beautiful body? Come, another kiss, me doxy.'

She snuggled up to him, and said, 'Information, Will.'

'How much is it worth, one crown or two, me sweetling?' he asked.

'Tis worth two, and a cut o' the profits – a third,' she demanded.

'Oh, a third, is it?' he said, changing his tone, and pulling her head back forcibly by the hair.

Quick as a flash, she felt the touch of steel on her throat, and screamed. 'No, Will, no, a crown, no more than a crown.'

He slowly released his hold and turned her to face him. 'Now,' he leered, 'tell me something.'

Suky, still shivering from her encounter, unfolded her plot. 'The visitor has a purse full of gold, and earrings of fine garnets. I heard her tell landlord that she would not eat at the inn, she is completely alone, and can be abducted easily down Bakery Alley.'

'She will scream,' said Will.

'Oh, yes, she will scream, but then we shall plant something on her and scream "Thief!" That will put paid to her voice,' said Suky. 'Meantime, I shall go upstairs and take her bag, whilst she is abroad.'

'The bag comes to me,' said Will. 'You can choose a dress from it, but I want the rest.'

Suky agreed, and the two of them sat down at the table together, his cronies having been dismissed previously. He listened to Suky's plan and said thoughtfully, 'Ah, it has merit, me sweetling, but we shall have to pay an actor from the theatre to prefer charges of theft.'

Suky clapped her hands with joy, for a new dress would soon be hers, and a crown to boot! Maybe then Will would sleep with her. She could even have her yearly bath, she mused. It must be due soon – June, she thought it had been the last time, or was it August?

Suky hurried on to the market where she bought the lawn sheets and pillow covers, returning as quickly as she could to the inn, in case Moll had left already. The signal for Moll's departure was to be a red scarf hung from the upper casement, which would put Will's companions at the ready.

Moll was tapping her foot impatiently as Suky returned with the bed linen. 'Odds bodkins, wench, what an age you've been. I swear, you could have woven them by now. Strip off these filthy sheets and remake the bed,' said Moll. 'I'm going out for a while – and don't take anything,' she added, 'or I'll have you soundly thrashed.'

'Oh, will ye, me fine jaybird?' Suky said to herself as Moll descended the staircase. The red hankie was duly displayed from the casement window. The signal was seen and acted upon, for Will had quickly sent a runner to bring over an actor he knew who readily agreed to accuse Moll of theft, at the same time holding her so that the runners would catch her. All was now ready, for Moll could be seen leaving the Mermaid and passing Bakery Alley. Taken unawares, she was no match for the two men. Will quickly and expertly relieved her of everything she possessed, including her garnet earrings and her rings. Before she could gather her wits, Will had scampered, leaving the actor screaming for help. Soon she was surrounded by sightseers, not understanding what was happening until she realized she was being accused of theft. The full horror of her situation dawned on her as she struggled hopelessly to free herself.

Rude hands held her as she was taken through the streets to a dark cell, and unceremoniously thrown inside, sobbing. When her eyes became accustomed to the gloom, she realized she was not alone. 'Settle down, dearie,' a voice said, pleasantly, 'no-one will heed ye. Not unless they hear the clink o' gold, they won't.'

Moll looked at the speaker, a once pretty woman of about forty, touched already with the French Pox, a sign which even Moll could recognize. 'Come on, dearie, it's not as bad as you think, I warrant.'

'Oh, it is,' cried Moll. 'I was robbed, then accused wrongly of theft. What shall I do, without money or possessions, nothing!'

'Your case comes up tomorrow. Let's hope Judge Casey Bell doesn't try you – they call him Newgate Bell.'

'Oh, no,' cried Moll. 'Dear God, no!'

Chapter 7

Moll's Disappearance

Roxanne's servants were soon aware that Moll had left, and set about celebrating in the only way they knew how – by opening every bottle in the wine cellar, lighting a candle, and there they sat, drinking and merry making. Only Robin was worried as to where Moll had gone, and left them in the dimly lit room drinking themselves into a stupor. He ran around the places where he thought she might be, and questioned the five sedan owners in the area. One remembered Moll a pretty wench in a cream sprigged frock, said one. 'Yea, we dropped 'er off in St. Martins, I believe she went to the Mermaid.'

'Ye Gods,' swore Robin. 'I must go, but first I shall call at Roxanne's lawyer for instructions.' Once he knew where Moll was, he decided to straighten up the affairs of the house first, 'before the slovenly servants left nothing but bugs and bare boards,' he muttered.

Stopping at Fleet Ditch, he came to the corner of Byrom Street, and recognized the sign as Roxanne's lawyer, Mr George Drew, Solicitor. He waked into the tiny office and stated his business.

'So you are Roxanne's coachman, are you not?' said Mr Drew.

'That I am, sir, that I am,' said Robin.

'Well, come into my inner sanctum, and we shall discuss Miss Roxanne's last requests.'

'You mean she left a will?' gasped Robin.

'Oh course she did,' said Mr Drew. 'I was her financial advisor and lawyer, was I not? And this is always my first instruction to my clients. Saves a lot of trouble, should the good Lord decide to call us home when in the flower of one's youth, which in this case, young man, is precisely what occurred, do you not agree?'

'Indubitably,' said Robin, wondering what it all meant.

'Well, now to business,' said Mr Drew. 'Now, where is Miss Moll Wakefield?'

'Well, as a matter of fact,' said Robin, 'that is why I came to see you. She left, and by all accounts, has forgotten to leave the key.'

'Left, left! Speak up, lad,' said Mr Drew, 'where is she? I have important news for her. Can you tell me?'

'No, I can't,' said Robin.

'In that case, here are my orders,' said Mr Drew. 'Chase all the servants away with a legacy of ten pounds each. Sell the horses, but keep one for the carriage; and you and a housemaid by the name of Kate are to stay in the house as caretakers until Moll Wakefield appears. You will, of course, come here each week for a stipend, plus all bills for the house are to bear my personal seal before they are paid. Now, here is the money for the servants. I shall, of course, need their mark. Miss Roxanne left me duplicate marks to compare, should it ever become necessary.'

Robin walked back to the house, wondering whether to rush over to the Mermaid, or clear the house of rubble. Knowing how the rest of the servants hated Moll, he decided on the latter, and turned back to the house in great haste. He heard the noise from the cellar and was appalled at the sight which met his eyes. Sprawled in the dimly lit cellar in various stages of intoxication lay the three servants. The smell was sickening. Knowing how difficult it would be to get them upstairs, he said loudly, 'Presents from Roxanne for you all! Come on, get all your things together, then you can have your legacies.'

At the word legacy they appeared to sober up considerably. 'Ye Gods, a legacy.'

'Come on,' said Robin. 'the house has to be locked up. Take a bottle of brandy each, or what you will, and go and pack all your goods and chattels up, straight away!'

Giggling and shouting, they fell over each other in their haste to get their come-uppance, as Grace called it.

Soon the unholy threesome presented themselves at the door and Robin told them to sign their mark on the papers, which they did. He handed the ten golden guineas to each of them and pushed them rather unceremoniously out the door.

Young Kate, the sweet young chambermaid, had spent the day at her sister's and returned to find the other servants gone, and the house a mess and unusually quiet. Robin explained the situation, and Kate agreed to stay. 'We'll soon know something once Moll comes back, and I'm glad those three doxies have gone – good riddance to bad rubbish,' she exclaimed. 'Tomorrow I shall clean this house until it gleams. I daren't do it before. Those servants would have taken it as a personal affront, "pleasing m'lady" – "m'lady" was what they sarcastically called Moll behind her back.

'Now I must go to the Mermaid and tell Miss Moll that the solicitor wishes to see her,' mused Robin. 'No time like the present,' and with a wave to Kate, he called, 'I'll tell the locksmith to change the lock. Won't be long. Put some wine to cool in the cellar, and we'll celebrate our splendid good fortune on my return.'

Kate wasn't really listening. She was beeswaxing the furniture and sprinkling lavender flowers all over the floor, humming away as pleased as a popinjay, thought Robin, and she looked very fetching in her big apron and white cap.

Robin walked out into the growing dusk, joining the throngs of people taking the evening air. Some would walk down to the river where the stalls would tempt them with cries of fresh cooked fish, sweet roast apples, hot venison pasties, hot apple toddies and myriad concoctions of sweet paste and marchpane. Others would take the boats out to the country, and walk the pleasant hills and lanes of Richmond, listening to the man playing the flute, or minstrels trying to earn an honest farthing or two in the lanes and byways.

Soon he came to the Mermaid, overflowing with revellers, some seated on the floor drinking porter from pewter tankards, others sipping wine from tin mugs. Robin swore an oath as he tried to catch the landlord's eye, but it was no use. Half an hour he waited, then, suddenly, he lost his patience and grabbed Suky, who was flirting with some gallants who were slumming in the corner.

'Here, wench,' he called, and pulled her to a dark corner. 'I'm looking for a visitor you had yesterday, a lady, Miss Moll Wakefield, by name.'

'Oh, yes,' said Suky, trying to hide the fright in her voice, 'she left, sir, in a carriage at about six o'clock with a handsome gallant, I warrant.'

'Where did she go?' asked Robin.

'Who knows?' answered Suky cheekily. 'She didn't tell me, sir, that's for certain.'

Robin was at a loss to know what to do, when suddenly Suky turned, and sparkling, unmistakably, in her ears, he saw Moll's earrings! He paled, and decided to leave this place to consider what he should do next. Nothing would come of threatening the girl here - she had friends about her, he was sure of that. Slowly he wended his way home and, over a glass of wine, told Kate the whole story.

'Well, perhaps what she said is true,' said Kate.

'No, Moll would never have parted with those earrings,' he replied. 'They were very special to her. Something is amiss, but how to find out? It is beyond me.'

With that, they lit the rush lamp and slowly climbed the stairs to their bedrooms, where a troubled night's sleep awaited Robin, carrying with it a feeling of dread which he found hard to discount.

Chapter 8

Moll's Sentence

In the dark cell, unaware of what was happening in the house, Moll curled up on the earthen floor, which smelled of faeces and stale urine. The air was dank and cold, and she felt vulnerable in this hostile world. Sleep wouldn't come easily this night, as she listened to the sounds of London pour in through the open barred windows.

She heard a baby's incessant crying, the neigh of a horse stabled nearby, the clatter of a woman's pattens on the hard earth outside, and the persuasive voice of a man accosting her. A price was agreed upon, and to her disgust, Moll was treated to a sound orchestration of a sexual act, followed by an oath as a householder above them found his sleep also being disturbed, he consequently threw a chamberpot and its contents over the copulating couple below. All this set a pack of dogs barking and Moll, feeling abjectly miserable, cried herself softly to sleep. She awoke to the sound and feel of rain, as it spattered through the window opening, and despaired because she badly needed to use the toilet.

In desperation, she banged on the door, which was duly opened by an evil looking jailer with one eye, and a three-day growth of beard. His gnarled hands turned the great key and he followed Moll to a privy which was nothing but an evil-smelling pit. To her horror, there was no door, and the man, obviously having no intention of doing anything decent like turning away, squatted down to watch. Moll, thanking God that the 'flowers' weren't upon her, did her ablutions as best she could, and quickly covered herself with her long skirts which got wet in the process. Quickly she followed the jailer back to the cell and waited for the next occurrence which she hoped would be her trial.

The day dragged on, and apart from a bowl of vile-smelling broth and some hard bread, no food was offered. The rain once again set in for the night. Her two companions, both female, were in fact old acquaintances and snuggled up together for warmth, ignoring Moll, for which she was extremely thankful. Two days turned into three; then seven, then the awful realization hit Moll that she was infested with lice! Her hair was matted, and the tiny three cups of drinking water barely satisfied the gnawing thirst which assailed her, let alone leave even a small cup for washing herself. 'Dear Lord,' she prayed, 'help me out of this place,' But she knew without money there was little hope of salvation and resigned herself to the possible fate of an even worse prison than this, or death.

On the tenth day Moll and the two other women were pushed into a hay-filled tumbril to be taken to the law courts for trial. Weakly, she hung on to the rail as the great horses lumbered through the rutted streets. The cart pitched and tossed as the horse sidestepped the worst holes, leaving the cart to follow as best it could. It was half past eight in the morning, and the London fog was just clearing as Moll whispered, 'Damn you, it's the first time I've wished you around, and now when I need a gray veil to cover my shame, you disappear.'

The morning was now clear enough for people to be abroad, and rotten vegetables were aimed, sometimes quite accurately, at the tumbril carrying the three women for trial. The law courts came in sight as the wagons joined the twelve others which disgorged their occupants into a great cell-like room beneath the court. There was a pump in the corner, where Moll thankfully washed herself and her matted hair as best she could. The prisoners were called, one by one, before being carried off to begin their sentences.

To Moll's horror, when she heard her name called for the court of Judge Bell, 'Newgate Bell', she knew that now her cause was lost, and that only death or a miracle could save her. Sadly she climbed the stairs into the dock and gazed around the sparsely furnished court room.

'Put her under oath,' snapped the judge, and a Bible was placed in her hand. 'Do you have anything to say in your defence?' the stern bewigged judge proffered.

'Yes, your honour,' said Moll. 'I am innocent.'

'Innocent!' snapped the judge, 'when this gentleman's purse was found in your possession?'

The actor, Gregory, loved a star performance and played the wronged party to the hilt.

Moll looked across at him, and said loud enough for him to hear: 'May God forgive you this day, Sirrah, and may his mighty sword be stayed so that his vengeance be not smited upon thy lying head.'

'Enough,' snapped the judge. 'Two years in Newgate, and should a second case of thievery be proven, I wish it to be recorded that she be taken to Tyburn, and her hand be cut off. This is to be recorded forthwith.'

Moll screamed and her voice echoed around the court as she was dragged, half swooning, down the steps into the waiting tumbril. 'Sweet Jesus, take me now,' she gasped, and with her hands tied securely behind her back and her feet chained to a post in the cart, she was once more jolted through the streets of London to cross the bridge which brought her to Newgate. The cart rattled and banged and Moll realized that this would be the last glimpse of London she would see for many a long year. Tears almost blinded her eyes, when she spotted a group of men turning to watch the cart negotiate over a pretty heavy piece of road. 'Mr Drew!' she screamed.

He turned in disbelief, and across the mêlée of noise he cried, 'Moll, for God's sake, what's happened!'

He barely caught the dreaded word Newgate, as the cart, lost now in the hodgepodge of horses, donkeys and carts, disappeared in the distance. With relief, Moll started to sob. Surely he would get her out of the place. Little did she know that once Judge Bell's sentence had been pronounced, little short of a miracle could aid her in her predicament.

Chapter 9

Newgate

Dusk was falling as the great forbidding fortress of Newgate came into view. The occupants of the convoy of wagons and carts crossed themselves in terror as its great black shadow enveloped them. The great iron-studded doors opened, and into the large holding area the vehicles drew to a halt.

An army of guards came asking names, and soon the eighteen prisoners' names had been ticked and they were locked away in their various designated cells. Once in the prison proper, the noise was appalling, so loud and consistent that no single voice could be heard. It was, thought Moll, like a great unending howl of a dying animal reaching a crescendo and dying back to a loud whimpering noise - unearthly and terrifying.

Crazy-eyed women with fingers like claws reached through the bars of the cells, eager to snatch the last remaining rags of decency which covered Moll, and she wrapped them tightly around her, dreading the clawing, searching fingers which threatened her very reason.

Soon she was hunched in the corner of a dark dingy cell with four women and two men; it was indescribably filthy, cold and extremely damp. Sheer exhaustion took over and she slipped into blissful unconsciousness, awakening only to the strange sounds of movement in the cell.

In a small compartment there was a trickle of water which ran into a sort of drain adequate for washing, which Moll very gratefully took advantage of, ignoring the curious stares of her compatriots. She mustered some sort of dignity and turned to take stock of the other inmates.

The two men were obviously old lags and settled down to some sort of routine. Two of the other women still wore the flashy clothes of their trade, whilst the last occupant, a middle-aged woman, was obviously a consumptive. None of them made any move to speak to Moll, and she was too involved in her own problems even to notice. She prayed that Mr Drew had recognized her, even in the Newgate tumbril. 'I'll die in here; it's not fit for a dog.' she thought. The food was brought every four hours, a disgusting mess, which consisted mainly of barley broth. Wisely, Moll left the meat and picked out the vegetables as best she could. The bread was hard and apparently had been gnawed by a rodent. This, too, Moll ate by breaking off all the outside parts and eating the uncontaminated centre. She was, of course, completely without money, and could only depend upon others, Sir Richard, perhaps. The servants, no, but Robin would surely try and discover her whereabouts.

Now, all she could do was to wait, wait and hope and pray, which she did for five solid days, at times feeling as if her reason was going, and that all feelings of decency were leaving her.

Each night was a nightmare; there was no way she could shut out the awful noise which permeated her very soul. Sick at heart, she prayed for deliverance, and hoped that when she did get her freedom she would thank God with every fibre of her being.

Chapter 10

Mr Drew's Quest

The conversation between George Drew and his colleagues ceased abruptly as they noticed his ashen pallor; when the girl in the tumbril screamed his name, and then disappeared, he couldn't believe either his eyes or his ears. The realization dawned on him that she was bound for Newgate. What or why? He would need information, and the best place for that, he ascertained, was the law courts.

He called his carriage over and was soon calling on his friends in the court offices, one of whom knew that Judge Bell's list was the probable one where details could be gleaned. For a few crowns, Mr Drew was able to sift through the many defaulters, none of whom escaped. 'A diligent judge,' mused George; ah, here it is.' The name Moll Wakefield stood out, and the felony – theft of a man's purse near Bakery Street.

'Rubbish', snapped George. 'Before calling on the celebrated judge I shall call on Roxanne's servants. Then, there's been skulduggery afoot, or my name isn't George,' he muttered.

He found Bakery Alley and dismissed his carriage, telling his coachman to return in two hours. Nothing untoward appeared in the small *cul-de-sac.* There was a cobbler's shop, long closed down, and a stray dog sniffing in the gutter. But, wait – there in the far corner was a daub and wattle hovel, with a small hole for a window. 'Surely no-one lives there,' he murmured, but found himself drawn to the place.

He called at the door. 'Anyone there?' and a voice called, 'Yes there is, come in, come in.'

He entered the tiny place, with its swept earthen floor; a table with a clean but well-worn cloth, a wooden stool and a few stones which was a cooker and fireplace. A very old lady came forward. 'Good morrow, ma'am,' he bowed, which impressed Sarah Dolby very much. He introduced himself, and explained the purpose of his visit.

'Ah, tis a long time since a gallant did that to me, sirrah. When I was young they did, but that was a few summers ago,' she smiled.

'I want to ask you some very important questions, Mrs Dolby, and before you answer me, I beg you to tell only the truth, for I shall pay well for the knowledge. However, I must warn you, that should you have the information I desire, we must hasten to the courts to put it before Judge Bell. A lady's life is at stake, and I must know the truth. Should you agree to my terms, and if I am satisfied that you have witnessed anything which may cast a new light upon this case, I shall reward you handsomely.'

Sarah Dolby looked him straight in the eye. 'I'm a God-fearing woman, sirrah, and if I am asked the truth, I shall tell it, with no fear of the consequences. Judge Bell holds no fears for me; neither does any other mortal on this earth. Ask me your questions, and in the name of the Holy Mother and all the angels, I shall speak only truth.'

He admitted that he did not know the date, but that Moll, the lady in question, was accused of theft and had been sentenced to two years in Newgate. Sarah Dolby crossed herself at the very mention of the place, which was well known from one end of the country to the other as a place only one stage better than the dreaded Tower of London.

'A lady, you say, sir, yes, a pretty lady in a sprigged gown. 'Twas on a Friday, I remember, before I lit the rush light. Such a commotion as never was! There was Will, the cut-purse, and a fellow from Thrush street, a street player he is, sir. Held the pretty lady, they did, and took all her money and jewels. Then, as I watched, Will ran off quickly, leaving the actor to hold her and call "stop thief"; but she was swooning. Then I saw him take a purse from his pocket and place it in hers. A crowd came, and they took her away. Sir, I don't know any more. I did find her scarf, though. Here it is.' said the kindly old soul, who placed a cream silk scarf, which George recognized as Moll's, on the table.

'My carriage will be here within the hour and with your help, hopefully we shall get Miss Wakefield released. Then my coachman will take you to my home on the outskirts of London for tea.'

He walked the two miles to Roxanne's house, delighted at this turn of events. But first he needed to know why Moll Wakefield was abroad alone. He came to the house and rapped sharply on the door, which was answered by Kate, enveloped in a large white apron, holding a duster, welcoming him. He was amazed at the transformation she had performed. The softly gleaming pewter glowed, the rugs had a new brightness, furniture shone till the ornaments on top appeared to stand on a mirrored surface, and the homely fragrance of lavender enveloped him.

'I'll call Robin and bring fresh sherbet and comfits,' she called. Meanwhile, Robin was coming from the garden where he was trying to hack his way through the neglected rose beds.

'Your servant, sir,' said Robin. 'How kind of you to call.'

'I wonder if you have news of Miss Moll.'

'No,' said Robin. 'We hope and pray every day for some snippet, but apart from the barmaid at the Mermaid telling me she had a secret assignation with a gallant, I have been unable to discover her whereabouts. One thing which puzzled me was that she gave her earrings, the ones which Roxanne presented her with, to Suky, the barmaid at the Mermaid.'

'Odds fish,' said Mr Drew, 'so that's where the evil plot was born, is it?' He explained to Robin all he had discovered, and Robin's face paled in anger and disappointment at his own shortcomings.

Moll in Newgate! He had been so busy looking after her interests he had let the thought of her being in trouble slip completely away. 'What can we do, Mr Drew?'

'Nothing now,' was the reply. 'Too many fingers in this pie could be extremely dangerous. I am going now to Bakery Street,' he went on, 'to take Mrs Dolby to the law courts. She knows that she can never live in Bakery Street again. They would kill her. We must take very great care.'

Mr Drew and Mrs Dolby climbed into the carriage. Soon the law courts came into view. They found Judge Bell's chambers and he sat listening to Sarah Dolby's witness of foul play with great interest.

'Astonishing,' he said. 'I am at a loss for words. But you must not judge me too harshly, Mr Drew, London is a place of thievery and we must at all times use the weapons we have to discourage it. Decent people should be able to walk the streets without being robbed of their possessions. I shall, of course, sign the Release, and,' he ruefully added, 'rescind the hand amputation clause.' Then, turning to Mrs Dolby, he said, 'And you, brave lady, are a credit to us all.'

Then he went on, 'Have no fear, sir, the three who planned this evil deed shall find themselves in Newgate before nightfall. Three for the price of one,' he said, amused at his own wit, 'three for the price of one.'

Chapter 11

Moll's Release

Armed with a signed, heavily sealed parchment from Judge Bell, George Drew called for his carriage and hastily headed in the direction of Newgate, stopping only to buy a new cloak and a hot roast chicken to take with him. He left Mrs Dolby at an inn on the road, with instructions that she be picked up and escorted to his London house on the morrow. Soon the forbidding prison came into view, its dark satanic form leaving him chilled to his very marrow.

The turnkey opened the gates and the Governor's office was pointed out across the yard. When all the formalities were over, Mr Drew waited in the carriage for Moll to appear.

Moll knew nothing of these developments. The six days seemed like an eternity, a nightmare from which there was no waking, and she was sick and feverish with an ague that shook her whole body. The turnkey opened the door of the cell and shook her roughly. 'Come,' he said, 'now.'

She turned over and tried to blot out the man who was pushing her, but gradually she dragged herself from the prone position and tried to stand. The jailer called for two men who roughly half-dragged her to the courtyard. Through a mist of pain and fever, she felt Mr Drew's arms about her, and the soft luxury of a wool cloak being wrapped around her thin wasted frame. A strangled sob escaped her lips as he carried her to the carriage, trying to stem the tears which flowed in unending streams down her cheeks. He tore the chicken into tiny morsels and fed her bits, with sips of malmsey wine in between.

'Where to, Moll?' he asked.

'Oh, I have nowhere to go,' she whispered.

'Yes, you do, my dear. You have a home. Soon you shall see.'

A grave-faced Kate was waiting with everything ready for Moll's arrival. Too weak to be bathed, Moll felt tender hands gently washing her unkempt body and a soft soothing voice comforting her, as if she were a child. As she lay on the small truckle bed which was always stored underneath the big four-poster, she felt her matted hair being washed in lavender, and soothing healing ointments applied to her many cuts and bruises. Kate wept as she administered these remedies, and made a potion of comfrey and heartsease, which Moll managed to sip slowly.

Robin lifted her gently onto the huge feather bed, warmed by the pan, and gratefully she sank into a deep sleep.

Twelve hours later, she awoke and called for a mirror. The deep hollows in her cheeks and dark circles under her eyes told their own story.

Mr Drew came to see her to bid her farewell, explaining all the events which led up to her release.

'Roxanne left me everything!' she exclaimed. 'I had no idea!'

'Rest, my dear, and get your strength back, and a little meat on your bones wouldn't go amiss, either.'

Moll's life settled back into the pleasant days she had longed for, despite the loss of her beloved mistress, who was never far from her thoughts.

Will, Suky and the actor were transported to a penal colony in Australia, and Sarah Dolby filled a niche as housekeeper in Mr Drew's home that was ideal for them both, giving her a joy and peace she had never known before. Moll's earrings were returned by the clerk of the court by special request of Mr Drew, and within ten days, Moll saw the former picture of herself return to the mirror.

'Now I shall buy some new clothes and start my life where I left off,' she decided. 'Robin can choose the servants. I warrant the reins are better in his hands. The hiring and firing, too,' she mused. 'What a story I will have to tell one day, perhaps to my grandchildren - who knows?'

The first thing Moll promised herself on her first shopping trip out was to visit Mrs Dolby at Mr Drew's country house, and take her a gift. This she did and they remained great friends, Moll never forgetting the debt she owed this kind, courageous lady. The ring she gave Mrs Dolby, with two hands clasped in friendship with a diamond on each, was greatly treasured, and Mrs Dolby was never seen without it.

Chapter 12

Moll's Return To The Social Scene

Sunday dawned. Dressmakers called at the house, perfumers, shoemakers, until Kate thought she would never get it straight again. Although she had ten golden guineas to spare, her legacy from Roxanne, she decided to save it for a pair of real gold earrings she had seen in East Chepe. 'The brocades are beautiful, milady,' she whispered, almost tempted to spend her all on one dress.

'Tush, Kate, I'll give you all the dresses you want. Go now,' she laughed. 'Choose what you will from my chest.'

Delighted at this, Kate did as she was bid, leaving Moll to wonder at her change in fortune. She had a house, good servants, money and a secure future. Now, all was well with her world.

She called Kate downstairs, dismissed the tradespeople after choosing all that she desired, and called Robin. 'Kate will accompany me to church,' she said. 'Call the coach in half an hour.'

Kate came down dressed in a lilac silk gown and matching bonnet, a sight to see, whilst Moll, a vision in cream silk, swirled around to show her pretty feet with silver buckled shoes all shining.

Her thoughts turned to the mysterious cloak which had been delivered to her on the day of Roxanne's death. Perhaps Roxanne had ordered it, destined never to wear it. Curiosity overwhelmed her, and with great trepidation, she went upstairs, opened the chest and took out the cloak. It really was beautiful, and between the soft folds of velvet lay a note.

'Kate,' she called, 'can you read?'

'But a little, ma'am,' answered Kate.

Moll handed her the note. The halting words brought back the memory of her spoiled dress. Ah! Yes, she remembered the gentleman's face, kind and full of concern, who had tried so hard to clean the soiled gown but to no avail. The cloak was a kind gesture which Moll greatly appreciated and without delay decided to send a message of thanks to her kind benefactor. Kate was dispatched to the scrivener to purchase a note of thanks which was soon delivered to Sir

Richard's housekeeper.

On her return, Robin ordered the coach and horses, for today was Sunday and Kate and Moll were to be driven to church in style.

As the coach rumbled up the cobbled courtyard, Moll grasped Kate's hands in hers and announced, 'My poppet, today we are off to church, a lady and her maid, dressed up like two popinjays.'

'Oh,' said Kate, 'you look so beautiful, you really do, madam.'

Taken by surprise at this spontaneous compliment, Moll laughed and looked in the polished steel mirror. Was this the dirty country wench who had been scrubbed so few years before in this very room? Steady green eyes gazed back at her, black hair, nay, blue-black hair tumbled in thick ringlets to her waist and her skin glowed like newly skimmed cream. Moll's eyes danced with delight at her new image and, like two happy schoolgirls, they glided down the staircase to the coach.

The new liveried coachman, Robin, slyly winked at Kate and helped the ladies into the carriage. The clip-clop of the horses' hooves echoed loudly on the cobbles, and gallants slowed down their carriages to catch a glimpse of the attractive ladies. Moll, however, did not know the language of the carriages, she was not *au fait* with the ways of courtesans who could signal by the raising or lowering of carriage windows, whether or not favours were available. Disappointed, the men bowed, for custom demanded they pursue no further without encouragement. On sped the carriage to the church, and Robin helped Moll and Kate up the great steps of St Martin's and returned to the coach to await their return. This time, the vicar himself escorted Moll and Kate up the aisle and, after making their genuflections, they gracefully seated themselves behind the empty front pew.

'Charles, Charles is here.' The whispers echoed in the church and Moll clasped Kate's hand tightly in anticipation. The tall figure in pale blue satin made his obeisance and turned, quickly, before taking his seat directly in front of Moll and Kate, followed by two members of the court. For this was His Royal Majesty, Charles Stuart of England! Moll was enraptured at the sight of this elegant and handsome monarch. The perfume from his gloves permeated the area of their pew, heavier than incense, and Moll could hear the rustle of his soft Spanish leather boots as he squeezed his long legs into a comfortable position. His hair was his own (of this Moll was sure) and she longed with all her being to snip one of the locks which fell on his shoulders in such luxurious profusion. The temptation rose like a tidal wave in her mind and, taking a small pair of pearl-handled scissors from her purse, she deftly snipped a lock of his hair! To her horror the scissors became entangled – Moll died a thousand deaths. Suddenly, above the chanting of the psalm, she heard a merry little chuckle and the same pair of twinkling eyes turned upon her. Covered in confusion, she felt a deep blush stain her cheeks. Kate, by this time, was stifling giggles as best she could in her 'kerchief, having plainly seen her mistress's misdemeanour. A whispered word to his companion and both heads bent as if in deep prayer below the height of the wooden pews. As Charles raised his head, Moll looked in vain for her tiny pearl scissors – they had disappeared! Moll wanted desperately to pick up her skirts and flee, but the church was full and she was seated in the front. What could she do now, but swoon? With a deep sigh she slid gracefully forward, and Kate, with a startled cry, and taken completely by surprise at this new turn of events, could not hold her. The young courtier seated beside the King leaped to her aid, and lifting Moll in his arms, carried her from the church. Cautiously peeping through a half-closed eye, Moll saw the look of concern form on Charles' face. The courtier climbed into the coach with his burden, followed by Kate. Moll, after a decent interval, was soon fluttering her eyelashes, and with heaving breasts (for Kate had loosed her laces), stammered her thanks to this gallant gentleman.

On arriving home, Robin and Kate escorted Moll to her room. Sunday at church had turned out to be much more exciting than it ought to be. She thought, and knew that the memory of Charles' face would burn forever in her soul.

The following Sunday Moll again attended church but was disappointed, for this time Charles did not appear. A broadsheet purchased from a street pedlar informed the people that Charles would be attending a special service at Westminster Abbey. Moll stamped her feet in annoyance. Why had she not thought of sending out for a broadsheet earlier? 'Odds fish. I really must learn to read.' It was quite improper for a lady of quality to request her servant to read for her. Without further delay, she sent for a scrivener and told the venerable old gentleman that she wished to be educated. The old man agreed to come each morning for as long as his services should be required, to be employed as Moll's private tutor.

She proved a quick and apt pupil, and the scrivener took pleasure in showing Moll not only how to read and write, but how to speak correctly. Quickly losing the country accent, her beautifully modulated voice, slightly husky, sounded more attractive than the squeaky high-pitched voices adopted by most of the fashionable ladies in London.

Now the broadsheets opened a new world for Moll, for she knew which church the King would attend each Sunday, and finally the great day came. This very Sabbath he would be worshipping at St Martin's-in-the-Fields. Oh, what a morning. Moll sang and talked and took quite three hours before she was finally satisfied with her appearance. Into the carriage at long last; she purposely arrived at the church slightly late, whereupon the vicar once more escorted her and Kate up the aisle to their accustomed pew. Five pounds a year to the vicar had safely ensured the pew as her own property. Her pomander perfumed the aisle as she followed the vicar - the fragrance of cloves, oranges and roses surrounded both ladies, and with a rustle of petticoats, they were seated sightly behind and to the right of King Charles II. A half smile flickered across his lips as he became aware of the ladies being seated, and then, sensing his duty, he gave all his attention to the service. Moll gazed at the handsome, swarthy man, every inch a gentleman, his foreign ancestry showing fleetingly in his profile. She sensed that somewhere in his heart lay a need to be loved. Many women had loved him, and each woman who dangled her charms before him knew that this man could not be faithful to just one woman, no matter how intriguing he was. Moll shrugged this thought aside and knew that nothing she could do now would avail her. The first intimation of Charles's intentions, if indeed he had any, must come from him. Had she time and patience enough to await the Royal command? Please, God, let it come.

It came sooner than she even dreamed. A messenger, bearing no cipher on his coat, gave a note to Moll's serving maid. The note read: 'His Gracious Majesty wishes to return the scissors you so gracefully bestowed on him. Charles R.' Nothing else. Moll searched the note for a hidden message, but nothing was there. The embarrassing memory of her lost scissors came back to her, and in her disappointment, Moll lay on her bed and wept.

The following week Moll decided to go by carriage to see the sights of London. She had seen very little since her arrival and her tiny world, although in the busiest part of the city, did not give her an insight to the King's London. This she felt a tremendous urge to see. Her visit proved fruitful, for as she gasped at the sight of the tall creamy Abbey, the seldom opened West Door swung back to a fanfare of trumpets and there, bowing majestically to the crowd, stood King Charles. Moll pushed her way through the crowd, having left her carriage some distance away, and she beheld him once more. Dressed in cream satin from tip to toe and wearing a beautiful cloak of brocade, she watched him bowing to the crowd, this beloved merry monarch. Moll swept a full deep curtsey, and the King's eyes fell on this beautiful creature again, unfolding like a rose at his feet. Without thinking, he proffered his hand, and helped her to rise. Turning, he whispered a word to his aide and walked from the Abbey to his waiting coach.

Moll turned to go, when suddenly the aide to whom the King had spoken only seconds before bowed before her. 'Madame,' he whispered, 'the King wishes you to sup with him tonight, at ten, at Whitehall.'

Moll's heart leapt within her breast, and she heard a voice, sounding no longer like her own, saying, 'Madam takes pleasure in accepting his Majesty's invitation.'

With a sweeping bow he left, to convey her answer to his master.

Picking up her skirts, Moll ran back to where Kate and Robin waited patiently in the coach, for Moll had wished to see the Abbey alone. She pretended not to notice Kate's tousled head, and the cloak tightly wrapped round her shoulders, but on alighting from the coach her cloak fell apart, disclosing her bodice – undone to the waist. Moll shrugged and decided that her own plans would keep her very well occupied from this moment on. She really must warn Kate to stop dallying with Robin in the future. Surely, in such a big city, a coachman wasn't the only fish to catch, and Kate was such a comely wench.

On arriving home Moll literally tore the bedroom apart, searching for a dress magnificent enough to grace the table of a King. At the very bottom of Roxanne's chest, wrapped in dark paper, a vision of such splendour was unfolded that Moll gasped in surprise. A gown of creamy cobwebby lace, festooned with crystals and pearls, glistened richly in the sunlight, but then Moll remembered that Roxanne had been smaller than she, and in trepidation, she tried on the gown. It was far too tight across the bosom. Moll called urgently for Kate, and taking the dress from Moll, hurried to the sewing room. Mrs Wilson, the seamstress, eased out the dress and cut it lower to give more fullness. Within an hour, Moll was trying on the dress once more – now cut much lower, leaving little to the imagination, but it fitted her beautifully.

Some time later, surrounded in an aura of creamy lace, her heart beating like a hammer, Moll slipped gracefully into the deep purple cloak, the white fur framing her lovely face, and the carriage soon pulled slowly away to the King's private apartments in Whitehall. She was helped expertly from her carriage by Robin, who then quietly drove away into the night. She was ushered quickly up a back staircase by the King's servant, where the door was opened by Charles himself, who greeted her in a charming, easy manner. He slipped off her lovely cloak and gazed in admiration at her gorgeous body clad in the cream lace.

Moll found him gay, softly spoken and easy to talk to. A natural grace and charm flowed about him and Moll knew she did not love him as a King, but as a virile handsome man. Her pulses quickened. Moll had never been a girl of easy virtue. In fact, she rather hoped the King would realize this and that she would be accepted as a trusted and loving woman, not some whore from the streets of London. Alas, for her fairy dreams, Charles had discovered the secrets of Venus very early in life through a succession of nursemaids and serving wenches. He was easily ensnared by women, and Moll knew he had been bedfellow to many. The city buzzed with the stories of Nell Gwynne, Moll Flanders and duchesses and countesses to boot – all supposed lovers of the King. Moll realized that she would have to play a clever game to keep this man interested.

Supper was delightful, with small portions of many different and tempting morsels. Moll felt she would not be able to eat for days after such a feast. The wine was heady and the room was comfortable and warm, and her only companion – a King! Charles drew her gently to him, and kissed her softly on the cheeks.

'My pretty darling,' he whispered. His tall frame bent suddenly and, sweeping her swiftly up into his arms, he drew back the large stump-work curtain of the great bed. Moll knew she must play her cards carefully, this must not be for one night only. The stakes were far too high. He gently caressed her cheek once more and kisses soft and gentle rained on her brow and cheeks. His fingers traced the perfect outline of her nose, lips and neck, then slowly she felt the warm caress of his hands upon her breasts. His hands quickly undid the bodice of her dress and caressed her breasts until her whole being cried out for him. She felt the urgency within him, and quickly and neatly she eluded his grasp and stood before him. The cream lace opened at the bodice, showing her magnificent figure. Her lovely face flushed with embarrassment, she dropped a curtsey, which threw Charles into utter confusion. 'Moll, Moll,' he begged, 'what is it? Are you offended?'

She turned her face toward him and said, 'No, sire, methinks the sweetmeats on thy table are too easily acquired.'

Charles, perplexed, suddenly knew that here was a woman perhaps unattainable, and this was new for his Royal Majesty. Women fell easily at his feet, but here was no common wench, giving favours to any man, nay, not even to the King! This was a woman in every sense of the word! Here was a Goddess, who actually refused to bed with the King. The humour of the situation struck him immediately, and with a merry laugh, he raised the silver goblet to his lips and murmured, 'Sleep well, my pretty virgin, our next meeting may prove thee more amenable.' Moll, after whispering a quiet goodnight, left Charles to ponder over this new experience.

Sleep came easily to Moll, perfumed, beautiful sleep which transported her into a magic fairyland. Charles, however, slept badly – he could not contemplate where he had erred. He had conducted his usual smooth performance well, in his own estimation, but, by God, the conclusion had never left him so bewildered and unsatisfied. The wench would wait for many days before he would lose any more sleep over her.

Forgetfulness did not, however, come to Charles, even though Nell Gwynne was her usual pert and pretty self, eager to please her Lord. Barbara Castlemaine, however, sensed in Charles something amiss. Her searching questions proved fruitless and off she flounced in one of her usual tantrums. Charles wondered why he had ever got involved with such a schemer. She really had led him a merry dance over the past few years and Milady Castlemaine, of course, would be the last person to realise that her figure had thickened badly with all the children she had borne Charles. His thoughts flashed to his poor misguided Queen. God's Blood, did ever a monarch have so many women on his mind? Perhaps more Tudor blood was necessary in an English monarch; at least Henry had disposed of his feminine troubles with less fuss, whilst Charles' paramours merely kept the coffers of England empty. After much serious contemplation, his thoughts once again turned to Moll, and try as he did to forget her, she was very firmly implanted in his mind.

Affairs of state kept him extremely busy for the next few days, and financial matters, brought to a head by Parliament demanding cuts in the Royal expenditures, angered Charles greatly. His fury at the pettiness of his government deepened by the end of the week, and at the next opening of Parliament, even normal everyday courtesies were in danger of being forgotten. After the ceremony, Charles, his face grim and angry, returned to his apartments and felt the heavy burden of Kingship pressing upon him.

Moll, meanwhile, was counting the empty days. So she had overplayed her hand, this would teach her to try to fool with a King, and feeling decidedly melancholy, she rang for Kate. Kate appeared, for after being with Moll for six months, mistress and maid felt a very strong rapport between them. Recently, however, Moll had wondered a little about her. She had not been her usual cheerry self, and seemed to be sluggish in the mornings. Twice Moll had called and quite an interval of time had elapsed before Kate had appeared. Now the door opened and Kate entered.

'Let some air into the room, please, Kate, it's very stuffy in here.' Kate reached up to open the heavy casement windows and Moll saw the swell of her stomach curving up to her breasts. With an oath, Moll tore open Kate's bodice. Moll knew only too well the symptoms – the sight of the white breasts, blue veined and heavy, told her the full story. '*Enceinte!* God, you little fool – who is it, Kate? Who is the father?'

The poor girl sobbed and between her tears confessed it was Robin, the coachman. Moll remembered the visit to the Abbey and Kate's dishevelled appearance. Why had she not questioned the girl then? What a fool she was. She ordered Kate to call Robin and waited until the two of them stood penitently before her. Moll was not lost for words – did the couple wish to be wed? They both affirmed that they did.

'Arrange the marriage to be in haste, then, and let's be done with it.' Moll gave Robin a sum of money to pay for the bans to be called, and they hastened off to the church to make the necessary arrangements. They were married quietly with little fuss, and life continued as before, with Kate growing larger and larger each day. Still capable of carrying on with all her household chores, she seemed to thrive, and seemed happier than ever.

August drew to a close and Moll guessed that Kate's time grew near. She was still awaiting word from the King, but none had come, and she had almost given up hope.

However, Charles had remembered her, but was skilfully playing the long waiting game until he knew that Moll would be eager and willing to fall into his bed. Towards the end of August, the awaited summons came. Moll, jubilant and with an eager heart, lovingly smoothed out the folds of her blush satin gown. She had planned to wear it weeks before, should the opportunity arise. Hours and hours of preparation to make herself beautiful, and faithful Kate, eager as ever to please, bustled about anticipating her mistress's every want.

Moll sensed something was amiss, and suddenly heard Kate moan softly. Almost ready to leave, she looked up in consternation at the girl, and saw she was quietly crying. 'Kate, Kate, what is it? Is it time? How long have you been in labour, child?'

'All day, milady,' was the answer.

Moll gazed in horror. Perspiration dropped from the poor girl's brow and Moll knew that the baby would be born soon. She called the servant to run quickly for the midwife, but back came the girl, alone.

'Where is she?' demanded Moll.

'Drunk, dead drunk,' said the young girl.

With an oath, Moll tore off her dress and bent over Kate. 'Hush, child, it won't be long now, be still.' She tied a sheet to the foot of the bed and undressed

Kate. The girl was slight, too slight, thought Moll, for her stomach was large and swollen and Moll could see the terrible contractions, flowing one after the other, bring tidal waves of pain with each surge. Kate screamed in agony and the young servant girl, her eyes wild and fearful, was sent flying to the apothecary's for laudanum. Kate drank the potion greedily and it seemed to have a quieting effect for a few minutes. Then the great pains tore into her body again. Moll gave Kate the end of the sheet and told her to bear down, but Kate was weakened, and a deathly pallor spread over her face. Moll felt the swollen belly and with a start, realized that the child's head was actually born. Blood oozed thickly over the sheets and Moll wiped a bloody hand across her brow. The child's face, now born, turned blue, then black. Kate twisted and turned at Moll's instruction, Moll trying her best to extricate the child, but to no avail. 'Bear down, Kate,' she screamed. 'For the love of God, bear down.'

With a superhuman effort, Kate did as she was told, and the baby was born. Everything possible was done to make this beautiful baby boy breathe, but the body lay limp and lifeless. After attending to Kate as best she could, and with a prayer on her lips, she sadly picked up the small limp form and softly whispered, 'In the absence of a priest, in the name of the Father, I baptize thee John.' With a strangled sob, she wrapped up Kate's son and took him downstairs for Mrs Wilson to dispose of. Since the baby had not been given life, an official burial was not necessary.

Kate flickered her eyes and asked for her baby. Moll held her hand and said gently that the baby had not breathed. Kate, blinded by tears, turned her face to the wall and sobbed uncontrollably. Robin appeared in the doorway, sad-eyed after his long vigil in the corridor, and took Kate into his arms.

Moll, her assignation with the King forgotten, crept silently away and left her servants to comfort each other as best they could. She fell, exhausted, on to her bed, and hours later suddenly awakened with a start. The King! How could she have slept, and worse, much worse, how could she possibly give an explanation such as this to him. With a sigh of utter despair, Moll slept heavily until late morning.

Charles was angry, justifiably so, as he had received no message and spent the evening drinking wine and cursing Moll, whoever she was. Odds fish, he did not even know her name, none the less her face – that beautiful face haunted him even more. He would not send a messenger – the apology must come from her. Days passed and no word came, and Charles grew morose. He tired of the court and the same old faces, he tired of the painted old jades who constantly bothered him with their stupid inanities, and he longed for a breath of fresh air. Quietly, he slipped away and covered his court clothes with a cloak of dark gray. His boots would do, he decided, and strolling unchallenged out of Whitehall, he roamed freely about the streets of his city. A beggar accosted him, and he discovered to his surprise, that he was without money, and sadly he turned the poor wretch away. The thought greatly amused him - a penniless monarch, trudging around the streets of his own Kingdom - why, he felt better already.

On he walked in deep thought until he came to a coffee house where he recognized Mr Pepys talking to his friends. Charles gravely swept off his hat, and with a courtly bow, passed the time of day. The good fellow acknowledged his greeting with a bow and a wave of his hand. Charles was quite delighted that he had not been recognized by such an intimate acquaintance. On he strolled until he reached the Thames. His footsteps quickened as he heard snatches of the Thames boatmen's repartee, clients riding in the boats were easy targets for their remarks and Charles chuckled at the earthy humour flowing blatantly across the river. Oh, what he missed by not mixing incognito amongst his people. He sat on the river bank, idly casting stones into the dark murky river, when he saw a lady, unaccompanied, and walking dreamily towards him. Something in the proud tilt of her head made his senses quicken. 'Twas she, Moll! She too, had felt the need for solitude this day and had walked on until she reached the river. Somehow, she felt this was a part of Roxanne, for her mistress had told her tales of the Thames waterfront and today Moll had decided she would see it herself.

As she drew nearer to Charles, he turned his head and as she came close enough for him to touch her, he swept her a graceful bow. In sheer disbelief, she could do no more than stare at him. Then, realizing that it was Charles in person, she dropped a curtsey and stayed, head bent almost touching his knee. He held out his hand to assist her to rise, as she kissed his ring. He gently took her arm and together, easily and naturally, they strolled in the grey dusk.

Neither Charles nor Moll spoke for some time. Then Moll haltingly poured out the sad story as to why she had not met him on that fateful evening. He listened with great patience and understanding, then bent and kissed her cheek, saying, 'My poor darling, now I understand completely.'

Charles and Moll strolled incognito through the streets of the City. Both felt the touch of a never to be forgotten experience lingering as Charles quietly whispered, 'Goodnight, and God be with you, my darling.'

She heard Charles' voice say softly, 'Tomorrow at seven, my apartment,' and Moll wondered if tomorrow would prove as perfect an evening as this.

Stars shone in her eyes as she sank gratefully into her soft down bed. Sleep, however, did not come at all this night, and as dawn brought the busy city to life, Moll listened to the awakenings of the household. The bright sun greeted her and, as she stretched luxuriously like a cat, she wondered if Kate would sing this morning. It was quite some time since the sweet melodious voice had echoed through the house and she realized she had missed the sheer happiness and joy of spontaneous singing. As if Kate had sensed her mistress's longing, the old medieval song broke from her lips and drifted sweetly into Moll's room.

'Summer is icumen in, loudly sing cuckoo.' Oh, how good it was to be young and desired by the greatest noble in Christendom. Moll lay and listened intently as Kate sang on. The song stopped, and Kate appeared quite her old self once more. 'Ma'am, good news! today, merchants from across the sea will be selling silks and damasks from the East; spices and new fruits, the likes of which have never been seen before in London, are pouring into East Chepe.'

'Odds fish,' said Moll, 'this will be a day of merry making; everybody will be there. Hurry, Kate, hurry, today we will buy some fine new clothes.

Quickly they made ready for the short trip which would show them new delights and fancies and both of them decided to walk the distance to the market. For such a street was East Chepe, shops with open wooden fronts, women bearing baskets of marchpane, peddlers selling ribbons from trays, pie-men carrying stacks of venison and mutton pies, all glazed and decorated with fancy patterns of leaves and flowers. Flower sellers calling to the ladies to buy fresh flowers, a country wench carrying medlars, apples, pears, cherries, all these wonderful sights and sounds combined to make shopping in East Chepe quite an exciting adventure.

The two girls, flushed with excitement and dodging the water and slops which were thrown down from upper casements on to unsuspecting passers by, laughed and jested together as if they were equals, instead of mistress and servant.

Soon they came to the beginning of East Chepe, where two men holding fighting cocks were having an animated conversation about their respective birds, whilst a small boy was holding the torn limp body of the previous loser. Its black and green feathers were bespattered with blood. The blood-thirsty audience eagerly and noisily awaited the next fight to the death, due to commence shortly. Bull Mastiffs, too, were held tightly on a long leash, all raring to go and growling fiercely.

A large brown bear, muzzled, stood quietly waiting for a prod from the pointed stick his master was holding, before dancing to an audience of delighted children. Beggars rattled tin cans by the roadside and dirty barefoot children played games, splashing in the mud, which very seldom dried up completely in the narrow street. Moll and Kate looked about them, trying to absorb this exciting cosmopolitan atmosphere. Crowds of ladies in brocades and velvets, hair piled in fantastic shapes, paraded past them. Old wizened faces showing black twisted teeth, smiling from red raddled faces, told the ageless story of courtesans, still believing they could attract the opposite sex by flaunting themselves openly in the streets. In complete contrast to these haggard old painted jades, stood a pretty country maid selling curds and whey and yellow buttermilk, hands red and cracked, but with a face as clean and bonny as the fresh milk she carried. In an open booth sat a wizened gypsy woman telling fortunes to the ones who would stay and be warned. The wise ones slunk away, followed by terrible curses and warning of bad omens which would surely follow. The crowd thickened and, as Moll and Kate pushed their way through the throng, there before them, like tropical butterflies in gorgeous disarray, were bales of the most wonderful materials they had ever seen. They rummaged through lengths of shot satin, pure silks, stroked lovingly the jewelled velvets, and purred delightedly over the threads of silver and gold bursting like stars through the heavy damask. Finally, Kate and Moll made their choices. Kate chose a dark blue, almost black velvet for a Sunday cloak. Moll, thinking of her many engagements to come, purchased six bales of material. White spangled with gold, sea green silk, white velvet, deep brown velvet and one magnificent length of pure cobwebby silk, shot with every colour of the rainbow; also some fine dark blue fustian for Robin to wear on Sundays. He would surely be the finest dressed coachman in London.

Chapter 13

Moll Becomes the King's Mistress

Flushed with success, they wandered on, having paid a young man to carry their purchases home. Kate knew he was trustworthy, having sent him on errands before. He did not belong to a master but freelanced his talents, doing anything he was paid for, and he made an honest but frugal living by his efforts.

Along the way they bought hot pippin pie, sweet and spicy, and they licked their fingers with pleasure, as they also purchased a small basket of black cherries. They were quite delighted with their morning's shopping. Kate touched Moll's arm. 'What a beautiful scent, m'lady!'

Moll sniffed appreciatively. 'What is it, Kate, do ye think?'

'Scent from the Indies,' shouted a foreign voice, 'spiced with oriental fruits and flowers. Come, my pretties, gallants will swoon at thy feet, never will you buy perfume like this again. Come and buy, come and buy.'

They hurried towards the dark Spanish face and gasped at the beautiful pomanders and jars at his feet. He moved a phial encased in gold filigree under Moll's nose – this was something new, certainly a great improvement on the lavender, roses and musk she was wont to use. 'How much?' she asked.

'One guinea.'

The price was appalling, still she could not shake off the covetous feeling to possess this beautiful phial of costly scent. After much haggling, the Spaniard came down in price, and clutching the precious new acquisition tightly, Moll decided it was now time to go home. Back through the busy streets they went, and on reaching the house they plumped down contentedly on Moll's bed.

'I shall rest for an hour before the evening meal,' said Moll.

Kate smiled and bade, 'Easy peace, milady.'

A small shiver of excitement ran down Moll's spine as she lay down contentedly to rest. As she closed her eyes, she felt a cooling lotion lovingly applied to her face, and then thin slices of cucumber soaked in witch hazel cooled her eyes, and soon she drifted off into a deep slumber. Kate awoke her gently two hours later, and told her mistress that her bath was prepared. Moll smiled and stepped out of bed, shaking her tumbled locks and standing on the small stool, stepped into the warm perfumed water.

Feeling refreshed, she dried herself and rubbed a sweet oil over her body and slipping into a night rail she requested a light meal to be prepared and brought to her bedroom on a tray. The meal soon appeared, chicken breasts and crisp salad, surrounded by chicory and marigold flowers, small unopened buds of nasturtiums and cherries made a pretty picture, followed by some excellent homemade elderflower wine. She now felt ready to face the arduous task of dressing.

Now, what should she choose to wear tonight? She decided to wear the dark green velvet gown trimmed with white ermine. A low-cut bodice and the tiny waistline accentuated her beautiful figure. A necklace of tiny white gold roses, each petal delicately enamelled, fell gracefully to her waist and long earrings made of tiny petals of gold tinkled as she moved. Time passed quickly and soon the watchman was calling his usual curfew greeting, 'A fine starry night, six of the clock, and all is we—ll.'

Moll tingled with excitement. In just one hour she would be in the arms of the King. Now she was ready, the new fragrance enfolding her whole being. She twirled her skirts and the perfume filled the whole room; her cup overflowed with happiness. Presently, Kate informed her that Robin was waiting with the coach. Impulsively, Moll kissed Kate on the cheek, who dropped a curtsey in reverent acknowledgment. 'M'lady looks like a queen,' she whispered.

The laughing beautiful girl hurried down to the carriage where Robin was waiting. He bowed gracefully, opened the carriage door, and tucked a white fur rug around her knees. With a crack of his whip, the two horses started suddenly, then off at a gentle trot down the court and on into Cheswell Street, heading towards the King's apartments at Whitehall. The coach came slowly to a halt in the cobbled courtyard. Moll saw once again the tall tower, overgrown with ivy. She waited for just a moment at the oak-studded door, which was immediately opened by a liveried servant wearing the cipher of Charles on his doublet. He walked slowly before her, bearing a lighted torch, and tapped gently on the door at the top of the stairs.

The door was opened by Charles himself, wearing a white lawn shirt with frills of frothy lace at his throat and wrists. His hair was free and flowing and, in the darkness, she could see no further detail of his clothes. He led her gently into the inner chamber where soft candlelight filled the room. Four large candelabra shed a dim light which enhanced her beauty even more. Supper was beautifully laid for two, with large red crystal goblets chased with silver and a centrepiece of fruit and grapes cascading down a large silver chalice. Napkins of white damask over a matching tablecloth completed the decor and Moll gasped in sheer delight.

Charles slipped the cloak from her shoulders and gently kissed the back of her neck, the heavy exquisite perfume pervading his very being, and he smothered the urge to kiss her passionately, for he had no intention of prolonging this waiting game longer than was necessary.

Moll smiled gently as he seated her at table; then, taking his own place, he filled the beautiful goblets to the brim with sweet heady wine. They chatted through the meal about everyday things, but throughout Moll knew that Charles' eyes drank in greedily every line of her body. Interspersed between the gentle chaffing, Charles charmed her with pretty compliments and, as he took her hand in his and kissed her pretty fingers, he pressed a charming miniature on a gold chain into her palm. Moll gasped with pleasure, for it was a water colour done years before by Nicholas Hilliard - a beautiful pair of eyes, nothing more, just beautiful blue eyes which seemed to be saying 'love me - please love me.' She handed it back to Charles and he placed it lovingly around her graceful throat as she lifted her thick hair with both hands, and he deftly fastened the clasp, at the same time undoing the fine chain of enamelled flowers she was wearing, and placing it on the table with an engaging smile. Turning quickly, he snuffed out all the candles, leaving only the ones on the table still flickering, and took both Moll's hands in his own. Taking her in his arms, he kissed her gently on the lips; enfolding her completely in his arms, he buried his face in the black perfumed cloud of hair. She moaned softly as his lips caressed her throat and she felt her hands moving softly upwards around his neck in a completely abandoned embrace.

They stood silently for a few moments, enjoying the sheer pleasure of such an intimate moment; then, with one gesture, he lifted her into his arms and carried her over to the large exquisitely draped bed.

Quickly, without fumbling, he undid the complicated fastenings of her gown, slipped the chemise down to her feet, and gazed with adoration at the exquisite form lying naked before him. Pulling back the silken sheets, she felt him slip her lightly and easily between the covers. Seconds later, she felt him, naked and burning, beside her, and without shame she drew him closer. His hands gently urged every fibre of her being to love him, to love him completely, if only for this one magical night. Tender words of love, interspersed with the familiar '*tu*' in French, poured into her ears. He caressed her, and adored her until her whole being cried out to him. A searing pain shot through her body. Charles murmured, 'Darling, my sweet darling.' A tidal wave of passion and then, in the stillness which followed, she knew that she had lost her virginity, not to a common yeoman, but to this magnificent man, the King of England!

Curled up in his arms she slept, until a tap on the door warned Charles that he must say adieu to this new love. For love her he did, with a jealous passion he had not felt for any of his other lovers. This one would not be taunted by the populace of London as whore to the King. Moll was different - she would live unheard and unsung, quietly and unobtrusively, in luxury. The thought of this beautiful creature whom he could not marry being hounded through history as yet another mistress of Charles II, appalled him. He must be extremely careful not to flaunt this beautiful girl at court. Quickly coming back to the present, he gently kissed Moll's fingertips, then her eyes, each in turn. She smiled and opened them, gazing up at the man whom she absolutely adored. He helped her dress, and whispered, 'Trust me, my darling, we shall meet again soon and remember that, as a man, I love you with all my heart, and as a King, I love you with all my being.' He placed the cloak around her shoulders and led her gently down the stairs to the coach which awaited her.

Moll drove away into the cold early dawn, and gratefully snuggled down into the warm folds of her cloak.

The King watched as the coach disappeared into the swirling mist of early morning. Upon arriving home, Kate quickly opened the door and drew her mistress quickly towards the warm kitchen fire, where Moll gratefully held her hands out to feel the comforting warmth. Kate wisely asked no questions, and for this Moll was grateful, but the bright eyes and flushed countenance told the story. Kate knew her well beloved friend and mistress was happier indeed than she had ever been before. Late in the morning, as Moll was lazily cutting flowers in the garden, a messenger called with a note. With eager fumbling fingers, she opened the envelope. 'My sweet darling. This note cannot tell you all that is in my heart, for no language would suffice. Only this my sweet, sweet, Maria (for I will not call thee Moll); tonight we shall meet at Hampton Court. Until then. Charles'

Chapter 14

Moll Meets Sir James

Life went on as before, and Moll found new acquaintances amongst her near neighbours. Invitations to Drury Lane, Shakespeare's plays and performances by strolling players all helped to fill Moll's life with new experiences. Days turned into weeks, and although sweet nosegays and messages arrived from the king, Moll heard tales in the city about the Duchess of Portsmouth and Nell Gwynne, and other ladies of the court, all bedfellows of the King, as she well knew. Jealousy tore at her heart until she pulled herself together and consoled herself with the thought that Charles loved her. Of this she was sure. The fact that he had royal blood and was merely following in the footsteps of his ancestors by indulging his masculine instincts partially allayed her fears. At last, a short and insistent message arrived asking that she attend his private chambers at nine o'clock that evening. Carefully she prepared her toilet, and arrived promptly, to be shown up to the Royal Apartments. They kissed, and Charles drew her to him. 'Listen, my dear one, I must talk to you.' Softly and earnestly, he expressed his concern for her well being. She should marry, he said. Moll recoiled in horror.

'Yes, my kitten, and soon, but first we shall arrange for you to stay nearer to me. Perhaps on the other side of St James's Park. I shall arrange an introduction to a friend of mine, Sir Richard Howard. He will give you the protection of his name, and you shall not be trapped by a conventional marriage.'

Moll gazed at him with tears in her eyes, and sadly she realized that nothing could be hidden from this man. He knew she was with child by him, and this was his way of protecting her from being labelled doxy, or worse still, because of the child she carried. Her child, fathered by the King, would otherwise be labelled bastard - how horrible! Sobbing, she clung to him and gently he comforted her with soft words and caresses until she felt herself drifting into oblivion in the strong comforting protection of his arms. She left at two in the morning, upset, but loving him all the more for the instinctive kindness and gentleness which never ceased to amaze her. Tears stung her eyes as she reached home, and sorely troubled, she waved Kate's ministering hands away, and fell heavily on the bed, only to fall into a restless but heavy sleep.

Two uneventful days followed, with no word from Charles; then a messenger came, bearing a note which told her to expect a visitor, namely Sir Richard Howard, Master of the King's Horse, who would be calling on her at seven on that very day. Her heart lurched within her for she knew that this would be no easy meeting. In trepidation, she prepared herself, sparing no effort to appear pleasing to this man.

Promptly at the appointed time, Sir Richard was shown into the long gallery where Moll greeted him with a natural grace and pleasure. Some years older than she, he nevertheless made an immediate impression upon her. His brown eyes gazed into hers, and suddenly he recognized her as the lady whose gown was bespoiled by his coach some time ago. With a gallant bow and a merry laugh, he recalled the former meeting to her. She joined in his merriment and was pleased that this first meeting had been so easy an introduction. Nevertheless, her mind instinctively recoiled from thinking about the real reason for his visit, and after serving coffee and comfits the evening went smoothly, neither of them alluding to the reason for his presence in her house.

Two hours later, Sir Richard bade farewell, and as she heard his carriage drive away, a feeling of desolation once more filled her being. With a half-strangled sob, she fled upstairs to her chamber and looked about her. The room, tidy and sweet smelling, felt comfortable and familiar after the ordeal of meeting her future husband, and though Sir Richard had eased them both through the two difficult hours, she did not relish the thought of accepting him without question. Her tormented brain twisted like a soul in hell, and for the first time in years, she felt her whole being crying out for the sweet scent of country air. 'Why not?' she thought. This very morrow she could be speeding on through the fields of Kent, for she desperately needed time to think. This was surely the right thing to do, for she must get away from London. Subconsciously, her agile mind began to prepare for the impending journey, mentally cataloguing the many tasks necessary in order to leave the house in good order. Once the idea had become firmly implanted in her mind, her soul lightened. 'Yes, Moll,' she thought, 'go back to your humble beginnings; surely things will look brighter on your return.'

After supper, Moll informed her servants of her intended journey, and on sheer impulse, she decided to travel by coach, unaccompanied. Kate's eyes widened as she heard her beloved mistress utter such a preposterous statement.

'M'lady, 'tis folly. What will become of you? The roads abound with cut-throats and highway men.'

Moll hushed her softly. 'Robin will follow later with the small coach, and meet me on Wednesday at the Tobard Inn. He shall carry all my money and valuables. 'Twill be safer. I shall have very little money with me, my sweetling, have no fear.'

Kate knew by the tone of her mistress's voice that further protestations were useless, and diligently directed her energies towards preparing for the journey on the morrow.

As she laid lavender flowers and powdered rose petals between the folds of Moll's dresses, Kate tried to dispel her fears. Even the fact of Robin taking her jewels and money appalled her, and quick as a flash, she darted over to the jewel box, and with a cursory glance over her shoulder, took out a heavy ruby ring and hurriedly stitched it inside the bodice of one of Moll's dresses. Laying other gowns carefully over her secret, she closed the heavy lid of the trunk and securely bound the leather straps tightly around it.

Morning dawned sunny and cheerful, and Moll was happily contemplating her journey. Her thoughts wandered back in time to her mother whom she had not seen for so long. Odds fish, was it four years? She could hardly believe it! Yes, it was time she returned home, if only for a short visit. Moll's daydreams were interrupted as Kate bustled in and attended to her toilet. Kate glanced down, and for one moment Moll thought she must surely have noticed the slight thickening of her waist, but, thank God, it had escaped her notice. She dried her mistress deftly, and placed a fresh robe around her shoulders, and arranged for the other servants to take away the water.

The London streets soon bustled with activity, and the mixed odours permeated the bedroom. Moll's nostrils quivered with distaste. 'Really,' she thought, 'Charles should hurry the new bill to forbid people throwing refuse into the streets.' London was turning into a cesspool; surely other people could see the havoc they were causing by slovenly living and foul habits.

Hurriedly she slipped into her travelling clothes and, with a swift farewell to her servants, climbed into the coach which was to take her to the Chepe where another coach awaited her and other travellers bound for the country. Holding a perfumed 'kerchief to her nose, Moll gazed out on the great city she had called home for almost four years and, like a bountiful mother, had showered her with gifts and blessings. Her starved soul longed even more poignantly now for the wholesome smell of the English countryside, and tomorrow she would be home to smell once again the sweet perfume of an English meadow.

Robin pulled up and helped his mistress into the larger coach which was already filling up. 'Servants on top,' roared the red-faced driver, soothing the large horses who were anxious to be off. 'Steady, steady,' he bellowed as his whip snicked the buttock of Rolf, the team lead horse who was now tossing his head and stamping his feet. The coachman held Rolf by the bridle, and fed him an apple. Flecks of juice appeared around his bit, and making noisy sounds of enjoyment, he nudged his master for more. The apple had obviously quieted the big horse, and with a quick glance, the coach driver checked that his passengers were now ready. Eight inside, and four aloft, quite a load, he mused, and with a loud shout to clear the road of urchins and beggars, the great coach trundled on its journey.

Moll eased her body into the not very accommodating curves of the hard seat, and took stock of her travelling companions. Two middle-aged ladies and their daughters, one quite pretty with bright eyes and a clear skin; the other girl, perhaps sixteen years old, had a heavy petulant mouth. She was obviously bored by the prospects of a long journey, and quite prepared to be objectionable to her travelling companions, should anything not please her. Four gentlemen seated opposite the ladies attracted Moll's attention. The first one was a pale, effeminate man who, Moll decided, was following the latest French fashion, a fop. Distasteful creature, she thought. Next, a saintly looking man in clerical garb, deep in concentration reading his Bible; then a red-faced but jolly fat merchant, wheezing badly, and a very refined looking gentleman, whose brown eyes gazed steadfastly and most disconcertingly into her own. She noticed particularly his hands, long slim elegant hands, on which a large crested ring flashing in the morning sun. She was reminded of Charles's hands, long and tapered though they were, they seemed coarse in comparison. The gentleman appeared to notice her gaze, and shrugging off these notions, she looked out the window to see the Thames swirling beneath the bridge, the dark water forming sinister whirlpools under the pier. As she turned her head, their eyes met yet again, and for miles Moll tried to avoid his gaze which she found fascinating, yet most disconcerting.

As each mile passed beneath the wheels of the lumbering coach, Moll hoped they would soon stop to change horses. Easing her aching body into a more comfortable position, she wished her laces were not quite so tightly drawn, for the heat was oppressive. God's teeth, when would this great trundling beast stop? Nausea welled up from the pit of her stomach, and with horror she felt an all embracing darkness creeping steadily over her. With a soft, barely audible moan she pitched forward into the arms of the brown-eyed gentleman.

The great coach ground to a halt outside a wayside inn, and strong arms carried Moll inside. Her first conscious moments were filled by gentle hands chafing her wrists, and the most beautiful masculine voice she had ever heard soothed her back into consciousness, but this was only a short stop to change horses. Quietly Moll thanked the kind gentleman for his assistance, but dreaded the thought that all too soon they must resume the long journey. Her travelling companions were afflicted by boredom, for a tirade of abuse tore from the elder girl and, quick as a flash, she snatched the knotting from the lap of her young companion and threw it contemptuously out of the window. The atmosphere in the coach was electric, and amidst the general hubbub which Moll was only too pleased to avoid, she drifted in and out of reality until she became aware only of the sound of horses hooves drumming her into a welcoming sleep. Her reverie, however, was soon over, for she became aware that the great horses were being reigned in for an unexplained stop.

The crashing of brakes jolted the occupants awake, and suddenly the door was flung open. Moll was forced back to reality by the harsh, loud voice of a man halting the coach. With horror, she realized that no coachman would halt on the main road from London for any traveller requesting a stop. Terrified, she found herself confronted by a pair of steely blue eyes, staring through a black mask. 'Highwayman,' she gasped, petrified. She glanced across to where a different colour of eyes remained calm and unmoved. The brown-eyed gentleman took in every detail of the scene as the passengers were hurried unceremoniously from the coach. By this time, the unwelcome visitor had dismounted from his dark horse which snorted and steamed in the half light. Moll could smell the heat from the hard-ridden beast, and once more felt the sickness threatening to engulf her.

She struggled and conquered, and with grateful thanks, felt the colour once more return to her cheeks. The highwayman ran his hands over the men, and relieved them of their valuables. He gave a curt nod to the ladies, who were by now fully aware of his intentions, and divested themselves voluntarily of their possessions, lest they meet with the same treatment as their fellow travellers. Moll's heart lurched. She had only three crowns and had purposely travelled without valuables. He glanced at her sharply, and waved his pistols impatiently. 'Do ye need help, m'lady?' he mocked.

Moll recoiled in horror at his coarse voice; her own falteringly told him she was completely without trinkets or gold, her white shaking hands holding out to him her three crowns.

With an oath, he reached over and ripped open the bodice of her gown, fumbling unnecessarily for valuables. The gentleman with the brown eyes, which were now narrowing angrily, kept silent, and with a loud laugh, the highwayman pulled Moll to him and kissed her, forcing her tightly closed lips apart. The brown-eyed gentleman expertly relieved him of his guns whilst this dalliance was enacted and instantly the highwayman found himself staring into the barrels of his own pistols. With a flourish, the gentleman signalled the intruder to return the valuables to the travellers and, with a resounding slap on the horse's flank, he sent the beast and its rider bolting over the dark hillside with two empty holsters and even emptier pockets.

Back in the coach, Moll quickly regained her composure, which soon turned to acute embarrassment, for the brown eyes did not this time meet hers – they were focused on her torn bodice. With a start, she realized just how much of her ample bosom was exposed to his gaze. Sensing her discomfort, he smiled. Faced with the hopeless task of covering herself, Moll prayed fervently for a safe and speedy journey home. For the rest of the trip, she deliberately avoided not only this fascinating man, but the rest of the occupants of the coach as well.

Familiar landmarks eventually hove into view, and Moll was delighted to see the old tavern where her great adventure to London had begun four years earlier. Everything was unchanged, even the dirty unkempt dog looked practically the same, perhaps a little mangier, and the old ostler, whom she remembered from her childhood, gave her a glance of recognition.

Presently, all the travellers, weary and dusty, entered the low-beamed tavern. Moll's trunk was dragged in by two stalwart youths, and carried up to her room. All that remained was to order water and herbs for her toilet, and thankfully she blessed the landlord's wife for her thoughtfulness in having these luxuries available.

The accommodation would suit her very well, she decided, until such time as she returned to London. The memory of the vermin-infested cottage where her parents lived appalled her, for she could not go back to live in such squalor, even for the space of a few days.

Moll enquired of the landlord if Robin, her servant, had arrived.

'No,' said he, "tis said there be trouble and pestilence in London, and talk of a plague outbreak.'

She blanched visibly at this news, and hoped that these awful tidings were not the cause of Robin's absence. With horror she remembered the three crowns confiscated by the highwayman, and realized she was completely without money. Inns did not offer free hospitality to travellers in those days, no matter what the circumstances. If Robin did not appear shortly, she would be compelled to ask her parents for shelter, and this she most certainly did not want to do. Surely he would arrive before morning, she hoped. Meantime, a change of clothing was her first thought; the rest she would think about tomorrow. Hurrying upstairs, she stepped distastefully out of her torn gown, and struggling with the tight leather straps, pulled open the lid of the huge trunk. Savouring the scent of the perfumed contents, she unfolded the sapphire blue gown before beginning her toilet.

As she brushed the tangles from her black hair, she decided to leave it loose around her face, with soft damp tendrils curling over her brow, and after rubbing a little cochineal powder into her pale cheeks, she slipped the voluminous folds of satin over her head. Lacing up the bodice, she felt something hard pressing against her breast, and on examining the lining, she felt the ring which Kate had sewn in two days before. With a squeal of delight, she held the flashing stone up to the light and knew that she could soon turn this trinket into cash. 'Ten crowns, at least,' she mused. 'Bless you, dear Kate,' Moll said to herself, appreciating once more her good fortune of having people around her who really cared.

Gathering up her skirts, she hurried to find the landlord. From room to room she searched, but he was nowhere to be found. Eventually, a blowsy serving wench, arms akimbo, pointed to a door leading to the cellar. 'He be down there, mistress,' she giggled.

Moll peered into the gloom, and taking a sputtering candle from the wall sconce, she descended haltingly down the steps. The faint glow from the candle picked out two naked forms in an intimate embrace; obviously, they had not heard Moll enter, and the revulsion which she could not hide flooded over her. There, lying on the straw was the naked serving wench and the gross flabby body of the landlord who was hastily trying to cover himself from the scathing gaze of his guest. The wench, however, had no such feelings of shame, for she faced Moll brazenly, angry at the intrusion.

Moll, however, had little time to bandy words with such a girl, and dismissed her with a sharp glance. As the wench was slipping a dirty shift over her head, Moll noticed the still young voluptuous body prematurely sagging with loose loving. 'A good wash wouldn't do you any harm,' thought Moll. 'Methinks the last time you had a good scrubbing was when the midwife did it.'

A very subdued landlord silently followed Moll up to the dining room. The ring quickly exchanged hands, Moll explaining very precisely that she would redeem it as soon as her servant arrived from London, so with ten crowns tucked away in her purse, Moll wended her way to the large dining room where the landlord's wife, a quick and neat little woman, was industriously plying her customers with food.

Once more she found herself gazing into two deep brown eyes, but this time he introduced himself as Sir James Waring of London. He glanced appraisingly at the beautiful creature dining with him, and wished with all his heart that he was free to carry on a lasting relationship with her. Alas, he remembered with distaste the fat, blowsy woman he called wife, and decided that for a little while at least, he would forget all the trying years of that marriage of convenience. Tonight he would remember this one evening with Moll, beautiful, dark-haired Moll.

His eyes followed the lovely line of her throat to the graceful shoulders, the blue dress falling in soft folds, accentuating her lovely bosom. He looked at her hands - zounds, this goddess wore no rings! He cursed the fates that had left this meeting so late. Why was life so cruel? No matter, for tonight the fates were kind and smiling gently. He poured her a glass of wine. Their fingers touched momentarily; disturbingly, Moll's whole body tingled. Was it so long since she had felt a man's touch?

The evening passed pleasantly, and Sir James's suggestion of a walk around the inn garden was most welcome. The evening fell balmy and clear, and as the night drew on, Moll felt that she wanted this man to hold her close in his arms more than anything in the world.

Moll, too dazed by her own feelings, realized that she was powerless to refuse him anything, and that the way the evening closed would be entirely up to him. All that she knew was that for the first time in her life she did not hold the upper hand, and that his wish was her command. They entered the inn which was now deserted, and climbed the stairs to their respective rooms, which Moll knew were in close proximity. He kissed her lightly on the brow, and whispered a low, husky goodnight. 'I can stay with honour no longer, my darling, I must leave you; until tomorrow,' and quickly he walked back to his room.

Moll gently closed the door and wondered at this man. ''Twas better we parted,' she mused, for a great tiredness suddenly overwhelmed her. She quickly prepared herself for bed, and slipped gratefully between the sheets.

Without warning a sharp pain tore at her vitals, and half-doubled with the onslaught, she dragged herself out of the bed. Time after time she called for help, but no one answered her cries, and the agony continued until the early hours of the morning. Bathed in perspiration, Moll found herself being torn asunder on waves of pain that she thought would surely kill her. Then Sir James's face appeared before her, coming and going with each new onslaught.

Out of the morass she felt sure she was slipping into came the blessed sound of a firm voice, which was like angels' singing to Moll's ears. The landlord's wife appeared, quickly roused from her slumbers by the cries of a servant. Taking in the situation at once, she sent the wench hurrying down for fresh towels and water. Drawing back the soiled sheets, it was as she suspected – her guest had had a miscarriage. Deftly changing the linen, she administered a potion of herbs, which stopped the dreadful contractions and softly she told Moll that her child was no more.

Moll laughed hysterically through her tears. Son or daughter of a king, to end up so ignominiously aborted in a wayside inn. Life was so uncharted, how could one foresee such a happening? Thoughts and images whirled in her mind, nothing making sense – her forthcoming marriage to give this child a name was now unnecessary. With this kaleidoscope running madly through her brain, she finally drifted into sleep. Unreal images forced their way into her dreams, giving her little rest.

Sir James was informed, tactfully, by the landlord's wife that Moll had taken a fever, and for three days he stayed near her bedside. Moll thanked Mrs Lightbody profusely for all her help, and felt sad that she could, at the moment, offer no more tangible token of her appreciation. She vowed that as soon as Robin appeared with her possessions, Mrs Lightbody would be adequately rewarded. When Moll felt able to sit for a little while, Sir James was ready to plump up her pillows and show in so many ways his respect for her by little kindnesses. Fresh flowers were brought in daily, and delicacies to please even the most jaded of appetites were placed by her bed, for nothing was too much trouble. He was extremely happy in her company and the next day, when Moll felt stronger, he led her into the garden.

He explained that soon he must return to London, and had decided to catch the coach leaving on the morrow. This was sooner than Moll expected, and her disappointment was obvious at the unexpected news. He noticed her distress and thought that the walk in the garden was perhaps too tiring for her. He offered his arm, and led her slowly back to her room, helping her back into bed and placing a wrap around her shoulders. Moll lifted her face for his kiss. He gracefully obliged, and bade her sleep and grow strong. He explained that after breakfast on the morrow he must leave, but asked if she would allow him to call at her home in London on her return.

Moll agreed that it would be pleasurable to meet again, and wished him a safe journey home.

She arose early the following morning, feeling much stronger, and joined Sir

James at their table for breakfast. Syllabub, followed by cold venison pasty, and washed down with fresh buttermilk made an enjoyable repast, but little in the way of conversation passed between them. Their silent intimacy was broken by two sluttish serving wenches starting a dreadful brawl. Moll could make out something about a ring, and the situation soon became volatile. One girl caught the other a resounding blow on her ear, their language coming straight from the gutter. Moll recognized one of the combatants as the wench she had seen in the cellar with her employer the night she arrived, and to her utter disbelief, she saw the other girl tear a ring from her finger. It was the one she had left with the landlord as surety against the ten crowns she had borrowed. It was becoming increasingly apparent that Moll would not see the ring again, which disturbed her very much, for it had been one of Roxanne's treasured possessions and held great sentimental attachment. Quickly, over the mêlée, she told Sir James the story of the ring. He spoke a few sharp words to the landlord, who quickly separated the two vixens. He whispered something to the wench, who then poutingly gave the trinket back to him with a scowl. Money in exchange for the offending ring changed hands, and Moll felt the ring being returned to her finger. Impulsively, she kissed Sir James on the cheek, and smiled as he ruefully touched the spot with his finger.

A commotion outside told them that their farewell must be brief for the coach was almost ready to depart. With tears in her eyes, Moll watched the great rumbling coach disappear into the distance on its way to London.

Chapter 15

Moll Journeys Home

Her thoughts turned now to her immediate problems, and unanswered questions crowded her mind, making her uneasy. Where was Robin? Had Charles sent messages for her, and what of her future husband - would he wonder where his prospective bride had fled? An early night was the answer, after a quiet day walking the countryside; tomorrow she would see her family.

She rose early in the morning, and was startled to hear the beat of hooves beneath her window. Drawing back the shutters, she peered out in the courtyard below. 'Robin, Robin!' she called.

He looked up searching for the face to fit the voice, shading his eyes from the morning sun.

'Oh, thank God,' said Moll, as she threw a cloak around her and sped barefoot into the yard. 'Robin, why the delay, what ails thee, lad?'

'M'lady, praise be you are safe,' he cried, his hands shaking with emotion. 'First Mrs Wilson, then Kate, then all the maids fell ill with the sweating sickness, and I could not leave them.'

'What news of Kate?' Moll heard her voice almost scream with frustration at his slowness of speech.

'She is well, m'lady, all have recovered now.'

Moll then noticed his weariness; the lad was exhausted. Calling the ostlers to attend to the perspiring horses, she ushered him into the inn where Mrs Lightbody fussed about him, attending to his needs.

When Robin was refreshed, he told her the news. Charles had sent a messenger, who had returned to his master with the unexpected tidings of Moll's departure, but no further contact had been made. Sir Richard had called many times, Robin said, but as the servants could give no news of Moll's return, his visits had become less frequent.

'Still,' thought Moll, 'I have no urgent need to return to London, especially since I now have money and jewels enough for a lengthy stay if need be.'

The thought of her jewels brought back to mind the kindness shown by Mrs

Lightbody during her illness. This must be put to rights, she thought. Immediately she carried the jewel box up to her room and searched diligently for a suitable gift. After much deliberation she chose a locket, delicately chased and studded with seed pearls and a long gold chain, the clasp of which matched the locket design perfectly. With this in hand, she rang the bell which brought Mrs Lightbody hurrying to her room.

'Are ye ill, ma'am?' asked the worried goodwife.

'No,' said Moll, 'but I wanted to have a few words with you in private. First, I wish to thank you for the many kindnesses you have shown me during the time I have been here, and to thank you so much for the way you nursed me through my illness.'

''Twas nothing, ma'am, it was a pleasure to nurse such a pretty lady, and little trouble,' was the reply.

Moll held the locket out to her and said, 'Keep this, with my thanks.'

'Oh no, ma'am, I couldn't, it's too fine for the likes of me.'

'Nonsense,' said Moll. 'I insist you take it, unless you'd rather have money.'

''Tis the most beautiful thing I ever clapped eyes on, and I shall treasure it always,' she replied as she pressed Moll's hands fervently between her rough work-worn ones, brushed a tear from her eye, and left the room holding the delicate locket tightly to her breast.

Robin was her next visitor, this time to inform her of his impending return to London. 'So soon?' said Moll.

'Yes, the house must be made ready for your return, and the maids find the furniture too heavy for them to move without me,' he replied.

Moll suspected that time spent away from his beloved Kate was time wasted, in Robin's mind, and knew that he was anxious to see her again.

'Do not be in haste to return to London, m'lady, the city is full of smallpox and sickness; as the weather cools the pestilence will abate. Kate yearns for news of ye, too, ma'am. I must not leave her fearing for your safety longer than is needful.' Excuses made, Robin bade her farewell, and Moll smiled at the way this uneducated young man had taken command of the situation. Yes, he was shaping up very well, she mused, so different from the gangling boy she had hired some months earlier.

Next morning she was off to an early start, for today she must let nothing interfere with her plans to visit her family. Dressing quickly, she crept quietly down to the kitchen where Mrs Lightbody was busy as always preparing the first meal of the day for her guests. Moll was greeted with a smile, as Mrs Lightbody said, 'Why, madam, you rise early as a milkmaid this morning.'

Moll returned the smile and gratefully accepted the light breakfast of boiled eggs, warm crusty bread with warm sweet milk fresh from the cow. The butter, newly made and still fresh from the churn, was brought in by the fresh-faced dairy maid, whose red hands bore the unmistakable scars of cowpox. All this made Moll realize how deep her roots were in the country. Even though she had no longings to return to live in the village of her birth, she knew she must return periodically in order to appreciate her good fortune.

After breakfast, Moll bade the landlady good day, and left the inn to walk once more down the lanes which led to her childhood home. Familiar country sounds refreshed her dormant memory. Peewits circling the fields, field mice scuttling in the hedgerows, and ambling slowly up the centre of the lane was a large, rotund hedgehog. Moll watched, enchanted, as he hobbled along, but suddenly he mistimed his rolling gait and slid helplessly on to his back, down a large rut in the road. Moll set him upright, turning to watch his progress, and smiled delightedly as he once more retraced his steps, and carefully skirted each rut in the centre of the road, exactly as he had been doing before she rescued him.

With a start, Moll realized that she was about to cross the field to her former home. Her footsteps quickened, eager yet afraid, for the cottage was now in sight, and appeared even more dilapidated than she had remembered. She knocked softly at the heavy door, which was opened by her mother. Looking older and very grey, she was surprised at the fine lady of quality on her threshold. 'Moll!' she gasped, 'Moll, is it really you? Oh, you have come back to us at last.'

'Mother, it's so wonderful to see you. It's been such a very long time.'

Moll cried as she embraced her mother, tears flowing uncontrollably down her cheeks.

Having heard the commotion, her father appeared, and was overjoyed at seeing the child he thought he would never see again. Tears streamed down his weather-beaten face as he embraced his lovely daughter. With her arm around them both, Moll swallowed hard to clear the lump which threatened to drown her once more in a welter of tears. Stories of her brothers and sisters poured into her ears. Then she became aware of the unnatural quietness in the cottage. Only the small children now remained; four others had died of a sickness, one after the other; the rest had gone to seek their fortunes.

Moll realized they were still desperately poor, and her first thought was to leave them money. She rejected this thought, because land was the only currency a yeoman farmer understood. The land in all the English counties was owned solely by gentry and, after paying rent, her parents had barely enough to keep them through the long hard winters. Moll left with the promise to return in the morning.

Moll marvelled at the fact that her long overdue visit with her parents had turned out so amiable and pleasant. She saw her parents in a new light and felt a respect and love for them that she didn't know was possible. She realized that in the four years she had been away, they had not really changed - it was she who had matured to see things differently now! She saw that her parents were honest, sincere and wonderful people.

'Meantime,' she told her mother, 'place everything of value,' which, as far as Moll could see, was nothing, 'to one side, and await my return.'

Moll returned to the inn for the night, but sleep would not come. Finally she came up with a wonderful plan. She arose very early, as she was full of enthusiasm, and had much to do in a short time. As she had foreseen, a word at the inn soon bore fruit, as a prosperous looking gentleman was introduced to her regarding a proposition for the sale of his house. The description sounded exactly suited to Moll's requirements, yet the price sounded exceedingly low. Moll soon learned how inflated London prices must be, and decided to see this house for herself immediately.

After a trip to the property, she decided the house was exactly right; a price was agreed upon, the finer points to be covered on the morrow. Unfortunately, the house purchase proved far more complicated than she had first imagined, and legal help had to be engaged to straighten out the complicated documents. Ancient land rights and tenants' privileges were incorporated in the lease. The furnishings, on closer inspection, proved to be in poor condition.

On second thought, she believed that her mother was probably not capable of furnishing such a large dwelling, so she decided to stay longer than she had first thought to put this house in order. The challenge of decorating it for her parents filled her with enthusiasm, and she knew it would be a fine house when she was finished.

The family eagerly awaited her return and amidst gay confused chatter interspersed with tears of joy, Moll explained that the big house, White Towers as it was properly named, was now theirs. They could not believe their good fortune, and Moll was deeply touched to see her father brush away a half-shed tear with his rough hand.

Supper that evening was a feast - never had Moll seen such food served at her mother's board. She glanced down instinctively at her mother's hand, and as she suspected, the one gold ring her mother had possessed had disappeared. Sold, to provide a supper fit for her daughter's return. Moll said nothing, but this sacrifice tugged menacingly at her heart, and she vowed that, come Sunday, her mother would ride to church in a carriage, and would vie in dress against any woman, aye, even the Squire's lady.

All too soon the carriage arrived in the lane. Moll could hear the driver sounding his horn, for there was no road leading up to the cottage, and with a merry adieu, she lifted her skirts, kicked off her shoes and sped effortlessly across the fields to the lane, watched by her parents who thanked God for such a daughter.

The Tabard Inn was silent, lit only by a dim guttering candle placed inside the porch. Moll entered, and the landlord's wife smiled at her as she busily cleared away the remains of supper, stopping only to take a note from her apron pocket and pass it to Moll.

Moll lit a candle from the wall sconce, and climbed the stairs to her room. With a thudding heart, she broke the seal, and in the yellow candle glow she read the beautifully written missive. 'My darling, so brief an encounter leaves me with much left unsaid, yet my heart tells me this is wrong, even to speak thus. I can bid my heart be still, yet my mind obeys me not. Some day, my dearest, I shall offer thee not only my love, but my life. James.'

Moll read the letter over and over again, and wondered why his voice still echoed in her ears, why she felt her heart lurch when she thought of him. Would those deep-set brown eyes burn forever in her soul? Lud, she was behaving like a lovesick calf. Wasn't her world so full at the moment that she didn't have enough hours in the day to cope with her affairs now? To fall desperately in love with this kind man was out of the question.

Thus, Moll talked to herself as she prepared herself for bed; she knelt humbly by the bed and repeated the old childish prayer – 'Now I lay me down to sleep, I pray thee, Lord, my soul to keep, and should I die before I wake, I pray thee, Lord, my soul to take . . . Amen.'

Slipping into bed she was suddenly aware of the dark shadows made more grotesque by the guttering candle and hurriedly, she gabbled the one Latin prayer she knew guaranteed to keep her safe through the dark night. Gratefully snuggling down in the comforting warmth of the great featherbed, she drifted into oblivion.

The next week proved to be a busy one for the whole family, including friends and neighbours, all anxious to help the Wakefields move into the big house. Choosing furnishings, accepting help from nearby villagers, arranging meals for the many people they required to put things in order, drained Moll of strength long before her family showed signs of tiring. However, by noon on Saturday, all was finished. Moll's eyes danced with delight at the result. Good taste and simplicity proved to be the correct foil for the house, and loving hands had restored the oak panelling to a beautiful lustre. Moll's mother and father hugged one another in ecstasy, and wine was called for to toast the occasion.

Moll twirled her skirts and whipped off the 'kerchief from her mother's head. 'Come and be cossetted into a lady,' she cried. Her mother, confused by this outburst, sought aid from her husband, but he pushed her back into Moll's waiting arms. 'Go, Sal,' he said, 'go with Moll. I wish with all my heart to see thee dressed in fine feathers.'

Moll, pulling her still protesting mother to the bedroom, knew that she was going to enjoy this transformation scene. Once in the bedroom, her mother disrobed, whilst Moll poured perfumed water into the large bowl. Moll discreetly turned away whilst her mother completed her toilet. She held out a blue petticoat, and slipped it quickly over her mother's head, doing up her laces quickly to stop further protestations. Next, a full-skirted gown of russet velvet trimmed with seed pearls caught up in soft folds to show the blue petticoat beneath, completed the ensemble. Moll applied a little make-up, which accentuated the rich colour of the gown, and was quite astounded how much she resembled her mother. She brushed her hair vigorously, and encased it in a long black snood, which detracted from the greyness. A pair of velvet slippers, and all was ready. 'Lovely,' breathed Moll. 'Mother, you look lovely.' She led her mother to the mirror and watched with pleasure as she touched her face, then ran her hands, disbelievingly, over the soft folds of the gown, and suddenly whirled and pirouetted, until Moll was sure she would collapse from sheer joy.

Proudly, they walked side by side down the wide staircase, and Moll watched fondly as her mother expertly handled the flowing gown, and strode gracefully to where her father, dumb with amazement, stood in awe at the sight of this elegant lady.

'Sal, Sal,' his voice was hoarse with emotion, 'you are truly beautiful.'

He glanced down, ashamed at his own humble attire, but Moll had foreseen this situation, and with a signal to one of the men standing by the door, he found himself being led upstairs to begin his own toilet. An hour later he reappeared, beard and hair neatly trimmed, and garbed in an elegantly cut suit of dark blue brocade with cream lace at his throat and wrists. Moll and her mother gasped with surprise at this change, and for the first time in her life, Moll realized what a splendid figure of a man her father was. Even his bearing was different. He held himself tall and straight, and the grey pallor of his skin was gone. 'Yes,' thought Moll, 'you will both do very well, very well indeed.'

Contented, the three sat together in the great garden and surveyed the beautiful vista of trees and flowers. Her father planned the vegetable garden and crops, while her mother talking endlessly of the great house party they would give for all their friends. It would be a big point of discussion for many months to come. Inside, Moll felt a warm glow, sure in the knowledge that her parents were happier than they had ever been before.

Later in the day, Moll talked with her father regarding the hiring of a steward, for she doubted that he had the knowledge or experience to handle a proposition such as this. She had infinite faith in his basic skills of husbandry, and knew that no man would overrule him. The man she chose was well known to the people of the village, and her father, after talking at great length with the man, decided to engage him. Moll said little, for she knew that her father must hold the reins, and she was well pleased at the way he conducted the interview, leaving the man in no doubt as to who was in command. Moll was delighted when, at the end of the interview, Mr Ralph touched his forelock to her father, and said, 'I shall try and give thee good service, squire, and will report at cock's crow for the day's instructions.'

It was obvious that the land would provide a substantial income for not only the family, but for many of the villagers too, who barely existed with no outside employment to subsidize their poor plots of land. Soon Moll would leave, and for the first time in her life, she was loath to go!

Sunday was a wonderful day, spent in happy and loving companionship. After church, they returned home to find the cook had prepared an excellent meal, but Moll knew that time was running short. She left the charming company to walk once more around White Towers, feeling sad that the time was near to say farewell.

This time, the coach drew up outside the great oak door, and amidst tears and kisses, she waved goodbye to her family. The coach clattered its way to the Tabard Inn, but the sight of Robin waiting patiently in the cobbled yard, drinking a large mug of ale and picking petals from the flowers in the tub, gave her a pang of remorse for tarrying so long. He was bursting with news of London.

The plague of sickness had now abated, and the city was back to normal. Kate was busy with the preparations for her homecoming and, in Robin's opinion, the sooner they arrived back at Great Swordbearers Alley the better. After her experience on the outward journey, Moll was inclined to agree.

Next morning they began the journey back to London, which was pleasant and uneventful. Both of them felt the change in the weather heralding winter, and already noticed the leaves changing colour under the darkening sky. Presently they drew up beside a wayside inn for supper, and a night's lodging.

By noon of the next day, the smoke pall which hung over the city was clearly visible and it appeared to Moll as if some grey spectre hovered in the sky. Sounds all too familiar crashed in on her, and, unused to the terrible din, she clapped her hands over her ears. The sun broke through, finally, and Moll marvelled at the change old Sol brought to the city. ' Perhaps the sunshine is a good omen,' she thought.

Familiar sights came into view; the bridge was the same, the huge stanchions proof against the great rushing waters of the mighty Thames, and Moll found herself loving this great river, dirty as it was, for she knew it gave life to this huge metropolis she now called home.

At last they reached the Court. Kate, hearing the clatter of the coach drawing up at the door, and flushed with excitement, hugged them both in turn, chattering and excitedly asking questions, one after another.

Once inside the house, Moll was pleasantly surprised at the results of the hard work Kate and the staff had put into making her lovely home so attractive. Even the bedroom was perfumed with sweet-scented herbs, and Kate had embroidered a new tapestry cover for her footstool to match the rose pink bedspread. Moll was delighted at these touches, and swept from one room to the next, purring with delight, to Kate's obvious joy.

During supper, Moll told Kate of the exciting moments of her journey, and saw the pleasure in her eyes as she thanked her for her forethought in sewing the ring into her dress. Kate wanted to know everything that had happened, but strangely enough, Moll found herself keeping her feelings for Sir James to herself.

Kate also had news to relate. Sir Richard had called many times but had left no messages. This Moll already knew, and was extremely concerned as to how she was to break the news to him of the child she had lost.

It was only fair to ask him if he wished to be released from the half-spoken engagement, but she was hesitant for perfectly selfish reasons. She was hoping that they would remain good friends and nothing more. Charles would be angry, of this she had no doubt, but she was not prepared to sacrifice herself on the altar of conviction, and would not be married against her will, nay, not even at the command of the King.

Kate was still chattering on, but Moll's head spun like a top. She really must go to bed, and perhaps in the morning would have some clear thoughts in her mind about how to handle her problems, not the least of them, Sir Richard and the King.

Chapter 16

A Letter from Charles

Sleep did not come easily this night. Although the court was normally very quiet, tonight proved to be the exception. A crowd of bloods were noisily challenging each other to a fight directly beneath her casement. It seemed never ending, and to her consternation she heard the sharp metallic clash of steel. 'Oh, the saints preserve us,' prayed Moll.

Death in the Court was unthinkable. She knew of streets in London called Duelling Alleys', where once a fight had occurred, the young bloods vied and often died to perpetuate the legend, and trouble flared night after night. With an oath she leaped out of bed and grasped the large pitcher of water, icy cold by this time, opened the window and poured it over the two duellists. A roar of shocked laughter came from the gallants, and plumed hats were thrown into the air. Moll opened the casement wider, her black hair cascading down to her waist, and sweetly called down, 'Good morrow, gentlemen, I trust you will all sleep well,' and with a wave of hands, they quietly dispersed.

Next morning, Moll came down to a fire burning in the inglenook. She soon realized how dreadfully cold the morning was and pulled the great heavy damask robe even closer around her shoulders. One of the maids brought her a warm glass of mint tea, and stirred the fire to a comfortable blaze. 'Where is Kate?' enquired Moll.

'Oh, she be out to purchase fresh bread from the baker, ma'am. 'Tis said there is a great frost on the river this day. Mistress Kate said we might be given time off to go later,' and with a grin, the young wench returned to the kitchen in order to finish her daily chores early.

Kate returned from the baker's, the aroma of freshly baked bread issuing from the large loaves in her hands, her nose red and shining like a ripe cherry. 'M'lady, news, news indeed! The Thames is frozen over, and they are roasting sheep on the ice. A great fair is being held and the people are already making their way to the river!' Breathless and flushed, Kate clapped her hands with pleasure. 'Oh, m'lady, we must go,' she pleaded. 'I have promised the maids that they too may see the fair, if madam so pleases.'

'Why certainly, Kate,' Moll replied, 'we must all go. Haste, then, and tell the household that the rest of the day is their own.'

Quickly, Kate raced away to tell the servants the glad tidings, and after a substantial breakfast, they climbed into the coach and made for the river. Such a sight met their eyes! The Thames was frozen to a depth of fourteen inches, and people were walking the full width of the river. Stalls were doing trade, selling hot roasted chestnuts, chitterlings, lark pies, and every conceivable kind of sweetmeat. Everything that was for sale normally in the markets appeared on the river. A man was even using a printing press, and for the three groats given, one's name appeared as if by magic. This was a great favourite with the ladies, in fact. The day was a roaring success and everyone enjoyed the outing immensely. As they returned to the coach, Moll was startled to hear a familiar voice amidst a gaggle of feminine squeals, and her heart missed a beat. It couldn't possibly be – she listened again, this time she could not mistake the merry chuckle – Charles, the King! The tall figure dressed in dark green velvet seemed suddenly to hear her thoughts, and for an endless moment, their eyes met. He winked, but did not speak since he had a charming female companion on each arm. One of them asked, 'Who is she?', but before anyone insisted on an answer he turned all his charm on the questioner, who nevertheless stared at Moll as she entered her coach.

They arrived home as darkness was falling, but the night was crisp and clear, the moon girdled by a ring of frost, full and bright. Moll's thoughts, however, were elsewhere. As they warmed themselves by the great fire, their reverie was interrupted by the sound of horse's hooves clattering up the Court. The sound startled Moll. Who would be calling at this hour? Her question was not long in being answered, for Kate returned from the door bearing a letter, on the back of which was the Royal Cipher.

The old magic flooded over her, and she wondered at herself. How could she be so affected by two entirely different men? First Charles and then Sir James . . . With trembling hands she broke the seal, and read a very short message: 'Tomorrow at seven. Charles.'

The next day was spent in preparing her toilet, which was even more involved than normal, since she took great pains to have everything exactly right. The dress she chose was beautifully cut and fashioned in yellow velvet trimmed in white ermine, and in her hair she wore a half circlet made of yellow enamelled daisies. Her black velvet cloak made a vivid contrast. At last she was satisfied with her appearance, and with a smile and wave to an admiring Kate, she climbed into her carriage. Moll knew that this meeting would not be easy, and felt great trepidation. She was going to rebel against the King's wishes regarding her forthcoming marriage. 'At the King's pleasure' – she grimaced at the words, but she knew that no matter how she protested, at the King's pleasure it would be.

The coach ground to a halt and Moll was once more discreetly shown up to the private chambers. Charles himself opened the door, and kissed her gently on the cheek. 'So long, my darling, so very long. I have missed you so dreadfully.' Taking her hand, he led her into the warm richly furnished room, where a light supper was laid. As the meal drew to a close, Moll found herself studying his face closely. Blue-black hair curled over his shoulders, his dark skin was tanned and unblemished save for a small scar on his cheek, the red lips parted to show perfect white teeth, and he had a small moustache which added width to his lean face. The sight of him fascinated Moll shamefully, yet his eyes were a mystery. She caught a glimpse of them in the candlelight, and decided they were dark brown, almost black, but surprisingly they seemed to change with each colour he wore. Nay, she decided the man's eyes would remain a mystery.

She spoke about her journey at great length, and Charles listened with sadness as she retold the story of the aborted baby. Only when she spoke of cancelling the marriage contract did his eyes lose their compassion. 'My darling,' he said gently, 'you will cause me untold embarrassment if you do not fulfil this obligation. I would ask you to wait until the spring before you make an irrefutable decision; only wait a little while, my darling, and if you still find the thought distasteful, come to me again and we will discuss it further.'

Moll knew then that the subject was closed, and to press his point, he drew her closely towards him, covering her warm mouth with his own. The kiss left her in no doubt that tonight she would be his. Eagerly, he slipped the fastenings of her gown, his hands caressing every line of her body, his voice murmuring endearments, and Moll found herself swept along on an all-consuming tide of passion, responding to his demanding touch. He swept her naked body on the couch, and eagerly, with no thought of possible consequences, they made passionate love. While she slowly dressed, Charles watched her with interest. 'Lud, Maria, you are a goddess, and as pretty without fine feathers as any woman in Christendom; aye, my sweet, you have captured the heart of a King.'

Moll chaffed him gently. 'Thy heart is like a bird, sire, captured for but a moment, only to fly away when the door is open.'

He laughed at this retort, and replied, 'Verily, thou art a wise old owl,' both knowing that a gem of truth was lurking somewhere beneath the banter, and not wishing that it should be different, for Moll understood that Charles would not tolerate chains, even if they should be cast of gold.

Time was growing late. It would soon be dawn, and pulling the warm cloak around her shoulders, she blew him a kiss and silently disappeared down the stone staircase.

Chapter 17

Betrothal

Life passed happily for Moll; visits to the theatre, plays, and masked balls made time speed quickly by. So much so, that she hadn't realized how long ago was her visit with the King. Lud, why hadn't she realized that Charles had been in Scotland for two months – what a fool she was.

Sir Richard had paid her many visits, and she was not displeased that she had postponed her decision regarding her marriage. Really, this had been no hardship, for he had not mentioned the so-called 'arrangements' since her return, and was obviously awaiting her pleasure.

Meantime, her visits had been interspersed with all the pleasures of London, and Moll enjoyed being escorted by this distinguished gentleman. Once more her thoughts flew back to her last visit with Charles, and the thought appalled her – two months, but it couldn't possibly be! How could time escape so swiftly? Feeling a bit jaded, she decided that a warm bath would be most refreshing, and rang the bell to summon Kate. Quickly, the hot fragrant steaming tub appeared, ushered in by Kate bearing white towels, already warmed by the quick application of a hot warming pan. Kate helped Moll undress and assisted her into the tub. Moll relaxed completely, enjoying the luxurious aroma and heat. After a soothing wash, she stepped out on to the tapestry floor covering, where Kate stood holding a towel. A sharp intake of breath involuntarily escaped from her lips as Kate rubbed her glowing body with a towel, for her breasts were extremely sore. Nothing was said until Kate, while folding the towel, asked a question. 'Does m'lady wish a soothing potion to be sent up? 'Twill greatly ease the soreness of thy breasts.'

Moll followed Kate's eyes, and realized with dread that the signs she had seen before were all too obviously apparent. Her breasts were large and swollen; the blue veins, which gentlewomen displayed with pride, were distended and of a deeper colour than normal. Added to this was the fact that she had ignored the lunar calendar – once again she was enceinte!

'Oh, Kate, what shall I do – I'm pregnant!'

Kate comforted her sobbing mistress as best she could, and shushed her as one would a child. 'I shall hasten to the apothecary's for a potion; I know of such a place across the river at Southwark,' and with no further ado, she summoned Robin, and soon the coach sped on its errand.

Two hours later she returned with a small phial of purple liquid and, without hesitation, Moll swallowed the terribly noxious draught. Her stomach rebelled at the bitterness, and blinded with tears she threw herself across the bed. The next few hours proved to be a nightmare. She had never felt so ill, but the artificially induced abortion was not to be, for Moll felt that this time the child would surely be born. Her agile mind, now free from pain, thought long and hard over the events of the past two days. What now? She decided Charles must be told immediately.

A broadsheet informed her that he had returned to London the previous day, and without delay a message was despatched to His Majesty. Moll fervently prayed that she had not committed a grave breach of protocol by doing so. The reply was swift, within the hour, in fact, saying, 'Meet me in St James's Park by the fountain at six.'

Time was leaping by and Moll urged Robin to bring the coach quickly to the door. With all speed, he complied and soon they were speeding through the great gates towards the assignation. Moll looked around for the royal coach, but she saw none. She was trembling with anxiety when the figure of a man suddenly hove into view. 'Charles!' she cried.

With a finger to his lips, he leaped quickly into her carriage, and kissed her gently in salutation. 'Well, my darling, you must have urgent news to summon me. What troubles you, my sweet?'

Moll found herself sobbing uncontrollably on his shoulder and, between sobs, poured out to him the story of her newly discovered condition. He soothed her gently and explained that she really must not distress herself so. He would see sir Richard and the long half-arranged marriage must now be brought forward. An hour later he bade her goodbye, explaining with regret that he had other important matters of state to attend to.

Moll was sad that she had burdened him with more troubles, for it was common knowledge the Catholic and Protestant elements were fighting for power. Charles had very sketchy Catholic leanings, but knew that the strict moral code of the priests absolutely forbade the sort of escapades he had indulged in during the whole of his adult life. After giving the matter careful thought, he decided to stay true to the English Church, consoling himself with the fact that should he decide to change his religion, it would be at the time of his death when all his sins would be abolished by the last remaining, all consuming rights of the Holy Catholic Church – the last sacrament. Surely the bigots of his kingdom could do little about this scheme. His Catholic wife, if she outlived him, would keep this secret, for she had stopped trying to enfold him with her faith since the early days of their marriage.

Still, he had clearly fooled them all. All this he had confided to Moll on the few times they had really talked about religion and politics, and Moll was impressed how well informed he was. Either that or he was fully versed in the Old Queen's ways of clever meanderings, never letting anyone, least of all her courtiers, delve into the inner recesses of her soul. Moll recalled all these impressions on her way back to the Court, and marvelled at the complexity of this man.

Moll recounted to Kate the events of the meeting, for she now believed that she could trust Kate with her life, if need be. She felt safe in the knowledge that she would not be the subject of gossip, and she thanked God for such a blessing.

Morning began badly, commencing with a bout of vomiting, and she feared the potion she had taken to procure an abortion had done some mischief to either herself or her unborn child. This was quickly dispelled, however, by Kate bidding her drink a soothing drink of raspberry tea, which she assured would guarantee an easy delivery. Her figure had altered little, which was no wonder, for Moll had little appetite for food. Kate tempted her each day with tiny dainty tidbits, but to no avail. Kate was driven nearly frantic with anxiety. Sir Richard called unexpectedly one morning as Moll was patiently embroidering some linen. Moll was surprised, for his visits were usually timed well, and an early visit by a gentleman was normally considered *contre nous.*

With a flicker of surprise, Moll greeted him with her customary curtsey, and on rising, called Kate to serve wine. But Kate had anticipated Moll's request, and was already placing a carafe of Madeira at her side. Moll poured the fragrant wine into the silver goblets, and as they sipped it, she sensed that this was no social visit. He spoke of Charles and of a supper he had partaken with him at Whitehall. Then followed a discourse of the plans he had to alter his house, asking Moll's opinion on the work of Indigo Jones, which had recently become fashionable amongst the nobility of London. Moll was nonplussed. Was Sir Richard leading up to a proposal? She could not tell, and her knowledge of Mr Jones, whoever he was, certainly did not allow her to offer an opinion as to his capabilities regarding the improvements to the great house. Giving an adequate if not intelligent reply irked Moll, and she realized that if she was to be the wife of such a well informed man, she must see her friend, the scrivener, who could be relied upon to come up with answers for her.

Sir Richard left Moll no wiser than when he came. In fact, so curious was she regarding Mr Jones and the other gentleman he had mentioned that she summoned the teacher to her house immediately. Seating himself beside her, he gently pointed out that Mr Indigo Jones was a famous architect, emphasizing the past tense. He had died some two years ago, he explained.

'But that's impossible,' vowed Moll, 'Sir Richard spoke of him as if he would employ him to alter his house.'

The scrivener continued, 'Patience, my child. He was famous for an architectural style after the Italian school. What is the scholars' term? Ah yes, Palladio. All London speaks of him as if he still lives, and his style is copied by many famous followers.'

Moll was pleased with the reply, and knew that the old man was a veritable well of information. She thanked God that her ignorance had not been so apparent and that her answer to Sir Richard, whilst not intelligent, had not followed her first line of thought and showed to her future husband, if indeed this he intended to become, that his future wife had been ignorant of the fact that he was speaking merely figuratively. She was quite sure that Sir Richard would not, or indeed could not, have overlooked a *faux pas* of that magnitude. Moll, however, had little to fear, for three days later he proposed to her, and with great misgivings, Moll accepted. They were to be married at the end of the month in St Margaret's Church, Westminster.

Moll, however, felt extremely guilty, since she was with child. Even though Sir Richard was aware that this was merely a marriage of convenience, she decided she must confess everything to him. Sir Richard had arranged to show her around her new home the following Sunday, and early in the afternoon she awaited expectantly for his call.

Moll's heart fluttered as they drove through the city near St James's Park, and the large stately residence came into view. Two tall grey stone towers guarded the entrance, and through these stately vine-covered portals they entered, stopping at the largest pair of wrought iron gates Moll had ever seen. A lackey, clothed in bright red, opened the wide gates at the coachman's bidding, and smoothly the carriage sped on until it reached a turn in the road.

Moll's eyes opened wide with wonder at the beautiful vista which appeared before her. The view was of a lake, ornamented with trees and flowers over which hung huge weeping willow trees, bowing gracefully, nearly touching the water. They rode past enchanting herb and flower gardens, and eventually drew smoothly to a halt in front of the great white mansion which was the home of Sir Richard Howard.

Moll turned expectantly to her fiancé. 'Sire, 'tis beautiful, what do you call this house?'

Sir Richard smiled and was pleased at the enthusiasm showing plainly on her lovely face. 'It is called Green Gables, my dear. Come.'

Taking her hand, he led her slowly into the great hall. In rapturous wonder, Moll gazed about her. The richness and beauty took her breath away, as if in a dream. She allowed Sir Richard to lead her into the drawing room. He rang for a servant who brought them Turkish coffee in exquisite porcelain cups, and small beautifully decorated cakes of marchpane and almond. They sipped coffee and Moll knew in her heart that she could not marry Sir Richard unless he knew the whole story, yea, even her humble beginning. Hesitantly she began to speak. He listened patiently and without interference until her whole life story poured from her lips; then he spoke softly and without emotion.

'Moll, my sweet child, many years ago my dearly beloved wife died childless. It is the wish of my family and my King that I marry and leave behind me a son to become my heir and to bear my name. I can give no woman a child, my dear, and my heart is often heavy for the very dear wife and companion who left me so suddenly. I know your heart can never be mine, and that the child you carry is of noble blood. I can at least ensure the child bears a noble name, and my lands and title I bestow willingly. I shall be proud, m'lady, if you will consent to be my wife.'

With a strangled sob Moll threw herself into his arms. He stroked her raven hair and quietly soothed her, gently comforting her as she clung so tightly to him.

Later that afternoon he accompanied Moll home. He understood she would need time to dispose of her home, and he made it perfectly plain to her that all she need bring with her to her new home were her most cherished possessions, or anything that she felt she did not wish to leave behind.

Moll felt drained and walked slowly up to her room. Her mind was too full of the day's events to even think straight. 'Oh, Charles, I need you,' she murmured to herself, 'I need you so badly.'

Pulling herself together, she rang for Kate and Robin. They appeared too quickly for her to rehearse a speech, and Kate sensed that her mistress had something very important to say to them.

'Please sit down,' she said, 'this may take some time in telling.' As briefly as possible, she explained that very soon she was to become the wife of Sir Richard Howard, and would be moving into his home. Tears welled up in Kate's eyes.

'Hush, child,' said Moll, 'there is more. I shall turn the house and servants over to you both, and pay you an annuity each month to live on. You, Robin, need no longer be employed as a coachman. Perhaps you could start a small business, like purchasing clothes from the merchant ships and selling to the ladies in town. Mrs Wilson, I'm sure, will be only too pleased to help you, if you care to take her into partnership. She is an excellent seamstress and knows everything about fabrics. A small sum of money will be given to the other servants and I am quite sure, if you work together, you will do very well for yourselves.'

Kate and Robin could not believe this turn of events, and with profuse thanks, they left Moll alone to contemplate her future.

Chapter 18

Wedding Plans

A messenger bearing a letter from the King called at the house one afternoon. This was the last letter Moll was to receive from him in this house, and with shaking hands she broke the seal. 'May I offer you my sincere good wishes, my dearest Maria, on your forthcoming marriage. Charles R.' A strangled sob broke from deep inside her and, holding the crumpled letter lightly in her hands, she broke down in a paroxysm of grief.

Some days later, Sir Richard sent a jeweller to discuss with her the details of her wedding ring. He suggested that a Tudor Rose motif, which was incorporated in his coat-of-arms, be engraved around a heavy plain gold band. Inside was to be inscribed – 'Sir Richard & Lady Maria Howard'. Moll was relieved he had not ordered the jeweller to engrave a token of undying love. The inscription chosen was adequate to the occasion.

The question of her gown troubled Moll. She felt the slight thickening of her waist, and knew that the dress would need to be cleverly cut to disguise the early signs of pregnancy. Mrs Wilson had been left to her own devices, and Moll hurried up to the sewing room to see the progress. To her surprise the dress was almost ready, fashioned in deep creamy brocade and embroidered with pale pink Tudor roses, the centre of each being a tiny seed pearl. A full skirt fell gracefully into a long flowing train. The head-dress was of pearls, copied in the old Elizabethan style, shaped to flatter the face. A wedding dress fit for a Queen. Moll was delighted at the painstaking work laboriously undertaken by Mrs Wilson and her helper. They both stood and watched with obvious pleasure as Moll slipped the lovely gown over her head. Moll turned slowly as they watched, enraptured by the beautiful vision before them. Moll thanked them graciously, and left the gown to be completed in time for the wedding in two days.

Sir Richard called each day to enquire if Moll required anything, and to keep her informed of all the wedding plans. The ball to take place at Green Gables was arranged and engraved invitations were now being replied to by all the aristocracy of London.

The day of the wedding arrived and the house was busy with preparations for this great occasion. Moll was ready, a vision of beauty, holding a nosegay of pink roses trimmed with silver ribbons flowing down to her silver shoes. Robin was late – where was the man? Nervous as a kitten, Moll waited impatiently. She could not hear the coach and there was still no sign of her coachman. At last Robin appeared in white livery, his face red with excitement. As he opened the front door, cheering crowds thronged the Court and Robin bravely fought his way through them whilst Moll turned and raised her face to see her servants throwing rose petals from the upper casement windows. With a start she noticed the coach, glittering gold and white, with four eager white horses waving white plumes from their tossing heads, and then she saw the Royal Coat-of-Arms emblazoned on the coach panel. This was the royal coach: 'Oh, Charles,' she murmured brokenly, 'my beloved Charles.'

To the sound of cheers and happy laughter, the coach drove to the beautiful church of St Margaret's in Westminster. She could see the great Abbey standing like a sentinel, its shadow softening the harsh medieval outline of the smaller church. With trembling hands she picked up her nosegay of roses and, as the door was opened by the white liveried lackey, she smiled and waved to the thronging crowds and walked gracefully down the red carpet to the strains of sweet music coming from the massed choir in the church. The congregation rose as she walked down the aisle to her waiting husband-to-be, and throughout the long Anglican service everything went perfectly. Sir Richard glanced down proudly at this beautiful vision standing proud as a Tudor princess – the new Lady Howard, his wife.

A sumptuous banquet at Green Gables followed the ceremony. Moll spoke quietly to Sir Richard and asked permission to change her gown. 'It is a custom here,' he said kindly, 'that brides wear their wedding gown until the festivities are over. I trust you will do this for me?'

Moll smiled and replied that she would be proud to do so. After the banquet, Moll was astounded at the sight of so many beautiful gifts. Sir Richard pointed to a wedding gift set high in a prominent position. The small gift was handed to Moll. As she opened it, a startled cry of surprise broke from her lips. Inside was a beautiful golden ball, studded with rubies and emeralds. As she held it in her hands, she unconsciously triggered a tiny spring and the ball opened! There, nestled on a bed of purple velvet, was a miniature pair of pearl-handled scissors, studded with diamonds.

Sir Richard chuckled, 'Quite beautiful, my dear – Charles has a flair for the unexpected.'

Moll discerned no rancour in his voice and marvelled at the man's control. The present was duly returned to its place of honour and she willingly acquiesced to Sir Richard's suggestion that she rest for an hour before the ball.

A maid led her up the beautiful marble staircase to a comfortable bedroom. Her dress was taken away to be freshened, and cool lotions applied to her face and neck. The ordeal was at last over, she thought, quite forgetting for a moment that it was merely the formalities which were completed. An hour later she was gently roused by the quiet-spoken maid, who led her into a small marble room to bathe. Greatly refreshed, she once again was arrayed in her wedding dress, hair brushed until it shone like the wing of a raven, and the French hood of pearls once more adorned her pretty head.

Sir Richard appeared, kissed her on the cheek, and with her hand resting on his they walked gracefully down the stairs to meet their guests. Moll had been too full of her own appearance even to take stock of her new husband. Whilst he was chatting amiably with his guests, she noticed his appearance for the first time. Tall and slim and dressed in pale blue brocade, a white lacy shirt showing at his throat and wrist and a dress sword buckled across his hips, he seemed taller than she had at first thought. 'Twenty years older than I, at least,' she thought. A brown periwig fell in curls to his shoulders. Nevertheless, he was quite a handsome gentleman, but he aroused no passion in Moll's heart.

As the dancing grew more boisterous a commotion was heard in the far corner of the large ballroom. Moll, busy chatting with one of her husband's friends, took little heed. A hush settled strangely around her and Moll turned. Her heart hammered until she thought it must surely burst, because before her, bowing gracefully, was Charles, the King!

The dance continued, and without a word Charles led her out into the garden. The scent of orange blossoms swirled about her, and as they reached the shadows of the rose garden his lips hungrily sought hers. 'My darling, my darling,' he murmured, 'oh, how I love you.'

The temptation to stay in his arms almost persuaded her to flee with him to his apartments across the park; instead she willed herself to say, 'This is my wedding night. I must return to my husband.'

'Your husband in name only, my sweet one; you will never belong to any man but me,' said Charles.

With a strangled cry, she picked up her wedding gown train, and hurriedly composed herself to appear calm and unruffled before her guests.

As the ball came to a close, the guests bade their hosts goodnight, and finally Moll was alone with her new husband. He held her warm hands between his and gently kissed each finger. 'My beautiful wife,' he murmured, 'come, we shall retire.' With her hand resting on his, he led her gently up the marble staircase to the white and gold bedroom. A maid servant awaited her, and Sir Richard left the room. As if in a dream, she felt the capable hands of the young maid wash her with perfumed water and slip over her head the lacy nightgown for the wedding night. An old woman came into the room with a bed warming pan, and slid it deftly between the sheets. The great curtains of the bed were drawn back, and with her hair loosely cascading around her shoulders, the new Lady Howard awaited her husband. Sir Richard entered quietly, his slim figure accentuated by a tightly fitting gown. He looked smaller without his periwig and she saw that his hair was brown and curled softly about his neck. He snuffed out the candles, and stepped soundlessly into bed. Moll stiffened as his hand gently caressed her cheek. Then, to her utter amazement, he kissed her gently on the brow, and quietly went to sleep! Moll could hardly believe it. Had Charles known this man so intimately that he had arranged this marriage so conveniently for both of them?' She would wait and see.

Sir Richard was a perfect gentleman in every way. They enjoyed a peculiar kind of love, which defied all explanation. A kiss and an affectionate embrace sufficed. No jealousies marred this relationship; neither did questions from either encroach on the other's privacy. Each day Moll grew more content as the child within her moved. At times she would walk in St James's Park and Charles met her there. As the time for her lying-in drew near, she walked less frequently abroad, but letters from her royal lover arrived each day, sometimes accompanied by exquisitely fashioned nosegays.

Christmas came and slipped by, and Moll was feeling tired and listless. One early morning in Spring, Moll felt sure that this was to be the day she was to give birth to the child of the King. Her labour was long and arduous and when she finally thought she could travail no longer, her son was born. No mistaking this child, he surely was the son of his father. A long baby, with elegantly slim hands, dark complexion and a wealth of dark hair growing low on the nape of his neck. He bawled loudly and was hurriedly scooped up by a very relieved midwife who, despite his howling, gave him the first washing of his young life. He was then placed tenderly in the arms of his beautiful mother. Moll loved this baby the moment she saw him, and wondered at Sir Richard's feelings as he softly tiptoed into the room.

'He is beautiful, my dear, I shall honour the trust you place in me.' He kissed both Moll and the baby gently, and quietly left the room.

A messenger was dispatched to Whitehall and late that evening, Charles arrived to pay his respects to the new parents. Sir Richard bowed as the King strode purposefully up the stairs to Moll's bedroom. Moll's eyes sparkled as Charles burst into her room. His genuine concern was still a great wonder to her and he questioned her closely about her health. As if she was a fragile piece of porcelain, he enfolded her and whispered, 'My wife, my beloved wife.' Moll clung to him, almost forgetting about her new son until a loud cry broke the spell. They both turned towards the child and, with a big hearty laugh, Charles picked up the squalling bundle and gazed for the first time into the dark eyes, so very much like his own. His son, who could never be king, who could not even be named Prince!

Moll was enchanted by Charles's obvious pleasure, and as he sat beside her holding her close, she whispered softly, 'Charles, what shall we call him?'

Without hesitation, he answered, 'Stuart Charles Howard. A noble name, my love, for a lad with Stuart blood.' He then took his leave, and Moll, tired now, left her son in the care of the nurses, who did not know that in their care was the son of the King of England.

Moll grew happily accustomed to her new life and the baby boy who was a joy both to her husband and herself. Their relationship grew warmer, until Moll found herself seeking her husband's company more and more, and this rather unconventional marriage filled a special kind of need for them both. It delighted her to see Richard's behaviour towards her child. He spoiled him outrageously, and was continually plotting and scheming to send the baby's nanny off on some trivial errand in order to have the boy to himself, knowing that on her return she would whisk him off, prise the forbidden sweetmeat from the baby's tightly clenched fist, and huffily bear the screaming child back to the nursery. This stopped Richard not a jot; in fact, Moll knew that his daily sorties with Nanna Pearson were a continual source of amusement to him.

Moll was far too amused to spoil his pleasure, but also found the formidable Nanny rather strong flesh for her taste, too. She consoled Nanna with the never fulfilled promise that she would speak very strongly to his Lordship on the matter. This common bond only strengthened the ties between them, and Sir Richard took the child with him on every possible occasion. Young Stuart revelled in these outings, small as he was, and cried with temper if his father deigned to cross the threshold without him.

Charles, too, loved the boy, and planned his future according to his noble birth. This distressed Moll deeply, for she knew only too well that favours from the King could point out to the world the indiscretions of the mother. The lad had noble lineage inherited from his legal father, who had already arranged for his coat-of-arms to be adopted by his son. The thought of her child bearing a coat-of-arms crossed by the black band of bastardy was beyond thought. The sinister band would never be worn by this boy, son of the King or not. With this thought firmly planted in her mind, Moll vowed that the King must know how she felt. To soften the blow to his pride, she could always suggest the Order of the Bath, which was justified by his father's rank, and would therefore cause no tongues to wag.

Other than these problems, Moll's life was extremely happy. She wanted for nothing, and her every wish was granted. Her joy was increased when she learned that her beloved Kate was to have a child. In the past, Kate had confided to her Mistress how much they desired children, and after the death of her first, Moll had often heard her sobbing quietly, night after night. As Moll read the letter from Kate, she whispered to herself the old prayer to help women in travail: 'God, stay with thee and may the Immaculate Virgin grant thee a speedy and safe delivery, for after pain cometh deliverance. Amen.'

Winter passed and the scent of Spring flowers filled the lovely garden where she often walked breathing in the fragrance, for Moll loved Springtime. This was the season she remembered as a child, recalling the old pagan festivals re-enacted in the village each year. The Morris dancers, heralding summer, the village maids dancing around the Green, portraying the half-forgotten fertility rites of long dead ancestors. The night when, unknown to the village priest, a cockerel was sacrificed under the full moon to appease the old gods. Yes, oh yes, Moll had her own memories of Spring, even the fragrance of the flowers now bending their heads in the breeze.

Soon it was early Summer, and although Moll still visited Charles in his apartments, she knew that they too had discovered a new relationship. Although the fire still blazed fiercely between them, this was a relationship they treasured beyond words. Moll demanded nothing from him and Charles was grateful from the bottom of his heart, for every woman he had known before had eventually requested personal favours. Here was a woman who asked only to be loved, not forever but just for the few precious hours they spent together.

Moll looked out over the vast grounds of Green Gables. Was it really only five years since she had first seen this great city? It seemed incredible. So many things had happened in such a short space of time. News had come this very morning that Kate had been safely delivered of a daughter, and Moll could hardly contain her impatience, for she was to be godmother to this already loved baby, and was even now awaiting the carriage to speed her to Great Swordbearers Alley. A great chest containing gifts for the child was placed in the coach by the two footmen, as they soon began the journey through the city.

Hardly waiting for the great wheels to stop turning, Moll leaped from the coach, to the great consternation of the footman. They then found themselves being ushered quickly into the warm kitchen by Mrs Wilson, and food and wine were pressed into Moll's hands before she was taken up to Kate's room. Kate was positively glowing, and as Moll entered, said not a word, but held out to her beloved friend the most beautiful baby she had ever seen. Silver down covered the beautifully shaped head, and great violet eyes stared up into her own. Moll gasped with pleasure, 'Oh Kate, she is exquisite.' And indeed she was.

'I shall call her Moll,' said Kate.

'Involuntarily, Moll cried, 'No, no, Kate, this baby shall not bear such a lowly name. I shall be undone to think that she will carry my old name through life, whilst I have discarded it. I wish to choose the child a name. Nay with your permission, I have already chosen it.'

Without hearing what she intended to call the baby, Kate agreed.

'Roxanne, my dear,' whispered Moll, 'we shall call her Roxanne. Her full name should be Roxanne Maria.'

This was fully acceptable to everyone, and the next few hours were spent in companionable chatter for it had been some weeks since the friends had last talked together privately.

The pleasant visit came to an end; the only disturbing news was that a plague was reaching epidemic proportions and Moll realized that Kate was extremely concerned for, as she was leaving, she noticed a strong smell of herbs and vinegar. With alarm she realized that Kate was using prophylactic measures to ward off the plague. The signs grew ominous for Kate was not a person to take things seriously if there was no need. Moll shuddered at the dreadful portent of these measures. Hurriedly, the coach drove back to Green Gables and Moll felt a sense of security as the great gates opened for them. This was dispelled, however, for on reaching the great white portals, a footman, white faced and agitated, told her that Sir Richard wished to see her immediately.

She hurried to the library where her husband who took her hands in his and whispered, 'You must leave here today, Moll, nay this very hour; sad news, sad news indeed. Two servants have fallen sick, and the physician is afraid they have the plague – the Black Death!'

The dreaded words crashed into Moll's ears. In horror she gazed up at him and felt her senses reel.

'Come, my darling, I wish you to travel with our son to your parent's home until this has abated; at least you will be safer there.'

'But you must come, too, Richard,' she cried, for the thought of leaving him in the plague-ridden city was too much for her to contemplate.

Sir Richard smiled sadly, and said, 'My dear, I cannot. Charles will need me, and I have grave misgivings regarding Clarendon. The Royalist Government have been circulating angry rumours that he has influence over the King, which is dangerous. Charles will need my help if the country is not to be plunged into civil war.'

Moll knew that she could protest no further, and that whatever else Richard might be, he was a staunch Royalist. Everything was ready for her journey, for her husband had previously given orders that all was to be made ready by the time her ladyship arrived. Such was Moll's hurried exit from London, and hardly was there time to bid the servants farewell.

Chapter 19

Plauge in London

The journey out of London was no pleasure for Moll this time, for she noticed with dismay the increase of traffic on the road. Crowds of people were hurrying from the great city, and the mass exodus filled the narrow roads for many miles. The journey was slow and laborious, and Moll felt sad for the people with no carriages who struggled on as best they could, heavily laden like beasts of burden. She could not offer help to these people, for Sir Richard had warned her that the roads would be crowded and dangerous, and pleaded with her not to stop the coach for any reason whatsoever. She must close her eyes to the mass of humanity so burdened. The inns were full, however, and by necessity Moll opened the great basket of food by the wayside. Children hovered as the cloth was laid on the grass, and Moll knew that they hungered. After her entourage had eaten, the rest was shared out to the hovering children, and the coach headed as quickly as circumstances allowed towards White Towers.

Moll was relieved to see the tall chimneys of her parent's house in the distance. A weary set of travellers arrived unexpected and unannounced at the great house. Her parents were surprised and delighted to see them, but their joy soon turned to dread at the news of the Black Death. Their first thought was for Moll's husband. Moll assured them he was in the best of health, omitting to mention the fact that two of the servants were dreadfully ill with the plague, for she could see that this news had already badly disturbed her mother.

A meal was quickly prepared, and they ate their fill. Stuart was enjoying his new surroundings thoroughly and had already adopted a fierce-looking sheep and a dog who instantly considered the small boy his master. Moll saw the boy had a way with dogs, and realized that his father too was very seldom seen without at least one spaniel puppy barking at his heels. His son was obviously an animal lover also, and Moll realized that his sheltered life in the big house had given the boy no room for natural boyish enthusiasm. There he was watched constantly, but now, freed from the trappings of nobility, he made full use of his newly found liberty. Moll saw it was good for the boy to run around free as the wind, for this child had never even known what it was to have dirty hands.

The days slipped pleasantly by, and letters arrived often from Sir Richard telling her the sad news of the plague, which by now had evidently reached alarming proportions. Thoughts of Kate and the lovely baby trapped at the centre of the city alarmed her, and with all speed, she dispatched a letter requesting that Kate and the baby be contacted and invited to White Towers for safety.

The reply, delayed somewhat by transport difficulties, informed Moll that Kate and her baby would arrive at White Towers the following Tuesday; but on that day no coach arrived from London, and Moll felt very concerned for her friend's safety. She waited each day for the sound of a carriage, until she felt sure Kate had changed her mind, for over a week had elapsed since she had received the letter of acceptance. She had almost lost hope when a sudden commotion in the yard told her that her guests had at last arrived, and a delighted Moll welcomed Kate and the baby with open arms. The two friends shed tears of joy as they strolled inside to meet Moll's parents. The gossip, of course, was of the happenings in London, but Kate's stories were dreadful to hear. Moll blanched as she heard the news; people they both knew and respected had been stricken down suddenly. The old shoemaker who fashioned such beautiful soft leather shoes, the buttonmaker from Great Swordbearers Alley, together with the whole of the Sibbering family and their workers had all perished in the same week, leaving only Sarah, the wife, to mourn alone.

Moll was desolate at these tidings, and listened with tears in her eyes, for these were the friends who had mourned Roxanne, and in their time of trouble, she had been unable to comfort them, and now they were all dead. Kate told her everything – the red crosses on the doors which filled the streets with evil tidings, rich or poor, heathen or Christian – all fell victims of this monstrous reaper – the Black Death.

With a breaking heart, Kate related the story of the great plague pits, and how graves could no longer be found to bury the dead; no-one could help an afflicted neighbour for they knew that if they did, they too would be in their in graves. She told of small children sobbing for dead mothers, yet no one daring to give them shelter; people demented with fever throwing themselves into the Thames to meet a hasty end by drowning.

No food was available from the shops, and what little there was in the market was soon sold. People placed their money in tins containing vinegar and strong aromatic herbs, for vendors would not touch the hand of any man, even to take money. Personal contact was avoided as much as possible, Kate went on to say, and both she and Robin had heard all these sad stories from the priest who spoke to them at a great distance, cupping his hands to his mouth to make his voice carry. They, too, had avoided contact with everyone, and on her way to White Towers all these stories had been confirmed for she had seen the terrible scenes for herself. Her one fear now was for her beloved husband, Robin. She had bade him travel with her to White Towers and flee the city until this pestilence was over. He had declined, saying that if he abandoned the house they would return to find it ransacked and looted, possibly even burnt to the ground.

With a sad heart Kate had known his words were true, and begged him to stay with friends on the south side of the city where the plague had not yet touched. This he promised to do, and Kate had felt a bit relieved, but had still been loath to leave him. At least she and her daughter would be safe, and she prayed to God that he be granted the same salvation.

After Kate had washed and changed she felt a little better and walked with Moll around the beautiful gardens. The house was now completed and very comfortable, and the two girls felt their spirits lift with the beauty of their surroundings, which soothed the memories of the great troubled city. Neither spoke for some time, for nothing could as yet wipe out the sad thoughts completely, and both girls missed their husbands sorely. Unspoken words echoed in each of their minds, both wondering if they would ever see their menfolk again.

Moll's son, oblivious of his mother's fears, was enjoying every minute of his holiday. He had never been in close proximity to a baby before, and the beautiful Roxanne captivated him completely. He would stand quietly watching her sleep, and played with her tiny hands, gazing in rapture at the shell-like nails. The baby, dog, chickens and birds all captivated this small boy from the city, and Moll watched his skin tan darkly in the summer sun.

Two months passed, and still there was no news from their husbands to return home. In fact, the messages they did receive only confirmed their worst fears – the plague was not abating. They now knew that many months would be spent at White Towers. Moll discovered that the country was as unfamiliar to Kate as it was to Stuart, and to pass the time tried to teach her the old ways of how to make butter, cheese, bread and wine. Kate's attempts at making bread turned out disastrously for it was rock hard, very different from the huge brown crusty loaves that Moll made.

As September drew to a close, Moll and Kate decided to pick the blackberries from the lane. Armed with large pipkins they roamed freely, choosing only large ripe berries for the next year's wine. Moll wandered away from Kate, for she knew where the finest berries were to be gathered, and realized that she was quite alone, close to the old Tabard Inn. Whatever possessed her to enter she knew not, but was soon greeted very cordially by the landlord's wife. They talked of the bad news from London, and Mrs Lightbody told her they had found it necessary to close the inn for their own safety. Casually she mentioned that one of the last visitors was the gentleman companion who had been so kind to Moll, Sir James. Moll's heart gave a lurch, and as casually as she could, asked if he was in good health.

'Well,' said the good wife, 'he appeared well enough to me, madam, but 'tis said his wife was taken early on in the year, not by the plague, mark you, the sweating sickness, 'twas.'

Moll knew she could tarry no longer for the night was drawing in, and she walked the two miles back home with her mind full of the landlady's chatterings. On reaching home, she found the family in a great turmoil and was very severely scolded by all for her tardiness and for going to the Tabard, which was no place for a lady to pay a social call.

Thoughts of Sir James welled up freshly in her mind as she bade her family goodnight. Guiltily, she also wondered how her husband was faring, and also her household in London.

Chapter 20

Plague Comes to Green Gables

Back at Green Gables, Sir Richard was desperately worried, and with just cause for he had walked alone into a strange city, a city of havoc and death, terrifying to behold. Unbelievingly, he had trodden the once familiar lanes and seen no-one. A strangled sob broke from his lips and, retracing his steps, he wearily entered the large gates of Green Gables, knowing that the great gates must be closed for many weeks on the outside world, making both himself and his household staff prisoners.

He was a pale and shaken man. He called his staff together to relate the situation and his decision to lock the gates in order to restrict their movements solely to the house and grounds. Their faces blanched, for they knew that they could not leave the house for many weeks to come. They quickly realized that these strong measures were for their own good, however, and gave promises that, no matter how irksome, they would abide by their master's wishes, for only by doing so would they survive. One fifteen-year-old serving wench, however, was not listening to these instructions. She had an appointment with her latest admirer in the park that very night, and neither Sir Richard nor anyone else would be any the wiser, she reasoned. As dusk fell, she quietly slipped through a gap in the hedge and spent the night with her lover.

Forty-eight hours later she was taken ill, and as the clothes were stripped from her perspiring body the telltale spots and buboes appeared before the eyes of her horrified friend who was caring for her. She alone knew of Seth's indiscretions. Her hysterical screams brought other servants to the door, but none ventured into the room, for the dreaded word 'plague' sent the whole household into panic.

Sir Richard was called as he sat writing to Moll, and looked up from his letter when he heard the commotion. As the dreadful story permeated his brain, he folded his arms on the table and laid his head down and silently and reverently prayed. The servants stood by, watching and waiting at the door, no-one moving, an ominous pregnant silence prevailing. When Sir Richard finally lifted his head, tears were trickling down his face, his whole being stunned, for he knew they expected him to issue orders. What could he do? He felt too drained and stunned to act.

The dreadful silence was broken by the strangled hysterical sob of a serving maid, which activated his mind, and questions formed themselves. Without realizing, he spoke his thoughts out loud.

'Who will nurse her?' he asked. A murmur of dread passed through the servants, but no reply was given by anyone. He could not send her to the pest house for then the whole city would know of the visitation, and the house was large enough to be commandeered as a pest house should word get around that it was already contaminated. This was too horrible to think about.

Finally, he rose wearily and, with heavy feet, headed towards the servants' quarters. Nobody else would enter the sick room, because death would strike at the most careful of visitors. Outside the small room he heard the sound of sobbing, and came across the young girl who had first discovered the plague victim, demented by fear, knowing she would be an outcast and eventually carried off to the plague pit.

Sir Richard called softly, 'Child, listen, follow my instructions carefully. Burn all the clothes you are now wearing, and cut off all thy hair. Use a large scrubbing brush, and scrub all the infection from thy body. Take strong vinegar and herbs and anoint thyself; after this drink a strong emetic; we shall save thee, lass, never fear!'

These empty words were spoken with such fervour that they gave the wench hope, for she had had none before, and she quickly hurried off to do his bidding.

He then held a 'kerchief soaked in vinegar to his face and entered the dreaded room to find the small body of the indiscreet serving girl quite lifeless. Leaving immediately, he wondered what he could do to stop this dreadful scourge from spreading. How futile it all was. The months of captivity, the endless care taken with food, the nightly roll call of all the servants – how had this minx fooled them all? From deep inside he felt a wild hatred and anger at this stupid girl. With an oath, he pulled a torch from the wall crying, 'No, we shall not all perish through the careless and selfish indiscretions of one girl.' He put fire to the bed and watched the flames engulf the whole room and choking with the fumes he left the servants' block.

He made his way into the courtyard and stopped the servants, who were even now carrying buckets of water to fight the roaring inferno. 'Do not quench it! Let it destroy the plague, there is no other way,' and together they watched the great fire light up the building that was their home.

A small voice brought him back to his next problem, for standing beside him, scrubbed and shorn of hair, was the one contact of the dead girl. She had a horse blanket around her shoulders, teeth chattering in the cold night air, and large eyes round with fear patiently waiting for him to speak.

'Listen carefully, child. I have but two choices. The first is that I can turn you out into the city where you will surely perish; the other is that you be confined in the old woodcutter's cottage, alone, for the next three weeks.'

A sharp intake of breath came from the girl, ending in tumultuous sobs.

'Hush, child, fresh food will be sent to you each day, but you will speak to no-one. Do not try to contact the servants, for I shall give instructions that anyone disobeying these rules will leave the house forthwith. Only in this way can we prevent the plague from spreading.' The young girl thanked him, and sadly made her way to the lonely cottage, grateful that she had not been sent out into the plague-ridden city.

The servants now realized what a narrow escape they had had, if indeed it should prove successful, and they knew that Sir Richard would not have to punish the next transgressor. A committee was formed who vowed that the next offender would die by their hands.

The three weeks passed uneventfully, and the girl was finally pronounced clear of infection. with great rejoicing, she was accepted back into the house by the other servants.

Time passed very slowly for Sir Richard and the rest of the household. Quarrels ensued between friends, which under normal circumstances would have been unthinkable. Summer came and left London bringing with it the peak of the plague, but by September people who would normally have died were now recovering. Perhaps a natural immunity had developed, who knows? But it was an established fact that the long siege was slowly coming to an end.

The first clue that Sir Richard had that things were getting back to normal came early one morning as he went to the gates to collect Moll's letter. To his amazement, he heard a voice shouting, 'Laces and ribbons, fair maids, what do ye lack? Come and buy, come and buy, my pretty ones.'

He opened the gates to find a pedlar with a tray piled high with fripperies, calling his wares. The pedlar saw the great gates swing open and stopped, thinking he had a customer. 'What news?' asked Sir Richard, 'what news of the plague?'

'The city is clear, sire,' came the reply, 'we have had no deaths from plague for three weeks.'

'God be praised, at last we are free!' answered Sir Richard.

He ran back to the house and told the glad tidings to the servants, who danced with joy, and ran to the great gates cheering madly. The gates swung open and the whole household emptied.

Sir Richard's first impulse was to send for Moll and the boy to return home immediately. But on second thoughts he decided that parts of the great house required freshening, so instead he requested that she delay her homecoming until the end of October. At least by then London would resemble the great city she had left many weeks previously. Merchants were already returning from their forced exile, and he knew that Maria would be shocked at the deterioration which had come about in so short a time.

The next day he called the servants together and spoke frankly to them. He realized, he said, the dreadful hardships they had endured, and under the circumstances would leave them free of duties until Monday morning. Monday, however, would be the beginning of a mammoth clean-up and masons would be called in to rebuild the burned-out wing. He gave instructions to his stewards regarding refurbishing, and instructed the coachman to have the carriage ready by noon.

The carriage gleamed as it drew up to the great stone portals. Sir Richard climbed inside and gave instructions for the coachman to drive to the coffee house in St Martin's Lane. Proudly, the driver cracked his whip and off they drove. The leading bays tossed their heads as if they too realized this new found freedom. St. Martin's Lane was almost back to normal, and Sir Richard was overjoyed to see so many of his old friends embracing one another with unashamed affection. He dismissed the coachman, for he knew that he could easily hire a carriage to take him home, and it was only right that this lad should enjoy the day off afforded the other servants. Sir Richard joined the milling throng on the pavements, enjoying the companionship of his friends whom he had missed so much. Questions were asked about absent friends who, thank God, were few, and as the optimists amongst them so rightly said, the day was yet young and perhaps they had been delayed in coming.

Conversation, strangely enough, was not of the disaster and tragedies they had all suffered, but instead of the new spirit of adventure and comradeship that had been born. 'The phoenix has risen from the ashes,' whispered Sir Richard to himself. How wonderful to hear them discussing shipping again, new routes to the Spice Islands and even snippets of talk regarding a new beverage called tea.

Laughter and gay banter thus returned to the coffee houses of London. The whole city looked forward to a rebirth, for once more, after so many months of misery and horror, it felt good to be alive.

Chapter 21

The Homecoming

The long awaited letter finally reached Moll, and she could hardly contain herself from hiring a coach there and then and dispatching both Stuart and herself back to London forthwith.

Calming down a little, she realized that her husband must have good reasons for imposing a delay such as this, and resigned herself to a further three weeks' stay at White Towers.

Kate, too, received a message on the following day asking her to return home to her husband as quickly as possible, and that all was well. She required no further bidding, and raced up to her room to begin packing for the next coach to London.

Laden with fresh country produce, Kate bade her kind hosts goodbye and, with great promises to write, waved a last farewell as the coach commenced its long journey to London.

Moll passed the long day of waiting by playing with her son, and was amused to find that he had quite a flair for mimicking the animals, even the rare goshawk cry poured out of his throat. Dogs, cats, hens, birds - even the poor old horse with the dreadful cough was not spared. Moll howled with laughter for his face was deadly serious and the sounds were so true to life that it seemed impossible for such a small boy to produce them. She looked at his dark head, his twinkling eyes almost black, enjoying every minute of their companionship. He really was a darling, she thought, and tickling him until he rolled over helplessly, she nuzzled his neck with her face until he shrieked with laughter. Moll knew that Stuart's nanny would never allow such goings on or approve of such behaviour. 'Bed, bed,' she shouted, and clapping her hands, chased him indoors where the hated sponge and water awaited him. After tucking him in bed and listening to his prayers she told him a story, but long before it was finished he had fallen fast asleep. Softly she placed a kiss on his adorable face, blew out the candle and retired into her own room to begin her evening toilet before dinner. Two days more, she thought, and then London. Oh, it would be good to be home, for as kind as her parents had been, she missed her husband and home.

She found things so dreadfully quiet; how she wished it were Saturday. The day dawned at last, and both Moll and Stuart had been packed and ready to leave a good two hours before the carriage was due. It arrived at last, kisses and hugs were exchanged and last goodbyes said. Moll looked back at White Towers and her family and hoped she would see them soon in London, for they had promised to come for the Christmas festivities. The coach rattled on and soon she lost sight of the house. Two miles further on, the Tabard Inn hove into sight, and that too was soon lost in the distance. There were no stops on the outward journey for the coach was not a public vehicle, but her own, emblazoned with the coat-of-arms of the Howards.

She snuggled down in the warm upholstery, wrapping the white fur rugs about them both, pointing out things of interest to Stuart as they sped through the countryside heading for the high road to London. On and on they went, until a brightly lit inn came into view, and the coach pulled into the inn yard, dogs barking at the horses' heels in welcome.

Moll gave orders they would tarry here for the night. Stuart was too young to stand the long journey in one day, and the horses required changing on the morrow. She, too, was feeling tired and travel strained. They alighted and she stretched her aching body in the cool night air before the landlord ushered them inside. She was delighted with the hospitality here. The White Swan had a good reputation in England and it was well earned for the landlord was extremely careful. A maid led her to an upstairs chamber, spotlessly clean and beautifully appointed with hangings of blue and white; the bed coverings were crisp and clean and the floor scrubbed to showy perfection and covered with sheepskin rugs. Ready for use stood a large bowl of water, clean homespun towels and a block of hard white soap. As she entered, a second maid was already running a large warming pan over the sheets and, just for a second or two, laied it between the towels to warm them also.

Stuart was tired and hungry but, before the words left her lips, the maid who had first shown them the room returned bearing a tray containing hot thick broth, a small piece of steamed fish with butter, and a sticky-looking pink sweet. Ruffling the child's head, she said, 'You're a fine big laddie,' then, to Moll, 'Supper will be ready downstairs in one hour, m'lady.'

Moll was astounded at the girl's quickness, and turned to find that her son was already taking advantage by starting on the sticky sweet, obviously hoping that his mother would not notice. Moll saw that it was too late to put the meal in the right order, and merely watched with surprise as the small boy ate everything before him. His black eyes drooped with tiredness, and she gave him a quick wash and soon he was asleep.

Moll realized she had no water for her own toilet, but as if her thoughts had been heard, the busy servant once more appeared bearing fresh water and towels. She prepared herself for supper, choosing a plain gown, but when she was finally ready to descend the stairs, she realized she would have to go downstairs alone. 'Perhaps the landlord will escort me,' she thought, nervously fingering her gown, but he was engaged in conversation with another guest and the kindly man did not notice her predicament. Her courage deserting her, she turned to retreat back to her room when a gentle voice startled her.

'May I, m'lady?'

Her whole body trembled, for as she lifted her head she met the steady gaze of Sir James. For an awful moment she felt her senses reel, but quickly she pulled herself together, placed her hand gently on his arm and in a daze, was escorted in for supper. As a myriad of thoughts raced through her mind, he drew her chair up to the table. In her panic she found herself speechless. He questioned her about her choice of food, but in her confusion she merely answered, 'The same as yourself, James.' She found she had no appetite for food, and ate little.

As they sipped a glass of wine, he whispered, 'My darling, at last; it has been so long, I have searched the country for you.'

Moll was at a loss for words for she knew that her whole being was captivated by this man, yet how could she explain that she was the wife of one man and courtesan of another – the King himself, to boot!

'I shan't,' she vowed, 'there is no purpose to it, 'twill avail him not.' With this decision firmly implanted in her mind she vowed to tell him simply about her marriage to Sir Richard, leaving out the intimate details of their marriage, for this she felt was personal and unnecessary to reveal.

He glanced suddenly at her across the table, as if intercepting her thoughts, and gently took her hand. He immediately became aware of her ring. 'A wedding band,' he whispered, and a hoarse 'no' broke involuntarily from his lips. Moll could do no more than nod her head numbly. His face was pale as he questioned her about her husband, who was, she discovered, well known to Sir James. At least, they frequented the same club in London, and sometimes discussed the business of the day together.

It was obvious he was dreadfully taken aback by the news, and even though she tried to talk with him in a normal manner, she could tell it had disheartened him greatly. The meal lay untouched before them; only the wine was taken and both of them had little idea of what they were drinking. A stony silence lay between them. Suddenly rising from the table, he placed his cloak about her shoulders and led her to the deserted annex, which led into the garden. Closing the door behind him, he took her swiftly into his arms, his whole body yearning for her.

'Moll, my darling, I have loved you for so long, and now 'tis too late.' His kisses rained down upon her wet cheek, a man's kisses telling her that he desired her more than anything in the world. Her pulses raced and she felt herself returning his ardour. Nothing mattered, they existed only in a timeless void. The perfume of her enfolded him complete. He knew that all the honour in the world was at this moment as nothing compared to this exquisite creature. He had never before experienced this all-consuming desire to possess a woman, and at this moment he would give his soul for one night with her. Moll had no resistance left. The only man she had ever known intimately was Charles, and as she well knew, any fidelity she had given to him was very certainly not returned. It was common knowledge he had slept with every aristocratic courtesan in Europe, plus a few not so blue blooded, to boot. But this was no time to think of reasons. All she could think of was that she wanted James as much as he wanted her. As she followed him through the now deserted inn to his room, her only thought was that she had waited so very long for this man.

He opened the door to find the candelabra unlit, but the fire crackled and shed a rosy glow into each corner of the room. He slipped his black cloak from around her shoulders and gently kissed the nape of her graceful neck. Turning her towards him, he teasingly kissed the tip of her nose and chaffed her gently, 'Come, my sweetling, a glass of wine and a kiss for the gentleman,' and he handed her a goblet of sweet red wine. She sipped it slowly, knowing that she too would play a waiting game.

For just a little longer she playfully shook her head as he bent forward to claim a kiss, her eyes twinkling in the firelight. 'Enough, enough,' he moaned, and taking the goblet from her, he held her once more in his arms, gently persuading, yet burning the very soul from her body. His hands, warm and gentle, caressed her face and hair, his fingers tracing the delicate line of her throat until she felt him undo the catch of her bodice. She felt his hands moving over her shoulders and slowly slipping down to where the King's locket lay in the cleavage of her breasts. He undid the clasp, and she felt it slip from her throat, and he laid it on the table behind him.

Her body melted into his, but he had waited too long to spoil this first evening with a hastily managed relationship. Moll was thankful that he understood. He kissed her over and over again, his hands caressing her shoulders and back, now urgently demanding. Her petticoat slipped to the floor, and as it lay in folds around her feet, he whispered, 'My beautiful, darling Moll, be mine, for I need you so.'

Her nipples grew hard at his touch, and quickly he carried her to the bed, looking down for a moment at her naked body. The sight inflamed him for her body was as a goddess – large pointed breasts, slim hips, and beautiful creamy skin. He bent down and kissed her breasts, utterly adoring her.

'James, I need you,' she whispered.

With all the passion of his being, he made love to her. She felt absolutely and completely loved. 'Moll,' he whispered, 'I must see you again – I couldn't bear to lose you once more.'

She hushed him gently, and said, 'No, my darling, it's too dangerous.'

'I'll find a way, sweetling, God's oath, I will,' he said, smothering her face with kisses.

Moll quickly jumped out of bed and wrapped a blanket around herself. She hurriedly slipped out the door, returning a few minutes later, after having checked upon her sleeping son. They slept together until cock's crow when Moll awoke with a start. 'Darling, I must go before Stuart awakens,' she said quickly. Playfully he tried to stop her, but sensing the urgency in her voice he realized that soon the coach would be ready to depart. He watched her dress, taking in every graceful movement as she stepped into her gown. He fastened the laces for her, and she brushed her long hair. He extricated the brush from her long slim fingers and brushed her raven locks until they shone. She held out her hand for the brush and received a kiss instead. 'James,' she scolded, 'give it to me, I prithee.'

'Not until you tell me when I shall see you again,' he replied.

'In the church of St Peter in Westminster on Sunday,' she replied, but he shook his head.

''Tis too public, leave it to me,' he vowed. 'I shall arrange it.'

With this she kissed him and quickly and discreetly returned to her own room where her son still slept peacefully. She awoke the sleeping child, and amidst violent protests, escorted him down to breakfast. He ate heartily and was soon scampering over to the coach, begging the coachman for a ride on the great horses.

The coachman was having a hard time trying to catch Stuart and rein in the horses at the same time, and Moll laughed as he swore at the boy, dragging him unceremoniously from beneath the carriage wheels. Duly reprimanded by his mother, and smarting from the hearty cuff over the ear which the coachman had craftily landed him, his mother climbed into the coach. Stuart quietened down, to gaze out of the window for at least five minutes. The memory of the chastisement, however, soon left him and as the coach pulled out of the sunny yard he passed the time by putting his tongue out at the little girl who lived at the farm next door. She, meanwhile, was pulling faces back at him. All this escaped Moll who was looking back at the doorway to where Sir James was standing, his brown eyes saying silently, 'I love you, I love you.'

The coach pulled quickly away and turned into the lane. The horses, refreshed, tossed their heads and lifted their feet which clattered noisily on the cobbles.

Off they sped with thirty miles to go before reaching London, but Moll answered the child's questions in monosyllables, not hearing his prattle for her mind was full of James. Stuart eventually realized his mother was not listening, so contented himself by playing cats cradle with a piece of twine, making up stories and planning how the very moment he saw his father he would ask for a dog and a horse, too, yes, a large black one of his very own. Both mother and son, each engrossed in their own thoughts, were startled to hear Dickon, the coachman, shout 'London Bridge, m'lady.'

Moll took Stuart by the hand on leaving the coach, calling back to the coachman to wait for her on the other side in one hour. Moll warned little Stuart to obey and be a very good boy, and she would buy him some sweets. He was enchanted with the bridge and the mighty river swirling below, with boats shooting the rapids and drenching the curious spectators. They passed the muffin man, the hot pasties sellers, and live poultry for sale. Stuart asked for a muffin, which he ate with relish; then he wanted a spinning top, which Moll also purchased for him. When they reached the church, which was situated in the centre of the bridge, Moll saw there was a wedding taking place, so they joined the crowd of well wishers, and the bride and groom threw money for the guests to squabble over. Moll was surprised at this custom being carried on in London, until she noticed the ruddy cheeks of the bride, which meant she was most likely a country girl, for London fashion thus decreed, 'Ladies wear roses on their dress, not in their cheeks.'

They strolled on happily, and suddenly a hand on Moll's arm surprised her. 'Spare silver for an old lady, m'lady. Spare a coin.' Moll rummaged in her purse and dropped a coin in the old lady's hand. With that, the old lady said, 'Tarry a moment, Maria. I must tell you something. You are in love with a man, not your husband. The next child you bear will not be the same father as the lad here. Tread warily, m'lady, tread warily.'

Before Moll could collect her senses, she was gone. How did the woman know her name, let alone such intimate facts about her? With a shudder, she swept Stuart up into her arms and ran the few yards to the coach, to find Dickon waiting for her. The horses were champing impatiently at the bit, anxious to continue the journey home.

Moll sat pensively in the darkest corner of the coach, absent-mindedly replying to the continuous chatter of the child, and missing the sights of the city as the coach rattled quickly through the busy streets. What could the future hold? Was any faith at all to be placed in the old woman's words? The incident had disturbed her far more than she cared to admit. When Dickon announced that they were nearly home, she forced thoughts of the fortune teller's words out of her mind, and came back to the present.

The tall white stone pillars of the drive entrance flashed before her, and in the distance she heard the entrance bell dinging the news of her return to the household. Richard appeared at the large portico and hurried towards the coach, almost losing his balance in his effort to open the door before Dickon had completely stopped the horses.

He bowed gracefully, and kissed her gently on her brow. 'Welcome home, my darling,' he whispered, leading her gently into the newly decorated entrance hall. Moll handed the tired boy over to the nurse, who fussed about him, wiping his grubby face with the corner of her apron, and complained loudly about small boys staying up way beyond their natural bedtime. Moll kissed the child goodnight, his howls of protest growing fainter as the nurse dragged him along the long corridor to his own room.

Turning, Moll realized how different the entrance hall looked. She was delighted with the beautiful alcoves, filled with lovely flowers and ivy. Sir Richard explained that the new gardener was like a magician, and could force flowers to bloom at will because of the new greenhouse that was just built. With delight, Moll noticed other wonderful changes in the house. Her pleasure at his efforts gratified Richard, and arm in arm they walked through the beautiful rooms. Gasps of delight rose from her lips, for her home was changed drastically, yet so pleasingly she was enchanted with its new image.

Moll sensed Richard's distress as he spoke of absent friends. For it was blatantly obvious as he re-visited his old haunts that the coffee bars of London would never be quite the same again. The evening fell quietly and silently as the footman lit the great candelabra. They enjoyed the intimate peacefulness of being together. As they walked upstairs, Moll slipped her hand into Richard's they retired to bed. Moll lay quietly on her lace pillow and glanced across the great bed; Richard's eyes met hers. Impulsively she turned and kissed him passionately. His arm slipped easily around her and he found himself returning the embrace. Moll knew that at least her husband was responding, and gently she coaxed him into consummating the marriage. Alas, it was not to be, and with a strangled sob, he wept like a child in her arms. All she could do was to comfort him and eventually they fell asleep.

Moll now realized that it was of little use to expect a sexual relationship with her husband, and vowed that never again would she torment him. Tossing and turning through the night, she woke early, hurriedly dressed, and went down for breakfast. Richard joined her shortly, and kissed her lightly on the cheek. No word was mentioned about the upsetting episode of the previous night.

Chapter 22

Tragedy

'What will you do today, my love?' asked Sir Richard.

'I shall go into the park for a walk,' she replied. 'Perhaps I shall do some shopping in the afternoon, for I fear I am no longer a lady of fashion.' Moll smiled, kissing her husband goodbye as he left for the city, and she hurried towards the nursery to see Stuart, before getting herself ready for her outing.

She took a shortcut through the grounds to St James's Park, where she sat idly tossing pebbles into the pond. She caught sight of her reflection and bending over, she said, 'Ginny Greenteeth, witch of the water, procuress of village maidens, where art thou?'

'Here,' said a voice, and Moll found herself breaking her image in the pond before turning sharply to meet the steady twinkling eyes of His Majesty, the King! Irrespective of their surroundings, he drew her to him and kissed her. 'Well, my darling, and how's my buxom country wench?'

She laughed gaily at his jest and putting one finger beneath her chin, threw an exaggerated deep curtsey. 'Oi be foine, ow be ee, 'andsome?'

He chuckled at her dialect for he hadn't heard her use it before. 'Zounds, Maria, we've a rival for that court jester, Nell Gwynne.' He swung her high into the air, kissing her soundly before putting her down. 'When shall I see you, sweetling?' he asked. 'Will you come to Whitehall on Saturday, before the ball?'

Moll looked at him in amazement. 'What ball, sir?'

'Why, you must have received my invitation by now,' he said.

But she only shook her head in wonder.

'Well, then, I will send the messenger this very day to the Gables. There is to be a great banquet and ball at the palace on Saturday, but why did you not know? I'm sure you and your husband are on the guest list.'

Moll then realized that she had been out of the house very early and in her haste had not asked for messages or letters. 'Your Majesty, your subject declines the first invitation, but gratefully accepts the second. Methinks I will have little time to accept both.'

With a chuckle, he kissed her cheek and walked across the park to the back entrance to Green Gables. They kissed again, and he whispered, 'Until Saturday, darling.'

She walked slowly through the gardens, losing all track of time. Heavens, she would be late for supper, and quickening her steps, hurried home where Richard awaited her.

'Come, my darling, we have guests arriving shortly,' Richard admonished.

Moll, flushed from hurrying, gratefully put herself in the hands of her very competent maid, and was soon beautifully groomed and ready for dinner.

As they walked into the dining room to meet their guests, Moll mentioned the ball. Sir Richard smiled as she prattled on. 'It will be a grand occasion, but I have been in the country so long that I have nothing to wear!' she exclaimed.

'The seamstress awaits your wishes, my dear; and the ship I own docked at the Port of London yesterday. Tomorrow you can go down and choose enough material for all the dresses you desire,' he said.

Dinner with Richard's friends proved entertaining, and the evening passed quickly. Oh, it was so good to feel that one's house was once again open to friends. The next morning Moll was on the wharf by half past nine, alighting from her carriage. She was shown into the warehouse by a jolly red-faced fellow who dropped his aitches in the most alarming places, and replaced them in the most fascinating fashion.

'Would m'lady follow me hin 'ere, please?' he bellowed. "Ere we 'ave silks from the Hindies.'

Moll stifled a giggle, for he really was most helpful and was trying his best to please. She gazed with wonder at the beautiful fabrics spread before her. Never had she seen the like. She chose five bales of velvets, and three of silk brocades for day gowns. She spotted some white satin embroidered with butterflies with sequins sewn on the wings. Greedily she took the whole bale, for it would be unwise to have a dress of such gorgeous material which might later appear on a market stall somewhere. Thanking the custodian for the great trouble he had taken, she had Dickon load up the coach and then drive quickly home, for time was flying. Upon reaching home, Dickon carried the bales of cloth to the seamstress, who was enthralled with the richness and beauty of the fabrics. Moll and the seamstress discussed styles, and it was agreed that even if she had to stay up all night, she would have a dress finished for the ball on Saturday. True to her word, the dress was finished in time – the most beautiful, fine-fitting gown Moll had ever owned. Moll looked at herself in the mirror. The white dress surrounded her like an iridescent cloud. Pressing ten crowns into

Mrs Baron's hand, she sped to her room to decide what jewellery she would wear with it. After careful consideration, she decided all she needed was her wedding ring and a pair of dangling diamond earrings.

All day Saturday Moll spent preparing herself for the ball. Her maid spent hours working on a fancy hair-do for Moll and fussing over every detail of her attire. When she was finally ready, she floated down the staircase, where her husband awaited her. He smiled in amazement at her beauty. 'Moll, you'll be the belle of the ball!' he exclaimed, as he wrapped her white ermine cloak around her and escorted her to the coach.

Arriving at the palace courtyard, Moll stepped lightly on to the long red carpet which led to the entrance hall. Hundreds of candles flickered and reflected on the huge crystal chandeliers. Their names were called, and King Charles, looking magnificent in turquoise and lilac brocade, greeted them formally, his eyes taking in every detail of Moll's exquisite gown. Sir Richard and his wife moved around the great banquet hall, and Charles appeared at intervals to introduce various people. The Queen was conspicuous by her absence. 'She is not well,' explained Charles casually.

A stir went through the crowd as a tall majestic woman sailed through the guests and curtseyed in front of the King. 'Barbara, my dear, how lovely you look,' he said, and deliberately steered her away from Moll.

A young black-haired lady with ruddy cheeks and an endearing cockney accent was kicking her legs high in the air to touch a palm held higher than her head by Lord Clarendon, whose wife soon bore down on him like a galleon in full sail to put a stop to the proceedings. Moll overheard her saying something about 'that doxey Gwynne'. With a start, she realized that she had just met Lady Castlemaine and Nell Gwynne, mistresses of the King! Moll, looking them over, was surprised to notice that Lady Castlemaine was getting too fat, and Nell Gwynne might be a dazzling enough player in the theatre, but she was certainly no lady! But what fun she must be, thought Moll.

The call came for supper and each lady was taken into the banquet hall on the arm of her escort. Beside herself with curiosity, Moll glanced over to where Charles was standing, trapped between both Nell Gwynne and Lady Castlemaine. Obviously, he was too much a gentleman to choose. The second call for supper was announced and, glancing over her shoulder, Moll moved towards the large double doors held open by the footman in white livery.

Sensing that every eye in the room was on the King, who was completely trapped by both protocol and breeding, a voice from behind him spoke to the King. 'Sire, I trust you will allow me to escort one of these beautiful ladies to dinner.'

With a loud laugh, Nell drew a deep curtsey and called, 'Come, me fine gallant,' and took Sir James's arm, laughing gaily. Together they followed Charles and haughty Lady Castlemaine into the great dining hall. Moll glanced at her husband, who whispered that once again Sir James had saved the merry monarch, and Moll felt her face flush at the mention of his name, for she had not expected him to be at the palace.

During dinner Moll and Sir Richard found themselves sitting opposite Nell and Sir James. Her rich cockney voice crashed into Maria's ears, but Sir James chatted along with her, his quiet voice hardly registering against Nell's raucous tones.

Richard was very quiet, which was little wonder, for as the guests drank more wine, the tongues wagged freely and louder. However, Moll noticed a peculiar pallor around his mouth and, upon questioning, he admitted he was not feeling well.

Moll asked a servant to have their coach brought around to the side entrance immediately. Moll and Richard discreetly slipped out unnoticed. The coach sped through the park and to Green Gables. Richard's manservant soon had his pale, sick master in bed, and it was apparent that Richard was desperately ill.

The apothecary came, and Moll winced as the knife was produced to bleed him. Memories of Roxanne flooded over her, and as the levy of blood welled up on Richard's arm, she fainted. Some time later, she awoke with a start and found herself lying on the long couch in the dressing room. She flew into the bedroom where Richard lay, and threw herself by the bed. His face was ashen and his breathing was laboured. With tear-filled eyes she gazed into the bearded face of the apothecary. No words passed between them as he sadly shook his head.

Picking up Richard's hand, she felt the clammy coldness of death already hovering, and with great effort he slowly opened his eyes. 'My beloved,' he whispered, 'stay with me.'

'Always, my darling,' she replied.

Without warning a great sigh fell from his lips, and his hand lay quite still in hers. The apothecary closed Richard's eyes. Moll's confused, shocked mind suddenly realized that her husband was dead. With a breaking heart, she fled into the guest bedroom and sobbed herself into a state of complete exhaustion. Her maid deftly slipped the lovely gown from Moll's body, and gently wiped the tear-stained face. She felt cold hands slip her between warmed sheets and spent the next twelve hours sobbing and sleeping intermittently. Upon awakening, she felt the nightmare of death in the house, and shuddered as the maid, unbidden, slipped a gown of grey silk over her head. The household was in deep mourning, and Moll was given sedatives to help her through this great sadness.

She went immediately to her small son who knew nothing of his father's death, and explained as well as she could what had happened. The child, never having experienced a death before, was wide-eyed with horror and confusion. Mother and child clung to each other, both sobbing, until the nanny gently led the boy to his room, trying her best to console him.

Moll felt numb to what was happening around her but pulled herself together when the Controller arrived for a meeting with her. He explained that the King had been informed of Sir Richard's death, and funeral arrangements would be carried out by himself. Moll, relieved, stood quietly gazing out onto the long sweeping driveways. Already carriages were arriving, and Moll found herself accepting condolences from politicians, friends and acquaintances. Later that evening, a commotion was heard as the servants announced 'His gracious Majesty, the King.'

Moll gazed into the black eyes of Charles. His words were clear and concise. 'Maria, you have suffered a great loss, as have I. He was my friend and loyal subject, and I can ill afford to lose either.'

She sobbed on his shoulder until she could cry no more. He stroked her raven black hair. 'I shall always be here, my darling, please lean on me; ask for anything and it's yours. I shall, of course, attend the funeral on Wednesday.'

She bade him farewell and somehow got through the next few days. With dread, she realized that tomorrow her husband's body would be locked in the private family vault and she would be alone with her son in this great house. Tears trickled slowly down her pale cheeks as she climbed the staircase to her room. Bereft of sleep, she arose early and washed her face in the rose water by her bed. Her maid, hearing her mistress stirring, hurried in to help her dress. Nothing was said, for words were useless; sorrowfully, the maid watched Moll walk to the great staircase alone. Wiping a tear from her eyes, she busied herself tidying up the bedroom before laying the fire in readiness for evening.

Mourners filled the large house, and a murmur of sympathy ran through them as Moll and her son walked slowly to the draped carriage waiting in the drive. Vaguely, she heard the service begin, and through all the pomp and ceremony of the burial, she spoke to no-one but held Stuart's hand tightly, as if he could help her survive such a loss.

After the service, blessed relief flooded over her as she found herself alone at last in the solitude of her chambers. The candles flickered, casting long shadows on the walls, and she imagined for a moment she heard his voice – Was he calling? 'Oh God, help me, help me,' she sobbed. Never in her wildest dreams had she thought of ever losing Richard. His kindness and understanding had brought so much happiness into her life, and now the suddenness of his death had brought home to her the futility of taking things for granted. Thoughts of her future welled like a spectre in her mind, for she knew that sooner or later she would have to face reality and make important decisions regarding the future, such as whether to keep Richard's business ventures, what to do with the house, and many, many more things.

The days passed and spring fell like a green mantle over the grounds of Gables and, sitting alone in the sunshine, Moll looked back at the great house. She decided she could not lose it, as this was her son's birthright and all that went with it. Poor lamb, she thought; he still couldn't understand that he would not see his father again. She suddenly realized that she must not mourn any longer, but instead use her time and efforts to keeping up the properties and business that her son was to inherit.

Next day, armed with papers and legal documents, Moll stepped into the coach and gave orders to drive down to the wharves. Her servants, aghast with horror that m'lady should do such a thing, tried in vain to deter her. But with a wave of her hand, she drove out quickly through the main gates. On glancing through the papers, she found that Richard owned ten large warehouses, scattered along the wide stretch of London's dockland; also, five merchant ships, three of which were anchored and awaiting sailing orders.

Her mind was full of excitement as she passed the wharves and warehouses, all busy loading and unloading goods. Aromatic scents and odours filled her nostrils; tar, rope, spices, and the indefinable smell of raw produce, all made her tense with excitement.

On reaching the first warehouse, she was delighted to meet once more the fascinating warehouse master who had shown her his host of materials before the ball. He wiped his hands on his apron, licked his palms and tried to slick down his hair. Thus satisfied with his appearance he walked with reverence towards her carriage and, with the courteousness of a born gentleman, helped Moll from the coach. He led her inside the warehouse where, to her amazement, he offered her a glass of excellent wine. Wiping the stool with his apron, be offered her a seat. 'Madam,' he spluttered with embarrassment, 'I wish to hoffer you my hexcellent condolences.'

Moll bowed her head, for had she spoken, giggles would have completely shattered these kind, simple, earnest sentiments. She sipped the wine slowly, and then said, 'Ralph, I need help.'

'From me, m'lady?'

She nodded. 'Tell me all you can about the warehouse business.'

Ralph's chest swelled with pride and Moll realized that this job was his whole life. The man was a mine of information and, apart from a few dropped aitches, he imparted his knowledge simply and accurately. So much so that, within the hour, Moll felt that this man could be trusted implicitly.

'I shall put you in complete charge of this warehouse. Can you read, Ralph?'

He nodded. 'Taught meself, ma'am, and I can write, too.'

'Each week I want you to write me a report, tell me everything that is happening in the warehouse, and I shall deal with each problem as it arises. Together, we shall continue to run this business profitably, as my husband has done in the past. As for wages, Ralph, you will find me fair and just in money matters and, on our first meeting next week, I shall inform you of my decisions regarding your salary and responsibilities.'

Moll visited the other warehouses, and was successful in arranging business matters and making decisions. She was grateful that her husband had chosen such reliable people to run the warehouses, and that things had been running smoothly for a long time. Hopefully, with her at the head, things would continue as they had in the past. She overheard one of the warehouse workers say, 'God help her, if any one of these cut-throats harms a hair of her pretty head, I'll swing on a gibbet myself for them.'

Gradually, the great enterprise took shape and Moll found that, by using her charm and beauty, even the dear old captains saw to it that she got a fair price for her cargo.

In the next few months her life changed completely. She was kept so busy with the warehouses and ships that she didn't have time to mourn for her husband any longer or to think about her appearance. One day the maid told her than a gentleman caller had stopped by. 'His name was Sir James, and he left a message that he would call this evening to see you.'

Moll's heart lurched, and it took quite a few seconds for her to trust her voice. 'Thank you, Sally, I can manage now.' She looked in her chest and found the dress she was looking for, blue, with a plain white collar and a graceful flowing skirt.

Satisfied with her appearance, she walked slowly down to the small drawing room and poured herself a glass of wine. The house was still and quiet and

Moll, for the first time in months, felt relaxed and peaceful. All her business worries seemed to vanish as she watched the flames flicker around the logs in the fireplace.

The footman tapped on the door. 'M'lady, Sir James to see you.' As she stood, arms outstretched to greet him, she felt tears well up in her eyes.

'James, darling James.'

He clasped her tightly in his arms and buried his face in the perfumed cloud of black hair. Suddenly she sensed something was wrong, and standing back, she saw the whiteness of his face in the firelight.

'Are you ill? Come, sit down and take a glass of wine, 'twill make you feel refreshed.'

His eyes held hers for a moment and, with a gesture of despair, he said, 'Moll, London is burning.'

Unbelievingly, she said, 'Come, we have not met since the great ball at Whitehall. Do not jest with me, James.'

He led her to the settle by the fire, and she noticed his long slim hands nervously picking at the embroidered cushion as he sat facing her.

'Why, James, you really are nervous.' She clasped his hand, stopping him from unravelling the exquisite embroidery. He was silent, and with dread Moll knew worse was to come. With a superhuman effort she waited patiently for him to speak, trying to stop the pounding in her breast.

'Moll, my darling, the fire started at the baker's shop in Pudding Lane.' Moll gasped, for she knew the jolly man and his pretty daughter who kept the shop. She often sent in a large order herself for the delicious pastries and marchpanes he concocted. Charles had first introduced her to the little shop, for he held the King's warrant and half of London patronized him.

'The fire has spread alarmingly, Moll, the dockside warehouses are burning. In fact, half the city will be in ruins by daybreak.'

Not waiting for further news, she sprang to her feet, grabbed a cloak, and both of them ran to the stables. Moll climbed on the large bay and James hurriedly mounted the chestnut. Down the long drive they galloped until the horses smelled the fire, which could be seen clearly like a monstrous thing destroying everything in its path.

The great beasts stopped, fear showing in every line of their muscular bodies. They tried spurring the animals on, but the horses could smell fire and death, and reared with fright.

Moll and James dismounted, and with a sound smack of their rumps, the horses raced to the warmth and safety of their stable. James took her hand in his, and they hurried into the city. 'Poor old London,' said Moll, 'she withstood foreign invaders only to be destroyed by fire. God help us, for we shall all perish.'

'Hush, child,' he said, 'let us see what we can do to help.'

Moll was feeling desperately afraid, for through the upper stairs of the houses little sky could be seen. 'God, they will fall like hay ricks,' she thought. The houses were much too close, for upper casements seemed but a breath apart. Shattering timbers crashed to the ground, making her tremble even more, and as they turned the corner where the old cobbler's shop once stood nothing but debris remained. People were running in all directions, smoke was thick in the air, and confusion was everywhere. Moll crossed herself and whispered the prayer for the dead, for she had heard a shrill scream as the shop collapsed.

'No-one could be alive now,' said James, 'no-one, darling.' He held her tightly in his arms, for he knew that this night much sorrow would be seen in the great city. Down Ladymill Court, women knee-deep in debris and mud helped their menfolk pass buckets of water to quench the all-devouring flames. Suddenly a woman screamed as a child appeared at the upstairs casement. Too terrified to jump, he stood like a small white statue. Moll reached instinctively for James's hand, but to her horror, she saw him disappear into the burning doorway. A hush passed through the crowd; only the crashing of timber could be heard and a cry of a dog in pain. A roar of relief surged through the tired people as James appeared carrying the small boy securely in his arms. Moll wept unashamedly as the mother, too overcome for words, kissed and hugged the child over and over again.

Quickly, they walked away down the court to the little square. This, too, was ablaze. Men had pulled down all the combustible material they could reach so that more fuel would not be added to the already blazing city. They pushed their way through crowds to Westminster, slowed by panicky people carrying what belongings they had save from the holocaust. It was impossible at this point to go further - panic was everywhere. In fact, people were already being trampled underfoot in futile efforts to escape the flames. The skyline was black against the vivid orange glow of the sky. A black pall of smoke hung low over the city, and too horrible even to contemplate, was the wind, which was howling around the few unlit buildings, whipping the fire into a frenzy until the flames were seen to leap across a space of fifteen paces, devouring the next building with increased ferocity. Although Moll's house was set in a thicket of timbers, to the rear of the property was a long road directly in its path. 'The wind will change, Moll, we must fell all the trees,' said James. He rang the large bell outside the grooms' quarters which raised the household. Most of the staff, however, were already dressed and watching the great city burn in the distance, and they were wondering just how long it would take for the fire to reach the house.

Sir James lost little time in speech. Quickly he ordered axes to be given to all able-bodied men, instructing them quickly to fell all timber surrounding the house. The great horses were used to drag the trees down to the lake, and men with hooks rolled the trees into the deep water. The small lake rose, flooding the ornamental gardens. James breathed a sigh of relief, for soon all of the gardens were flooded with a few inches of water. Moll wiped the grime from her face in relief, for now at least the house was safe - but what of the warehouse and the ships?

They did all they could possibly do, and the house now appeared safe from the fire. Everybody was exhausted, and hot Malmsey wine was passed to all. As James was preparing to return to his home for the night, Moll asked if he would stay, for her whole being longed for the comfort of his arms, but she felt that he would not tarry.

Since the staff knew of his presence, he must be seen leaving in order to protect her reputation. Since the death of her husband, she was especially vulnerable to gossip. Society could be extremely cruel. With tears stinging her eyes, she bade him farewell and wearily climbed the stairs to the quiet of her chambers. He had been so distant - why? She knew he must use the utmost discretion, but why had he not contacted her before now? With this worry on her mind and all the excitement of the fire, she found difficulty in sleeping.

In the morning, London was still burning. Smoke filled every nook and cranny of the house. Her footman handed her a message, and with a start, she noticed the royal cipher emblazoned on the note. Opening the letter, she read quickly, 'If you need help, Maria, please do not hesitate to ask. Charles.'

Her spirits lightened somewhat, and she was able to enjoy breakfast. The day was dark and smoky. Now she could see flames where before all had seemed safe. Sounds of crying coming from the corridor disturbed her, and gathering her skirts she sped quickly to the door. A maid, sobbing controllably, cried 'We shall be burned alive, Oh God, let the blessed saints save us.'

Gathering the frightened girl in her arms, Moll rocked her, murmuring words of comfort until the sobs subsided. She stiffened, for through the girl's sobs, the words penetrated Moll's brain.

'Oh, ma'am, the sparks are falling on the roof like rain; soon we shall all perish.'

Moll rushed out, and saw for herself that the girl spoke the truth. She pulled with all her might on the great bell, summoning all the available staff to her aid. Sparks dropped on them as Moll ordered, 'Place wet sacks on all thatched roofs, leave pitch forks on each building to pull down the thatch if it catches fire.'

The men rushed to do her bidding, when suddenly a small fire fanned by the wind cracked into a blaze which threatened to engulf the stables. A roar from one of the men brought others to his aid, and soon it was brought under control.

Moll was feeling the pressure by now, and ordered the men to stand a four-hour watch each. Great cauldrons of soup were brought into the courtyard. The fires were packed with wet peat as soon as they were discovered to stop any further spreading.

Men slept wherever they could, some leaning up against the houses and dogs for warmth. Moll felt dirty, tired and a little sad for she knew that she couldn't leave these tired men alone. Through the night they toiled and still the strict vigil was necessary for the sparks became more threatening. The wind was playing with them like summer midges, whirling and swirling them into nooks and crannies where the slightest puff of smoke heralded fire. Later in the afternoon the wind dropped and the sparks stopped.

Moll left two men on watch and retired to her bedroom for a well-earned bath. As she gazed from the turret window she saw with horror that London still burned, and wearily she slept as she had not slept for weeks. By evening, the ominous glow still hung over the city but the howling wind was still! 'Why not rain?' prayed Moll. 'Oh, Lord, send rain,' but the choking dust blackening everything was her only answer.

The weekly meeting with her warehousemen, master and ships' captains was to be held in three days. The place she had chosen was the large room in the Spanish Guinea near the wharves. 'Whatever happens I must be there,' she promised herself. When the day dawned the coach arrived at the front of the house to take her through the city.

With horror, Moll witnessed the devastation. 'Holy souls and martyrs, will a phoenix ever arise from ashes such as these?' she wondered. She saw some children badly burned and lying on the roadside. 'Stop the coach!' she cried. The four great horses wheeled to a standstill. Moll took a small boy of six, crying with pain and shock, in her arms.

A woman, sobbing with her own sorrows, said the three children had lost their parents in the fire. 'All dead, m'lady, all dead.'

Moll bustled the children into the coach and ordered the coachman to drive them back to her house, where they soon came under the gentle ministration of her kitchen staff.

The carriage drew up at the Spanish Guinea about a half hour late. Hurrying from the coach she coughed, for the air was badly polluted with smoke and quickly she hurried inside. Proudly she gazed around her warehouse staff. Each man was standing with hat in hand, a gesture of respect for their female employer.

'Good evening, gentlemen,' she said. 'Please be seated.' The room was very warm, and the men were perspiring. They opened the window for air, but it was futile for the air was even more polluted outside than in, and the smell of smoke was oppressive.

'Bring ale,' she ordered to the serving wench, and a sigh of relief swept around the room as the men sank tankard after tankard of the bitter brew. Then each man reported on his domain. One ship had been lost in the fire and one warehouse had been burnt to the ground. Moll breathed a sigh of relief. Things were better than she had first thought. It was suggested that they desert the warehouse that was burned, sell the land, and use the money to extend the small but busy warehouse near the wharf. As they were leaving, each man showed respect for their leader with a few kind words, and Moll felt relieved that her financial future would soon recover and perhaps even grow.

Life was very busy these days for her, such a lot of things had happened. Looking back, she realized even more how easy her life had been with Richard in control.

Chapter 23

The Meeting with Nell Gwynne

Finally the air of London cleared. Architects sprang into action, and rebuilding was going on everywhere. The great fire was now history. Masons and labourers now found their service in great demand, for Parliament had decreed that an even greater city should rise from the ashes; a London equal to Florence, Rome or any other capital city would grow. Streets were to be broader, wider and paved. Ramshackle houses would be replaced with attractive dwellings of stone and brick. Never had such a clean-up taken place in London before, and with a sigh of nostalgia, Moll knew that this modern new city would not have the atmosphere of the old one. Things had needed altering, but the plague and the fire, so close together, had robbed London of much of its character, and more drastic changes would surely leave London unrecognizable.

She decided this would be a good day to take her son on an outing to explore the city. Stuart prattled on merrily about birds, the fire, and any and everything he saw. 'Mama, look, I have a pet!' Startled, she turned to find him holding a large, very surprised, hedgehog, who promptly curled up into a ball with shock.

'Sir, put that creature down this instant,' she cried, and with a merry laugh he opened his jacket and pushed the prickly creature inside, darting up the lane shouting, 'Catch, as catch can.' Moll knew that hedgehogs carried hosts of fleas and other parasites. She picked up her skirts and, in vain, tried to catch the small boy. He was quick as lightning, running backwards and calling, 'Catch me, catch me.'

Breathless, Moll was wondering if she had been right to take this imp out without servants. He turned suddenly and collided with a young woman who quickly grabbed him by the scruff of the neck and laughed, 'Now, me fair laddie, gotcha!'

He wriggled in vain and Moll smiled as she saw the unknown woman whisper something in his ear and miraculously, the dirty old hedgehog was returned to the roadside. As Moll drew closer, she recognized the lady as Nell Gwynne. 'Oh, thank you, Miss Gwynne, he really is a rascal,' said Moll.

With a smile she said, 'You can call me Nelly. I recognized you as a friend of the King. The Lady Howard, are you not?'

'Yes,' smiled Moll, 'but Richard, my husband passed on some months ago.'

'That I heard, too,' said Nell, 'come, we shall be friends and spend the day together.'

Stuart looked up at this lovely vivacious lady and found her entirely captivating. Nell smiled, as the small boy slipped his hand quite naturally in hers, and whispered something obviously quite outrageous to him so he chuckled with delight. Nell looked at the child on hearing his distinctive chuckle, and noticed particularly the black curls and dark skin.

'Zounds, Moll, it seems we have the same sire, but different dams!' Now Moll knew her long-kept secret was a secret no more.

Nell invited her into the coach, which was but a short distance away. Her broad cockney accent reminded her so much of Kate, and quickly she decided that she really liked Eleanor Gwynne, in spite of her earlier opinion of the woman.

The three acquaintances climbed into the coach and Nell invited Moll to a coffee house in Drury Lane. The naughtiness of the suggestion surprised Moll, but quickly she found herself nodding assent. Drury Lane soon came into view and laughing merrily, they walked into the coffee house where all the actresses and ladies of London held court. Moll had never heard such goings on, but she thoroughly enjoyed the excitement and fun.

'Zounds, it's like four Christmases rolled into one,' she exclaimed.

Nell's laughter could be heard above the noise. Everyone knew her there, and introductions came so fast that Moll could not remember them. Stuart was enchanted as an actor carrying a monkey sat the child on his knee, and not a word or sound broke from his lips. He hadn't seen a monkey before, and this one wore a little black hat and a red jacket.

'A song, Nell, a song,' came a cry from the crowd, and Nell rose to the occasion by hiking her skirt up and pulling her blouse down low so that most of her bosom was exposed, and she leapt on to the nearest table top. 'I'm alone in a wicked world,' she sang, which brought screams of laughter from the crowd. When she finished she jumped off the table and draped herself suggestively around each man in turn, moving only when searching fingers tried to expose even more of her pretty person.

'What a merry lot they are, Moll,' Nell exclaimed breathlessly. Moll was chuckling happily at the very jolly entertainers who came on to perform one after the other, until she thought her sides would surely split. Midnight drew near, and with a start Moll saw Stuart being carried out.

Nell put a small hand on her arm and quietly said, 'I have a house close by. Ray will take him there, he's in safe hands, so don't worry. I think Lord Beauclark will find himself a half-brother in bed in the morning. Zounds, Moll, they are as alike as two peas in a pod!'

Moll said nothing, for she had never seen Nell Gwynne's two sons by Charles, and she was certainly curious.

'Come, Moll, we will sup together. My appetite gets fearsome after midnight,' and with a laugh Nell kissed her and did a theatrical exit towards the door. Breathless with laughter, Moll followed her outside to their coach. From the warmth of the tavern, Moll and Nell felt the chill night air bite deeply into their bones, and the effect of too much wine quickly wore off.

'On, driver, into the city to the pastry cook's in Well Lane,' ordered Nell, and off they went, presently coming to an abrupt halt. Moll became aware of the most succulent aromas she had ever experienced in her life.

Wrapping their shawls tightly around them, they bustled into a large, sweet-smelling kitchen. Pies of every description stood on white scrubbed trestles, waiting to join the lovely baked ones cooling on wire trays. Moll's mouth watered as the big motherly cook, Mrs Baines, cut a large beef pie into slices. They eagerly ate the succulent pastry with murmurs of delight as the warm juice dripped on to chins and gowns. After the beef pie they had some hot plum pie, which was hard to refuse. They drank hot thick chocolate which made them both feel like two stuffed porkers and gratefully they curled up near the great ovens watching the staff produce a fantastic amount of bread and confections ready for sale at six o'clock the following morning. As the great ovens expelled their delicious wares, Mrs Baines found time to place her ample bulk on a chair at their table and they chatted pleasantly – nothing malicious or spiteful, just happy women talk. Mrs Baines was every lady's friend and Moll found herself curiously drawn by her warm and motherly nature. Nell was completely at home here, and what little remained of the night they spent enjoying each other's company.

As daylight penetrated the bakery the tinkling bell of the shop door heralded the first customer. Wearily, Mrs Baines rose to attend the summons, but her husband patted her arm and said, 'Sit still, dearie, I'll see to them.'

'Moll asked Mrs Baines when she managed to get any sleep. Mrs Baines laughed, as two wide-awake girls tripped down the steps from the bedrooms. 'These are my daughters, Heartsease and Violet. They work in the shop until dusk while my husband and I sleep.'

Moll and Nell left the shop so that the sweet old couple could get to bed, with a promise to return soon. They shook the coachman from a deep sleep, and the sun was well up by the time they reached Nell's house. They tiptoed into the boys' room and Moll could not stop the involuntary gasp of surprise as she gazed on the three boys. Brothers, or at least half brothers, they surely were, and Nell bustled Moll from the room before she woke everyone up.

'Aye, lass, our monarch is a merry one to be sure. We shall enter the history books as ladies of pleasure. What an uncomfortable thought!' said Nell. Moll nodded in agreement. 'Come to bed, Moll, we shall leave our future to the gods.'

Moll found herself being ushered into a large ornate chamber grossly overfurnished, with a huge brass four-poster around which hung curtains in brilliant shades of purple and gold. Moll climbed gratefully into bed, and was asleep before her head hit the pillow.

Moll awoke to the raucous cries of the street sellers below. She thought how different it was from her home where everything was very quiet. The company and excitement of Nell's life far surpassed the gracious living she was accustomed to. She stretched like a cat and was startled to hear a tap on the door.

'Enter,' she acknowledged, and the smallest lady she had ever seen laid a beautiful tray of hot bread and cold meats before her. Moll noticed her tiny, exquisite child-like hands, and she gently questioned the girl. She said her name was Melanie and she was employed by Mistress Gwynne. 'I was an orange girl in Drury Lane, m'lady, and Mistress Gwynne brought me here; she is very kind, ma'am.' With a graceful curtsey she was gone, and Moll wondered what other surprises would greet her this day. Quickly she finished her meal, and put on the gown she had worn the night before. She noticed stains on it which had caused her such great hilarity the previous evening, showing up greasily and perfectly horrible in the morning sunlight. Uselessly she mopped at the stains with water, but this only had the adverse effect of making them a lot worse, so in frustration she stamped her foot on the floor. As if in answer to her ill feelings, a second tap was heard on the door. Melanie entered bearing over her arm a beautifully sprigged muslin day gown. Moll was delighted and changed quickly, arranging her long black hair into an attractive style, and went downstairs to start the day.

Nell greeted her warmly, if not genteelly. 'God's oath, Moll, we caroused all night. How's your head?'

Moll laughed and found herself answering in the warm country accent of her youth. It was far too good an opportunity for such an actress as Nellie from

Drury Lane, who replied in the vernacular and both of them practised each other's accents. Aching with laughter they collapsed on the floor, Moll feeling years younger than she had for a very long time. Nell, vastly encouraged by such a wonderful audience, did a life-like caricature of m'lady Castlemaine and a true-to-life repartee between his Royal Highness Charles the II and his courtesans requesting more money. Moll knew little of this aspect of Charles' domestic affairs and was not a little shocked. She still could not control her laughter. Nell quickly realized that Moll was no courtesan and that her relationship with Charles was not a casual one, neither was her own, and thus the final barrier between the two girls was broken. Friendship was born, one which would last a lifetime, much to the annoyance of Charles who would be appalled at this situation. Moll realized it was time to leave, and promised to return on Friday evening to taste once more the pleasures of London's night life.

Bustling a strongly protesting Stuart into Nell's coach, she closed her eyes to the resounding slap he received from the coachman, who was used to wayward lads, for Nell's two boys were no small handful. This worked wonders for he seated himself quietly in the corner and waved like fury to the two boys standing in the doorway.

Gables soon came into sight, and Moll was ashamed to feel the sombreness of the great house closing in on her. It wasn't the decor, which was beautifully bright and airy. It was the atmosphere. At Nell's, it seemed almost a Christmas atmosphere permeating each nook and cranny of her townhouse, so much lacking in her own.

Chapter 24

James's Ultimatum

As the carriage drew to a halt outside the great doors, Moll was surprised to see Sir James hurrying in front of the Controller to fling open the coach door himself. 'My dear, where have you been?' he gasped. 'I have been here since yesterday, wondering what had happened to you.'

Moll decided not to go into details but quietly held her hand out to his. He kissed her ardently and escorted her into the house, but Moll hadn't banked on her chattering son who poured out the story to his 'Uncle James'. With horror, Moll knew that James was shocked, for he listened in stony silence.

Completely at a loss, she found herself stammering, 'But James, she really is very sweet.'

'A King's mistress!' he spat.

The words clashed around her ears, and with horror she realized that her secret relationship with the King had not yet reached his ears. His wrath tore her soul apart. To make excuses to James seemed intolerable, but she knew it must be done. He was so very dear to her, and she desperately needed his gentle quiet strength. This fairy tale pertaining to her secret must be violently destroyed.

'James,' she whispered, 'sit by me, for now I must speak. Perhaps it will be the end of our relationship, I hope not, but now the truth must be told.'

She started by asking him to look closely at Stuart, who was awaiting the coming of Mrs Pearson. His eyes looked searchingly at the small boy, and Moll knew that he now had seen the father in the boy. Mrs Pearson entered and hurried the lad up to the nursery for his daily scrubbing. Slowly Moll turned towards James, dreading to see the reproach and torment in his eyes.

'No,' he stammered, 'God's oath, tell me it isn't true, Moll.'

Moll could only nod helplessly. His eyes blazed and she saw the white of his knuckles showing through the skin, as he bowed his head over the table. In a low husky voice he asked her for the whole story and Moll slowly unfurled the truth, beginning to end. As she spoke softly and gently about Charles, he stiffened. 'The man has the morals of a monkey,' he yelled.

She continued her confession. His high respect for her was shattered and he finally realized this woman he had held in such high esteem was no goddess after all, but a mere woman. For a few minutes neither of them spoke and then James, in a low husky voice said, 'Moll, this is the bitterest pill I have ever swallowed; please forgive me, but I must say goodbye.' With a look of deep disappointment he bowed and left.

Wearily that night, Moll watched the moon drift peacefully across the sky. Sleep was impossible, for she believed, sadly, that James had now gone from her life forever.

Next day the maid brought up a tray bearing a card. She eagerly tore it open and a smile flickered fleetingly across her face as the uneducated scrawl met her eyes – 'Wot cher oim ere. Nellie.' Grabbing a gown, she raced downstairs to see Nell already cuddling a delighted Stuart and popping great lumps of marchpane into his already over full mouth. Mrs Pearson girded her loins and was desperately trying to extricate her charge from this strumpet, which was too much for Nell. With an oath, she trimmed Mrs Pearson's reddening ears to a wick!

Mrs Pearson fled in horror, and Nell continued spoiling and adoring the little black-haired boy, so like her own son. Moll had felt like discharging Mrs Pearson long ago but had never had the courage of her convictions. She was surprised and delighted when Mrs Pearson reappeared, dressed in her Sunday best, and 'wiped the dust of Gables from her feet forever'. Moll knew that the other household help would take charge and things would probably run more smoothly once Mrs Pearson had gone.

Moll showed Nell around her gracious mansion. Nell 'oohed' and 'aahed' and praised the decor and furnishings and, so typically, said, 'Gawd, Moll, 'tis like a bloody great museum.'

The two friends once more laughed and chatted until Nell, sympathetic creature that she was, realized that Moll was upset about something. 'Come into the garden and tell "Nell, confidante of the King".' They sat under the willow sipping warm buttermilk, and Moll told her story of her break-up with James, leaving out the part where James scolded her for forming an acquaintance with Nell.

Nell listened thoughtfully, and asked, 'Do you love him, Moll?'

'Yes, very dearly,' she replied.

'Then sleep with the damned fellow and be done with it,' reasoned Nell.

'Oh no, Nell, it isn't that sort of relationship. I could not cheapen myself anymore than I already have.'

Nell could see that her friend was extremely distressed, and decided to cut her visit short until such time as Moll felt more sociable. As she was tying the ribbons of her bonnet, she said, 'Moll, think, my dear, of all the things we could do together in London. You have seen little since living in this part of the city. Come to Drury Lane as planned on Friday, and we shall sup together.'

As the day dragged on Moll felt that her life was surely over. 'Oh, James darling, please, please understand,' she repeated to herself. At four in the afternoon, she was astonished when the maid announced the arrival of Sir James! She tried her best to straighten her unruly looks before he was shown in the drawing room, but it was too late.

He stood before her, still very stern and serious, and Moll steeled herself to hear the worst. His brown eyes smouldered and she could feel no warmth pass between them.

'James, how nice to see you again.' The words seemed empty and curt, but she knew that the words needing to be spoken must come from him. He seated himself before her on a footstool, and quietly said, 'Moll, I knew you had contracted a marriage of convenience, for I knew Richard well. This I can understand, but to join the legion of Charles' mistresses and bear him a son seems so alien to your sweet nature that I still cannot believe it!'

She felt herself stiffen and quickly decided that she would not be judged by him or any other person, for that matter. Drawing herself up to her full height, she spoke gently, but firmly. 'James, I have no wish to wear sack cloth or ashes to appease your ego. My past life is done, you had little part in it. Say your piece and go, for I have little humour for this conversation.'

Startled by this new turn of events, James stared at this beautiful proud creature before him, and jealousy tore at his very soul. 'God's oath, Moll, 'twill be spoken of no more, but one thing I ask of you before I say what is in my heart. I am no milk-sop who would share his wife with any man. You must choose between the King and me. It is impossible for me to compromise and I will not be a cuckold, not even for one merry monarch.'

Moll knew she would need time for breaking off the long-standing relationship with Charles, and gently she kissed James on the cheek. 'You shall have my answer by Friday,' she whispered. There was really little else to say, and as they stood together in the half light, Moll felt she wanted to throw her arms around him, but she knew that the answer to this problem was not going to be easy. Unfortunately, Charles was obviously going to be terribly angry at the thought of one of his subjects dictating a thing so personal as the end of an amorous relationship.

They parted with James promising to call on Sunday to discuss her decision. Her life seemed complicated beyond words. James wanted her, but only on the condition that she break ties with Nell and the King. Her business was also in jeopardy. Would James agree to its continuing? She felt trapped by events, and sitting quietly alone with her thoughts, wondered if she was sacrificing too much. A marriage with James held many unanswered questions. She had not seen his home or how he lived, nor did she know his friends or anything about his business. The day passed slowly, her thoughts outpacing time. She did not feel capable of coping with any more, and with a deep sigh she wearily retired for the night.

As the bright sunshine lit up her bedroom, she thought, 'Courtesan or wife. I wish I were as free as a bird.'

Suddenly she knew she was! 'I am free! James must do as he wishes, but marry him – no! Not yet, anyway.'

Tossing her black hair back she ran downstairs to play with Stuart, feeling lighter and happier than she had for weeks. Her worries seemed to have fled with the birds, and her day was spent walking in the garden until the evening meal. Early to bed, she mused, and gratefully sank into the warmth of her bed, eagerly awaiting tomorrow and the scintillating companionship of Nell.

Early next morning she bustled Stuart into the coach and swiftly headed towards Nell's townhouse. Nell waited patiently as she alighted from the coach, smothered Stuart with kisses and produced a large sticky sweetmeat for her 'little blackbird.' Stuart rammed it into his mouth, gave her a sweet sticky kiss and ran upstairs to join Nell's two sons in play.

'Come, Moll,' said Nell, and clasping her arm around Moll's waist, led her friend into the garden where the tiny maid brought fragrant wine and sweetmeats for their delight. Nell looked at Moll quizzically. 'Well, you have obviously come to a decision. Will you marry another fine gentleman, love?'

'No, Nell. I have decided to wait twelve months before I consider marriage. I hope he will be patient until then.'

They spent a very pleasant afternoon on the Chepe buying perfumes, ribbons and fripperies, laughing and enjoying the early Summer weather. From the Chepe they went on to Mrs Baines's shop, but found that it was too early in the day, for the small shop was bustling with activity and customers were jostling one another for service. They decided to come back later, but for now they would go backstage at Drury Lane.

Soon they were standing behind the stage, and Moll was watching the performance eagerly. The orange sellers carried baskets of oranges, teasing the men with their low-cut bodices. When the performance ended, they joined the actors. In a confusion of chatter, Moll found herself watching Nell's antics with great amusement, for she easily surpassed the regular performers. Her voice was sweet and high and her vivacious singing tempted all to join in the chorus. Moll, too, found herself singing clear and true, not realizing that her rich voice drowned even Nell's sweet voice. With a start, she noticed that everyone had stopped singing and the whole company was listening to her!

Enraptured, she carried on and finished her song to tremendous, spontaneous applause. Blushing, she dropped a curtsey and smiled. They partied with the Drury Lane Company at the tavern until midnight, and then once more went to the warm comforting portals of Mrs Baines's pastry shop. This time they ate a portion of a rib of beef straight from the ovens, the pastry casing used to seal the meat melting in their mouths.

'Oh, what a lovely evening,' Moll said. 'But, Nell, 'tis late, we must be away, for these good people must sleep.' Nell agreed, and wishing the Baines a pleasant good night they quickly climbed into their coach and headed home.

Next morning Moll pondered over her predicament. She must give James her answer by the morrow, and even now she was in real torment as to what her answer should be. To her horror, a message was brought up to her in great haste by the maid. 'Tonight at my apartments. Charles.'

It had been so long since he had summoned her. Then she realized that he was following tradition and showing respect for her period of mourning, which was now over. The old excitement poured over her. Tonight, for the last time, she would meet Charles alone.

Her toilet took her many hours, and as seven o'clock drew near, she looked magnificent, dressed in black velvet from head to toe, relieved only by the miniature which Charles had given her.

From the courtyard at Whitehall she tripped gaily up the steps to visit Charles's private apartments. Eagerly Charles opened the door to her. 'Maria, Maria,' he whispered, and enfolded her gently in his arms. His lips sought hers and hungrily she responded to his passion. She wanted him as desperately as he did her, and the thought flashed through her mind that she was a courtesan at heart. Horrified, she pulled away from him, but he held her tightly. 'Maria, what is it?'

Her passion drained from her, and whitefaced, she stammered, 'Charles darling, please do not be angry. I must talk with you.'

'A glass of wine, my dear?' He proffered a large silver goblet, and she sipped it gratefully.

'Charles, it has been too long,' she whispered.

'Aye, Maria, too many hours, too many problems,' and with a merry twinkle in his eye, 'and too many women!'

Relieved at his calmness, Maria spoke about her marriage proposal from James and her conflicting emotions and confusion, and asked his advice.

'Well, my darling, shall we drink a toast to a new friendship? We shall wine and dine together, but not bed together. 'Tis time I put old Roley to sleep anyway. I haven't the stamina for long passionate evenings any more.'

With a start, Maria saw that the lines of his face showed a great weariness, and how tired he really looked in the glowing candlelight. He kissed her hand and said softly, 'Adieu, sweet maid of my youth, no more shall we sport 'neath these merry portals.' He kissed her on the lips and with a pang of regret, Moll said goodbye.

Riding home, the thought occurred to her that she had broken her relationship with the King for no apparent reason. After all, she wanted to be free to make her own decisions. She wondered if the King had grown tired of her, and if he felt this was a convenient way to cut the ties. Tomorrow she would give James her answer, and everything inside her screamed caution. She had thought she had made up her mind to tell him to wait one year, but now she was undecided and confused.

She rose early next morning and attended church, finding St Margaret's stuffy and unbearable. Her thoughts drifted back over her life as she sat here in God's house trying to pray for guidance. Unfortunately, none came during the service, so with a sigh she entered the coach to commence the short drive home, unprepared emotionally to face her meeting with James.

She waited expectantly for his knock, yet was startled when finally the footman announced Sir James had arrived. On entering, he bowed low, and she held out her slim white hand, which he gently kissed. They seated themselves on the settee, and she could feel him trembling.

'James darling.' He turned quickly towards her. 'I promised you my answer today, but before I give it there are certain things we must discuss. My relationship with Charles is over. In fact, it has been ended for some time due to my husband's death. I would like to continue in Richard's business ventures, and I want to keep this house for ny son. As for my friendship with Mistress Gwynne, I value this friendship and will not give it up.'

He stiffened, but forced himself to acquiesce to her requests.

'Also, James, I cannot consider marriage for at least twelve months – in fact, maybe never.'

Moll saw the disappointment in Sir James's face, and was sad for he was well beloved in her eyes. Yet she knew her life was now fulfilled with her many projects, and to be treated as a loved yet pampered wife was not entirely wholesome to her.

Sadly he made his farewells, and said that he hoped this would not be the end of their friendship.

'No, James, we shall dine together often. I just need time to adjust and, although it may be hard for us both, perhaps we need time before either of us marries again.'

He mounted his horse and galloped swiftly up the drive, leaving Moll to think over her rather harsh decision alone. Slowly she walked back to the house and waved to her son who was playing in the upstairs nursery with his friend. She saw his nurse draw him away, and she also waved a greeting to her mistress.

Picking up her skirts, she entered the large house and sat at her desk, shuffling through the ship's manifest that she knew would soon be docking with a cargo of spices. A lot of her money was tied up, but she had been most fortunate in her dealings, and also Captain Caleb would be reporting soon. News of the sightings of the great ship gave Moll a thrill, for her investment would soon be in port, and she would see for herself how prosperous she had become.

Two days later came the exciting news that the *Elleray Queen* was in port, and with all haste Moll ordered her fastest horses to carry her to the dock. The great ship, its timbers creaking, lay at anchor clean and sharp in the morning sun, with her personal flag flying at its staff. With her heart thumping at the sight of such a majestic ship bearing her flag, she hurried to where the great hawsers tied the ship to the dock. Captain Caleb saw his visitor long before she caught sight of him and was already halfway down the gangplank to meet her, his huge hand outstretched, and his even white teeth shining from his tanned smooth face. His blue-green eyes swept over her like a fire, and she felt a terrific attraction for this captain, but hushed the inner voice which threatened to put desire before business. This, she was determined, would not happen.

He showed her to his cabin in the high prow of the ship. A warm, rich redwood lined its walls, and the furniture, although rough hewn, was mellow with use. He pulled up a chair at his side and placed a neat portfolio of papers before her with a neatly drawn up profit and expense account.

According to Captain Caleb her profit was handsome, even after taking into account his cut and the crew's share. He turned to a cabinet on his right and produced two handsome goblets with silver trim. From a matching heavy based crystal decanter, he poured them both a ruby-coloured drink, deep and robust.

Moll sipped hers, and felt a fire and a warmth as never before steal through her whole body. She relaxed casually into the chair, and took the opportunity of surveying Captain Caleb at close quarters. Her long hair flowed gracefully over her shoulders, and she gazed steadily at his handsome features. He smiled at her, once more showing a flash of white even teeth, obviously finding her extremely desirable; yet as the captain of one of her ships, he felt it seemly that he keep things as proper as he could.

Moll sipped her drink and picked up the profit and loss sheet. Why, she really was on the way to being a very wealthy young lady, she thought. It was time she began to enjoy herself a bit.

The decanter was at the ready filling up her glass, and Captain Caleb pulled off her cloak, placing it reverently over a chair.

'Let me congratulate you, Captain, on a successful voyage.'

'Why, thank you, ma'am,' he replied. 'I have it on very good authority that, from a deep sample taken today, the merchandise is classed as "A" condition and should bring perhaps even higher prices than I first thought. Your congratulations are very kindly accepted, ma'am. May I also congratulate you on an extremely seaworthy vessel. She was a pleasure to handle, and we had an accident-free voyage, one of the first on the trade routes.'

By now, Moll's eyes were sparkling and she knew that her feelings made it dangerous for her to tarry. She rose and reached for her cloak. He came behind her and placed it gently around her shoulders, allowing his hands to brush across her briefly, but enough to send a thousand pin pricks up Moll's spine.

He walked with her to her carriage and kissed her hand as neatly as any gallant. On impulse, she turned and said, 'Captain Caleb, be at my house with the bills of sale for the cargo on Sunday, and we will have supper together.'

With that, she waved to the coachman to drive on, and with a clatter of hooves the black bays pulled the coach steadily up the cobbled slope to the bustling London beyond.

On her return, the housekeeper handed her a note. The Royal cipher told her it was from Charles, who was passing through by coach and wished to call upon an old friend. The following evening Moll realized she would have to be very careful, for she would even now be hard pressed to refuse Charles's sexual advances, for another pregnancy, even by him, was not in her scheme of things for the future.

The following morning Moll went to the nursery and played with her son. So like his father, she mused, even his mannerisms told the world he was different. His nurse adored him, and the love was mutual, but his beautiful mother obviously held the throne in his tiny kingdom, and their daily playtimes gave immense pleasure to them both. After a light lunch, Moll bathed and rested, and called Bessier, her personal maid, to press her dress and do her hair.

By dusk she was ready, sitting by the great window in the library looking down the long drive to where Charles' carriage would soon be seen. The glimmer of torches heralded his coming and the servants had been primed to show no surprise at their important guest, but Moll could sense their excitement. For the first time in their lives they would meet their king!

The knock on the door by a liveried coachman goaded everyone into activity, and Moll rose to spread her skirts in a low graceful curtsey. Charles raised her gently and kissed her hand lightly, tossing his gloves to the groom behind him.

'Come, my dear, we have many things to discuss,' and with his hand supporting hers, he was shown into the large comfortable drawing room. The door closed behind them as he caught hold of Moll and kissed her passionately, forcing her mouth to accept his. Moll knew she was on dangerous ground. She broke away from him gently yet firmly, which only served to inflame him even more. His hands fumbled with her gown, and his breath became laboured.

'Charles,' she murmured, 'don't complicate my life further. We have already been lovers, now let us be true friends.'

He looked at her in amazement! 'By the Holy Grail, Moll, you're the only woman in Christendom who would refuse a King's advances; more than my bevy of Royalist mares would do, my beauty.'

He gazed at her white cheeks and slowly bent to place a chaste kiss on each one. Laughingly, she fastened her dress and poured him a glass of Caleb's wine.

'Zounds, Moll, you eat and sup like a queen. This is the best wine I've tasted since I left France.'

'I shall see to it that you receive a supply from Captain Caleb,' she said.

'We shall dine early,' said Charles, 'for it seems this night I shall only have my dreams for company.'

Supper was easy and light. Moll's cook prepared a roast capon, with peaches and fresh beans in a sauce. Dessert was a platter of fresh fruit with dairy cream, and the toast of the evening was Captain Caleb's wine.

Breakfast the following morning was bread, cheese and light beer, which was all Charles usually had. Moll, surprisingly enough, enjoyed it with him, although usually for her an egg lightly boiled sufficed.

Charles proffered to buy a quarter share of her ships, which Moll agreed to, providing the money was placed in an annuity for their son. 'Done,' said Charles, 'my share plus half the profits, but don't you tell those women at court or they'll take the coffers of England and share it equally between my bastards.'

With a laugh, he made for the door and with a cheery wave from the coach, he bade farewell to Moll and her household.

Chapter 25

Captain Caleb

The day started bright and balmy and Moll worked absent-mindedly around her spacious garden, fingering a flower here and there, yet not really feeling a part of anything. The sound of a horse startled her momentarily. Shading her eyes, she could just barely make out the form of a rider bearing a dispatch case, and knew without a shadow of a doubt that the longed-for letter from Captain Caleb had arrived.

'God's teeth!' she whispered to herself, 'I hope the second voyage proved as fruitful as I had hoped. So the Captain's back ashore, bearing gifts, I'll warrant.'

With a laugh she tossed her straw hat back, and with ribbons flying, ran helter skelter to the front driveway, pausing briefly to tidy her fly-away hair and to tighten her laces, and smooth her dress.

John, the footman, came to meet her, smiling broadly. 'Ma'am. 'tis news from the good Captain. Good news, I hope,' he exclaimed, as he handed her the letter. 'We've given the rider ale and cheese, ma'am, and Dickon is watering his mare.'

'Good lad,' said Moll, and smiled at the flush which formed on the boy's cheek. The Captain's ship docking always meant a day off and a get-together for the servants and crew, paid for jointly by Moll and Captain Caleb. Everyone loved this affair, and downstairs there had been talk of nothing else for weeks.

'Zounds,' said Moll, 'I hope he's let the crew out on London for a night or two. The London whores can cope with the lusty sailors who've done a long trip better than my poor countryfied serving wenches. He found quick husbands for two of my maids on the last spice run that I'm thankful for,' she laughed ruefully.

'Anyway, to the drawing room, my girl, let's hear news of Captain Caleb this instant.' Refreshed and rested, the rider smiled, and bowed low to Moll.

'Your servant, ma'am. Captain Caleb send you his news and instructs me to say he must see you at your earliest opportunity for there is much to discuss, and the ship, even now, is due for scraping, painting and is to be stocked up for a new voyage within six weeks.'

'Capital,' said Moll as she opened the carefully sealed letter with bated breath. Eagerly, she read the letter.

> 'Madam: your obedient servant, who is even now at the Post of London with the underwriters, is assured by them of successful bargainings with the warehouse men, who are licking their lips at the booty I have lain before their eyes. Never have silks shown so richly, nor velvets so bejewelled. I bring perfumes from the Orient and pearls from the Gulf, and spices from the Indies.
>
> But now I have business with thee that cannot wait. The ship needs attention, ma'am, and although the booty is rich, some must be laid aside to put the ship in order. Therefore, ma'am, I pray leave to meet you, either on the ship or in a place of thy choosing. The first choice of the merchandise is, of course, yours. Your obedient servant, Capt. Caleb.'

'Bring quill and parchment, quickly!' called Moll, and soon a hurriedly written letter was being fastened into the leather pouch, telling the gallant captain that Moll would meet him at the Popinjay Hotel on the Dover Road at eight p.m. on the morrow.

'Dickon, I shall need the fast coach and four tomorrow. I do not want to be on the Dover Road at night. 'Tis said the highwaymen are fierce, once night has fallen. Therefore, we must leave early,' said Moll.

Her mind was now racing with thoughts of what she should wear, for Moll knew that her emotions were once more being stirred by thoughts of the white flashing smile and bronzed skin of the captain. Would he be thinner, she mused, or maybe even more muscular than before? She squirmed with excitement.

'Holy Mother,' said Moll to herself. 'I only hope my new dress will be ready on time. Hannah,' she called, 'do send someone to Madame Farley's to pick up my new dress. It should be ready by now.'

'No need, madame,' said Hannah. ''Tis all ready. 'Twas delivered an hour ago. It is so beautiful! I am having it pressed for you, and shall bring it up for ye to see presently.'

Once the servants knew that Moll was leaving to meet Captain Caleb on the morrow, a new spirit of excitement pervaded the house, and each person did his allotted task to the best of his ability so that by nine o'clock the next morning, after a hearty breakfast of roast pheasant, homemade bread and ale, Moll was waved off by all her retinue, bound for the Popinjay Inn on the Dover Road. All the servants hoped for news of the big event of the year, the sailors and servants 'thank you party', which Caleb and Moll usually arranged to celebrate a successful voyage.

The day proved fine, and Moll and her maid servant smiled at the children who waved as they passed. Moll, enveloped in the fragrant aroma of her perfumed pomander, lay back across the silken cushions and smiled at the young girl who enjoyed accompanying her mistress in the best coach. Reaching over occasionally to straighten a fold of Moll's gown, or to wipe away a fragment of dirt, usually imaginary, from Moll's person, made the young servant girl feel very important.

'Oh, what a beautiful day,' said Moll. 'I shall have time to bathe and change before Captain Caleb arrives,' and thinking to herself that she could wear the lovely pearls Roxanne had left her, the perfect foil for the plain yet exquisitely cut gown she planned to wear that evening.

The driver stopped the coach at a wayside inn, and opened the door, letting down the folding steps and helping Moll and the maidservant to alight. He smiled and said, 'Only a horse changing stop, ma'am, we'll pick the nags up on the way home. Wouldn't leave old Dandy and Clarion any longer, would we, me beauties?' he laughed as he slapped the horses good naturedly on their round sleek rumps.

The ostlers ran out to attend to the horses, and Moll stretched herself like a sleek cat enjoying the smells of the pretty countryside, and laughing at the cockerel who tried gallantly to tread a loudly protesting hen, who with feathers ruffled, left the frustrated bird disconsolately pecking at the gravelly road. 'Poor old Chanticleer,' she laughed. 'Never mind, 'tis the same the whole world over, "only the brave deserve the fair". 'Tis as it ever was.' The landlady, a round, jolly red-faced woman, wiping her rough hands on her apron, bustled forth to greet them.

'Good day, m'lady, what news of London? Is m'lady Gwynne still mistress at court, do you hear tell, ma'am?'

'Aye, that she is,' laughed Moll. 'A fine one, our Nelly, and she never changes. That I'll warrant.'

''Tis a long time since she graced my table,' said Mrs Perkins. 'She was an actress and played at a masque at one of the big houses along the Dover Road. Stayed here, she did, three times. Such a bonny lady. Anyway, enough dalliance, come in, my lady, I have vittles prepared.'

Gratefully, Moll sank into the cosy chair by the fire and sipped happily the pale yellow homemade wine, sweet and perfumed with rose petals. A cooked chicken breast with fruit and salad plus a great bowl of black shiny plums, served with thick clotted cream, was a feast fit for a queen. The shadows lengthened, and Moll knew they must be off before dusk, so rising to her feet she called for her servants to make haste and leave. The bill was paid, much to the landlady's joy at being rewarded so generously, and soon the coach was rattling noisily along the Dover Road to meet Captain Caleb at the Popinjay Inn at Little Medford. By four o'clock the coach had rolled safely through the large portals of the inn and came rumbling to a stop. It was a pretty place, with an inner courtyard surrounded by a double balcony where the servants were encouraged to grow flowers in tubs and crocks. The colours were enchanting, and Moll was fascinated by the vines that curled around each portico and handrail. With a smile a pretty serving wench dressed in brown serge homespun, with a snowy white apron and cap, showed Moll up the highly polished wooden stairs to her chamber. A great bowl of flowers and herbs stood on the hearth, and although the room was simply furnished, it was clean and cheerful, and as the last rays of sunlight fell across the bed, Moll sank gratefully into the soft down coverlet.

Soon Hannah came to help her bathe and to put her long hair in rag twists and by eight o'clock she was ready. The long oyster-coloured satin gown fell in soft folds about her feet, her firm breasts framed in a froth of cream lace were a perfect foil for Roxanne's beautiful pearls. The soft light of dusk added magic and atmosphere as, candlestick in hand, Moll carefully picked her way downstairs, across the slate floor in the passageway to the long dining room, where she could see the strong handsome figure of Captain Caleb, legs straddled and holding in his large hand a tankard of the landlord's best foaming home-brewed ale.

Chapter 26

The Assignation

Hearing the sounds of footsteps, Captain Caleb placed his tankard of ale on the large oak table and looked expectantly across to the open doorway. A vision in cream lace holding a pewter candlestick appeared before him.

'Moll, my beauty,' he breathed. He smiled, bowed low, but with a kiss of salutation, addressed her as 'your servant, ma'am.'

'Ah, Captain Caleb, how good it is to see you again, after so long and such a successful voyage.'

'That it was, m'lady, that it was. However, I am pleased to be back in London and shall now rest up a little and generally enjoy being a land lubber for awhile, once the ship's refit is underway,' he replied.

'Come, ma'am, let us now drink a toast to our successful business venture together.'

Moll smiled, and looked searchingly at him over the rim of her tankard. Lord, but he was a handsome brute; strong face, clean shaven with a deep cleft in his chin. 'Oh, I could cover him with kisses and drown in those green eyes,' she mused. Then, 'enough, girl,' she said to herself, 'or he'll throw you into the nearest four-poster and have his wicked way with you, even before you've drunk a toast.'

He gently led her to the table where a light meal had been laid, but neither of them could do more than pick at a morsel or two, for the attraction was both instantaneous and, as far as Moll was concerned, quite devastating. Moll flirted with him so outrageously that he could hardly control himself. The thought of kissing her lips, her eyes, her white breasts barely covered by films of cream lace, almost drowned him with longing.

'God, you're beautiful ' he whispered, as he tried to hide the strong sexual urge which threatened to engulf him. Months at sea, then temptation such as this! 'I should have gone with the men to the London doxies before meeting this object of my desire,' he said to himself.

'Captain Caleb,' said Moll, 'if we are friends, as I hope we are, I surely should be allowed to use your given name. I do not even know it.'

He stammered with annoyance. 'Well, yes, m'lady, but 'tis a name I never use.'

'Well, then,' Moll smiled, 'I shall be the only one to have the privilege. Please tell me what it is.'

'Jacob,' he mumbled.

'That's a very masculine name. I shall call you Jake.'

'That will do,' said the Captain.

Moll turned her face up to him provocatively. 'Yes, it suits you perfectly,' she said.

He gazed down at her face, even more beautiful than he had remembered. A rosy blush stained the soft curve of her cheek, barely visible in the mellow candlelight. She floated into his arms so naturally that his intentions of holding back his emotions were gone. Her action took him completely off-guard, and he was soon showering her face and neck with kisses. His lips, hot moist and demanding, took her breath away, and without protest she tingled as his hands ran expertly across her back and tiny waist, and over the soft voluptuous folds of her gown. Seconds later, she felt his warm hands caressing her naked breasts as urgently, compellingly, he murmured endearments, as he tried to disrobe her. 'No,' said Moll, 'not here. 'The servants may come.'

Gathering her robe about her, she picked up the heavy candlestick and led the way across the hall to her bedroom. Jake Caleb cursed this masculine urge which threatened to spoil this first meeting, but was helpless to do anything but follow Moll to her chambers. He undressed quickly in the flickering light of a candle, and Moll gasped as she looked for the first time on his nakedness. 'Ye Gods,' she breathed. 'Charles would ban ye from his kingdom had he sight of such a body.'

He stood and faced her, proud of his masculinity. Moll, pulling back the bedclothes, said, 'Darling, come.'

He came to her strongly and urgently, without love play or tender words to soften his need of her. Moll was perplexed. It was too quickly over and left her feeling disconsolate and unsatisfied. He turned to sleep, but Moll would have none of it. Shaking him gently, she said, 'Jake, you must leave now. I do not want my servants to find you in my bed on the morrow. Hurry, please.'

With a nod of assent, he quickly dressed and was gone.

He must be tired, thought Moll, and silently cursed herself for being led to the altar of Venus like a common whore. 'It shan't happen again,' she thought to herself. 'He'll beg for me before I give myself so easily. Moll, you've behaved no better than a common doxy. Now sleep, if sleep will come easy after such a night.'

She slept badly, and awoke feeling ashamed. 'Ye Gods,' she breathed, you've behaved like a doxy and you look like a doxy.'

It was a blessed relief when Hannah came in at seven o'clock to help Moll prepare for the day. The bath was filled with warm water and she stood as Hannah washed her down with sweet smelling herbs and lavender-perfumed soap. She changed into a rather demure lilac-sprigged dress and went into the garden for a walk before breakfast. The morning was fresh and bright, with that special perfume that only an English garden has in the height of Summer. She breathed in the heavy aroma, and bent to pick a sprig of lavender which she tucked into the bosom of her dress. Jake watched her from his bedroom window, and quickly donned a white full-sleeved shirt, pulled on his boots and strode down the narrow polished staircase to greet her.

'Good morning, m'lady, Moll,' he smiled. And once more she felt her heart lurch at his handsome face and rich deep voice.

'Good morning,' said Moll, 'shall we walk a while before breakfast?'

'Capital,' said Jake, as he offered his arm. 'We'll walk down the lane a little way. 'Twill sharpen our appetites somewhat.'

The mood for both of them was calm and easy, and if either felt regret at the culmination of the previous evening, it was not mentioned. Together they walked down the pleasant country lane leading to the village, hearing the countryside's special sounds which, to city dwellers, were a source of wonder, with the promise of a beautiful day to come. They returned to the inn for breakfast, and although a hearty one was laid, Moll did no more than nibble a piece of cheese and a morsel of crusty bread. Jake pulled a leg from a large capon, together with a portion of white meat. This, washed down with a pitcher of ale, was a pleasant start for the day.

'I cannot tarry long,' said Jake. 'The ship must be inspected after the repairs and painting have been done. I have yet to go to Exeter to see my mother, and then to Cadiz in Spain on Tuesday.'

Moll's face fell. 'So you will be in London but a short time,' she whispered.

'Aye, that is so,' he said. 'A captain's task is busier ashore than at sea, I'll warrant. But come, let us discuss our next voyage. Where will it be, ma'am?'

Moll thought carefully about his question, for this was the only ship she had free rein on. This agreement had been firmly adhered to and Ralph, her well-trusted adviser, kept his mistress's coffers reasonably supplied with gold through his expert knowledge of merchant shipping.

'Spain, I hear, has some rich pickings. On your next voyage, I shall come with you.'

He appeared startled at her suggestion, but stammered mildly, 'Moll, m'lady, the cabin is not fitted out for a lady's sea journey.'

'Then get two cabins fitted, one for myself and one for Hannah, my maid. Yes, Jake, I have decided we shall buy laces and paintings in Spain and sell them at a great profit in London this Christmastide.'

Jake knew she would not be gainsaid, yet the thought of women on board gave him the shivers. The old mariners' superstitions of women aboard a ship held fast, and he knew he would have great difficulty in signing on this next crew.

'Damnation to all women!' he cursed inwardly, but forced himself to smile disarmingly at Moll and said, quite charmingly, 'Madam, your wish is my command.'

Moll had been aghast at her swift decision to sail on board with Caleb, but this voyage was the only way she knew of getting to know this fascinating yet elusive man. Her common sense, nevertheless, told her that yet again she might be clutching at straws. Having no man in her life made her cling all the more to someone as dashing and handsome as Captain Caleb. Why then, did she find her thoughts racing to Sir James, while still wanting to be possessed by this rough mariner? Sometimes Moll hated herself for the spur of the moment decisions she made, and quickly brushed the thoughts of Sir James out of her mind.

'Stuff and nonsense – nothing more,' she said to herself. Hannah had tidied up the room and packed her clothes and there stood Moll's coach, clean and sparkling at the front door. The horses' hooves sparked as they impatiently stamped their feet on the cobblestones.

She turned to see Jake leap on to his horse, his black boots pushed firmly into the stirrups. He threw his long black cloak over one shoulder, doffed his white plumed hat, and said, 'I shall call on you once I return from Cadiz, ma'am. The ship, by then, should merit your inspection. Good morrow, m'lady,' and with a smile he waved, and wheeled his horse around and galloped swiftly through the gates heading towards London.

Moll settled down into the soft interior of the coach, and waved the driver on. Hannah, as usual, was fussing over Moll, making sure her mistress was comfortable for the thirty miles or so journey. She produced a silver fruit knife, and deftly cut a pear and some plums into tiny tidbits to refresh them both.

On her return, a note from King Charles gained her rapt attention. It was an invitation to a dance at White Hall, a masked ball. Immediately Moll's spirits rose, as she gazed through the lattice windows at the rolling hills before her. 'I shall go as Spring,' she murmured, and hummed gaily to herself as she planned a filmy pale green outfit cut like a boy's costume, with tight breeches and a flower-strewn jacket.

Hannah tried to get as close a picture of the costume her mistress had in mind before going down to East Chepe to tell the sewing woman of her mistress's wants.

'A pox on Jake Caleb!' she said. 'This night I shall sleep easy in my bed, and think about everything tomorrow.'

Chapter 27

The Masked Ball

Soon the day of the ball would arrive, and Moll looked as pretty as a picture trying on her Spring costume. The tight breeches clung to her well-shaped legs, and a fitted jacket sprigged with flowers, topped by a tiny flowered cap, added a touch of whimsy to the costume.

'Odds fish,' she laughed, 'this should turn a few heads, including Nell's. I can hear her laughing now. She always said I had a nicely turned calf, which was a shame to be hidden. Wonder what she'll be wearing? Masked, 'twill be difficult to tell one lady from another, I'll warrant.'

Meanwhile Nell was thinking about her own costume, and wondering what she should present herself as at the King's ball. 'Barbara Parker, or M'lady Castlemaine, will surely try to impress Charles by going as Britannia. Pox on 'em!' laughed Nell. 'I'll go as something more to my liking, but the devil take my mind this day. I can't think of a suitable costume.' Suddenly an idea came to her. 'The very thing,' she said, 'I'll go as a soldier with boots, tight buskins, and a white silk shirt with gold braid! Maybe the palace guards can loan me a uniform. Methinks that would amuse Charles! I'll go to White Hall this very day.'

Calling for her horse and carriage, Nell settled herself to drive through the London Streets to the Palace. Suddenly her coach was rocked violently and she saw to her horror that there was to be a public hanging. She tapped for the driver to stop, as he was lashing about him with his whip to discourage the people from clambering on to Nell's coach. She looked out of the window as a woman's voice screamed, 'Look, it's the King's Catholic whore!'

Nell pushed hard against the coach door and held up her hand to still the crowd. 'La, no, madam,' she laughed, 'I'm the King's Protestant whore.'

With roars of laughter, the good-natured Nelly blew kisses to the crowd, who laughed delightedly as she made her obeisance through the coach window as if she was the queen herself. Nell hated public hangings, and was relieved not to have to face a blue-faced man hanging from a gibbet. Nelly had seen enough of the sleazier side of life growing up in the back streets of Drury Lane not to dally on this occasion, and she impatiently tapped on the window for the driver to hasten from the scene before the tumbril cart arrived with the condemned man. Quickly the coach rumbled on towards the palace, and Nell arranged to meet the Captain of the Guard in the inner sanctum of the guardhouse. Sipping daintily on a glass of best malmsey, Nell's eyes twinkled as she placed her request before the guard's officer. His response was to throw his head back and roar with laughter. 'Madam, the guard's officer's uniform would reach to the floor on you. Not even the Army tailors could make you look like a king's guard.'

'Tell you what, ma'am. How do you fancy being a calvary officer? We do have some old, fanciful hussars' uniforms that would do nicely.'

Nell clapped her hands with pleasure. 'When can I try them on?' she cried. 'Oh, do tell me when.'

'I'll have a servant bring a few to your apartment tomorrow, ma'am.'

Nell was delighted, and rattled home at a fast pace, pleased to solved her problem as to what to wear to the ball. 'Only two days to go,' she murmured, for there was nothing gay vivacious Nelly liked better than one of the king's 'fancifuls', as she called them.

The two days sped by quickly until the morning of the twelfth; half London was agog at the festivities the King had planned for the evening. Crowds waited to watch the fireworks display and the roads were lined with poor people striving to get a glimpse of the rich company heading for White Hall. Fully masked, Moll entered the palace, and was pleased that no one recognized her. She was delighted also that she had shed a few pounds; otherwise, her curves would have given away her secret. With all the flowers and leaves wrapped around her, no-one recognized her. Maybe even Charles himself would be fooled. Not easy to miss Charles, however; his tall figure was head and shoulders above his contemporaries and his sensual mouth could never be disguised beneath a mask. He was dressed as a bowman in Lincoln green which suited him so much that Moll felt she could easily have opened up the long-standing affair with him, but decided against such a scheme. Charles was a better friend than a lover, for he soon tired of his favourites. Nelly, too, she knew, was getting vibrations of another love who had charmed her way into Charles's life quite suddenly. But Nell, in her own inimitable way, chose to ignore his dalliances.

Completely at a loss as to whom the revellers were that surrounded him, Charles caught sight of Nell Gwynne, splendidly dressed in a red and white Hussar's uniform.

'Bless you, Nelly, I knew the backside was familiar.' With a hearty slap on her rear end, the King roared with laughter. 'What sort of a mount do you have, my little Hussar? A Shetland pony, I'll be bound.'

This remark started up the musicians, who played a resounding cavalry-like dance, as the King and Nelly tripped a measure. The first dance to Nell. Wouldn't the court favourites be livid at the orange seller from Drury Lane stealing their thunder yet again! For the first dance with Charles meant supper and bed later, which gave Nelly a sparkle telling the world that, yes, she really was Charles's favourite mistress.

Moll laughed heartily at these goings on, when to her surprise a tall figure gently kissed her hand. 'Your servant, ma'am.'

She looked up into the dark eyes of Sir James, dressed as an Eastern potentate in a rich bejewelled costume, embroidered with pearls. Moll could feel herself blushing, as he escorted her to the dance floor. 'Come, Moll, we used to dance well together.'

Moll longed to throw herself into his arms, but remembering his conditions of marriage which chose her friends for her, and forbade contact with Charles, her resolve held fast. No, she would fight this weakness that threatened to engulf her. 'He shall not chain me like a chattel, and I shall, by God's teeth, make him acknowledge dear Nell this day.' Moll dropped her mask for an instance to show Nelly her disguise, and as they walked across the ballroom, Nell made a point of confrontation. Kissing and hugging Moll, she flatteringly turned to Sir James. 'Salaam Alaikum,' she said, bowing low. 'How handsome you look.' Sir James was lost in admiration. Why, she wasn't the ignorant street urchin he had been led to believe. She was a beautiful and vivacious woman. Very prettily, in good French, Nell introduced herself. Moll, who so wished these two to be friends, turned, excusing herself, leaving Nell in animated conversation with Sir James.

'Now, me beauty, what are you supposed to be?' asked Charles.

'I'm Spring,' said Moll.

'Good Lord,' said Charles, 'I thought you were an overgrown garden.'

With a twirl he danced her over to the floor for the second dance of the evening to the consternation of the other ladies present, for to dance with the King was a privilege they all wished to share.

Later Moll and Nell met over supper, and laughed long and hard over the merry revellers as all the London gossip flowed between them. Moll found herself confiding to Nell about Captain Caleb. 'I'm to sail with him to Cadiz on the evening of August the ninth.'

'Oh, how lovely,' breathed Nell. 'A sea voyage. Will you take your son?'

'No, 'twill be safer for him at home,' said Moll. 'Hannah and the servants will guard him well enough. He is spoiled outrageously as it is.'

'Speaking about sons, Nell, how is Lord Beauclerk these days?'

'Oh, bright as a button. Now he knows who his father is,' laughed Nell. ''Tis a wise child who knows his own father, especially when it's the King, and a king with so roving an eye. Never mind, I have one or two irons in the fire myself, and this arrangement suits me well enough.'

Soon the evening drew to a close, and as Moll left in her coach for home, Nell sped swiftly to the King's apartments.

Chapter 28

Moll Sails on the Gloriana

Once the dance was over, Moll's life settled into rather a humdrum routine, which quite frankly got on her nerves. One thing Moll loved was variety. She was bored with the house, bored with the garden, and generally more out of tune with herself than she had been for some time.

Nell was busy refurbishing her new apartment and there had been little communication from that quarter, and no scandal from London for almost two weeks; and nothing from Caleb upset Moll more than she cared to believe. God's teeth, the man was infuriating, she thought. Why didn't he send a message? A long silence, also, from Sir James, whom she knew still felt very strongly about her, wayward as she was. 'Devil take the pair of them,' she swore, and rang the bell for one of the servants to bring her a large glass of hypocrass wine to lighten her thoughts a bit. The day wore on agonizingly slowly. Dinner alone - damn, damn, damn!

Just then a servant tapped on the door and brought her a glass of sweet wine. 'Your wine, m'lady, and I am to give you this.' He handed over a folded parchment, which bore the unmistakable red seal of Captain Caleb showing vividly against the cream paper.

'Thank you,' said Moll, as her trembling hands opened the long-awaited letter.

> M'lady, I shall be calling upon you at seven sharp this evening to discuss our forthcoming voyage. Your obedient servant, Jacob Caleb.'

'Zounds,' muttered Moll, ''tis almost six o'clock now.'

She rang the bell for the housekeeper. 'I know it's very short notice, but can you please serve dinner for two with the best china service and silver candelabra and cutlery, to be served at nine o'clock? Dinner should be something light, perhaps a cooked capon with salad greens and a hot pippin pie with clotted cream. Fill the table up with flowers and marchpane and serve the French wine as cool as possible in this heat.'

The housekeeper nodded in agreement, knowing that all this was possible, even on such short notice. Her beloved mistress always eased the burden whenever she could, and this request was unusual. She would, therefore, get the very best response from the kitchen staff, who could spit roast a couple of capons within the hour. 'Call Hannah to lay out my pink silk, and ask Thomas to fill my bath.'

'As you wish, m'lady,' came the reply, and within minutes the house was a beehive of activity. By seven o'clock Moll was bathed, dressed, and at work on her tapestry as Captain Caleb was announced.

Gracefully she rose from her chair and with hands outstretched, welcomed her guest, lifting her cheek towards him for a chaste kiss. 'Welcome, Jacob, how lovely to see you again,' she smiled. Dropping her outstretched hands, she rang the bell for Thomas. 'Wine, please, Thomas, and a glass of French brandy for the Captain.'

Jacob nodded assent, taking into account the beautiful furnishings in Moll's home, and enchanted by her tasteful collection of china and books. He settled himself down for an enjoyable evening in such richly amiable surroundings. Dinner was served promptly at nine, and the conversation turned to the approaching voyage.

'The cabins are not yet completed, but by the evening of the third, I expect to have the upholsterers in to complete the soft furnishings. Moll, do you have any colour preferences for the upholstery? I ordered a rather deep cream colour, which I hoped would be to your taste.'

Moll nodded assent, and replied that cream damask was to her liking.

'The maid's cabin is in another corridor. Mine is along the same hallway as yours, but all are on the same deck. I trust this will meet with your approval?'

'Certainly,' said Moll. 'I shall be ready to sail on the third at noon.'

Dinner passed pleasantly, and the wine made them both a little mellow. Jacob walked over to Moll's chair and kissed her on the cheek, obviously looking for a sign to press his advances further. Moll smiled and stood facing him.

'Well, thank you, Jacob, for all you've done. I shall be on the dockside at the appointed hour to sail on the evening tide.'

This dismissal angered Jacob, and he wondered if once more he had pressed his suit too soon. 'She's a damned attractive woman, rich too, by all accounts.' Although Captain Caleb had been in command of four ships, he had not accumulated riches such as these. 'Must slow down,' he mused, 'or I'll scare the pretty bird away.' He left the house early, without further advances, and took leave of Moll in full view of the servants with a chaste kiss on her hand and a low sweeping bow. 'Adieu, madam, until we sail.'

Ten days hence they would sail on the evening tide. The ship had been repainted and named the *Gloriana* in honour of Moll. Moll called Hannah, and told her that they would be taking a trip together on the ship, and Hannah was overjoyed.

'I can't tell you how I feel – how wonderful!' exclaimed Hannah, and with this she cried tears of joy.

'Come, Hannah, we have much to do. I must set about leaving my affairs in order, and make arrangements for my son; the clothes and packing I shall leave in your capable hands, and the housekeeper and Controller will deal with the rest.'

The days sped on, and soon the great chests were loaded on to the coach, and it rattled over the cobbled streets of London to the dockside. The wharf was a hive of activity, with bolts of bright cloth, huge jeroboams of wine, and other merchandise being unloaded on to the wharves. Vendors did a roaring trade in selling roast chickens, pasties, boxed beverages, in fact, anything edible, flesh, fowl or fish, and Moll found the atmosphere both refreshing and exciting. The newly painted ship looked regal and Moll was proud to be the owner of such a beautiful vessel. She led the way up the gangplank to be greeted by Captain Caleb, the name Moll planned to call him on this voyage, and they were shown into the Captain's cabin to partake of wine and comfits. Hannah was shown to her mistress's cabin, and straight away set about unpacking and tidying things. The wine, combined with the excitement at the goings on about her, almost proved too much for Hannah, and she collapsed, exhausted, on her mistress's bunk.

Moll sipped her glass of wine and looked at Captain Caleb. She admired how he stood tall and straight in his uniform; but then, a fashionable man was a successful one, as the old adage went, and it was obvious he didn't have any manual work to do in those clothes, she thought. 'Dinner will be served in my cabin at eight sharp. We should be underway by then, and there may be some rough weather ahead, so we'll eat lightly, m'lady.'

'Until eight o'clock,' said Moll brightly, and left the Captain's quarters to walk the short distance to her cabin. The ship was soon underway, and Moll could feel the tug of the great sails and hear the activity on deck. She opened the door and saw Hannah dozing on the bed. The girl, startled, jumped quickly, and looked shamefully down at her shoes. 'I'm sorry ma'am, it was the excitement made me dizzy.'

'Never mind, come, Hannah, help me wash and change. Where's the tub?'

'That's it,' said Hannah, pointing to a tiny footbath.

'Ye Gods, I can't bathe in that,' said Moll.

'Well, if you wish to complain to the Captain, ma'am . . .'

'That I don't!' yelped Moll.

'Come, we'll try,' said Hannah. The bath proved to be the merriest occasion for them both, and they laughed uproariously. The small amount of water it held was far too shallow for a bath, and Moll scratched her way as best she could with the most unladylike loofah, which, if it did not leave her clean, left her glowing.

Dinner with the Captain was pleasant enough, but Moll kept to her original plan to keep him at arm's length for a while. Unfortunately, Captain Caleb was a very highly sexed young man, and the frequent callings of his masculinity left him frustrated time and time again. He took cold showers at times to ease his problem, but decided that Moll was playing hard to get, and that he must use more forceful tactics with her.

The atmosphere aboard the *Gloriana* was a strange one. The sailors, as Jake had already foretold, did not appreciate a woman aboard, and two were even worse. 'It bodes ill,' as one old salt whispered. 'Bodes ill, it does.'

Both Moll and Hannah tried to be as pleasant as possible to the crew, and kept out of the way as much as they could. Jake came down to chat at least once each day, and Moll was invited to dinner with him, usually alone in his rather cramped quarters. Still, she resolved not to be the one to offer herself to him, although it was hard to be in such close proximity and remain aloof.

The night was calm as they hugged the coastline of Spain, and Moll was excited at the prospect of sightseeing in Cadiz. She walked down the corridor towards the Captain's cabin, and was astonished to find the Captain had been drinking. He drank, of course, but usually in a very controlled way. In fact, Moll felt she had to curtail her own consumption in order to appear as moderate as himself.

'Come in, Moll,' he called, and tried to pour her a drink, but the decanter missed the rim of the tankard and spilled out in a steady stream across the table on to the floor. Finally, he managed to pour her a drink. Lurching to a chair with a large slug of French brandy, he downed it in one. Moll cautiously sat on the edge of the chair, hoping he would at least be sober enough to talk for a little while. Instead, his garrulous attitude became worse, which prompted Moll to excuse herself and call for Hannah. There was no reply from the servant, and Moll was extremely worried as to where she could have gone.

Hannah, however, once her mistress had entered the Captain's cabin, had gone visiting herself. Unbeknownst to Moll, she had met a very handsome ship's carpenter, and was deeply infatuated. Such dalliance of this nature was new to the lass, and she was making hay while the sun shone, as she put it. After this trip, she might not see him again, ever, and he was quite the handsomest man she had ever seen. She wanted to be with him at every opportunity.

Thomas was the ship's carpenter, and a good one. After this trip, he planned to take his bonus and go back to Tiverton where he had a small house; true, it was in disrepair, but the bit of land surrounding it was beautiful. It could become a very nice home with some work, and he hoped to find a suitable, industrious, wife to help him. Hannah was both - a farm girl by birth, and she dearly loved the country.

This proposal would be welcomed by Hannah, would he but only speak. He was exactly the man she had dreamed of finding - honest, handsome, hard working and loyal. But Thomas's idea of romance was a peck on the cheek. He had no notion as to what to say or do with a maid, and tonight Hannah vowed she would teach him a thing or two. 'But not everything,' she smiled to herself.

Down the stairs she crept into the carpenter shop where Thomas was working diligently. The spoke-shave he was using added curly shavings to the great pile in the corner, and as he heard Hannah's footsteps, he turned to greet her.

'Hello, Hannah. How nice of you to be early. I haven't much more to do, be with you in a trice,' he said, smiling.

Hannah spread her skirts around her on the shavings, and twirled a brown ringlet around one of her fingers. Her bodice laces were loose, and Thomas was uncomfortably aware of the swell of her ample bosom.

'Oh, do put down that silly piece of wood, Thomas. I haven't come to see you work. This is a social call.'

He laughed at her formality, washed his hands in a bucket, and after drying his long sunburned fingers carefully, sat down next to her. His tanned flawless skin appeared even darker in the candlelight. Black curling hair, snow white teeth, and well over six feet tall, he had completely captured Hannah's heart. The only fault she found with him was his shyness. He could hardly look her in the face without blushing, he was so full of love for her.

She gently took his face in her hands, and kissed his closed eyelids, then his cheeks, then the cleft in his chin, before kissing him long and passionately on the mouth.

His blue eyes widened in astonishment! 'My lord, Hannah, what are you doing?' he stammered.

She boldly opened her bodice and pressed his strong warm hand against her breast. For the first time he felt a woman's naked skin. It was something he had dreamed about many times, but this was no dream. This was real. Her breasts felt beautifully strange, warm and alive. He wanted to give way to the tremendous urge which consumed him. He gently forced Hannah on to her back, pushing his leg between her knees and burying his face in her breasts, covering them with kisses.

'Stop, Thomas, this would be the first time for me. I'm not a doxy, much as I feel the need for you.'

He stopped immediately, covering her face with kisses as he clumsily fastened up her bodice for her. 'Hannah,' he whispered, 'I'll love you as long as life itself. I've made you a ring as a betrothal token. Will you have me, my dearest?'

He brought from his pocket a highly polished wooden ring with the initials H and T intertwined, and with a kiss, placed it on her finger.

'Oh yes, I'll have you, Thomas.'

'I'll be true to you all my life, Hannah. Not like our Captain with Lady Moll, while his wife and four children exist on a pittance in Spain.'

'Are you telling me that Captain Caleb is married?' asked Hannah.

'That he is, Hannah, that he is.'

Hannah could do no more than wait with this awful news, for she could not disturb her mistress, even though this shocking news disturbed her greatly.

Moll, however, unaware of this piece of information, was having a problem dissuading Jake that she was not in the mood for drunken love-making, and was trying desperately to find a way to escape from the confines of his tiny quarters. Infuriated at her lack of cooperation, Jake grabbed at her dress and tore it open at the bodice. Her naked breasts inflamed his passion even more, so much that he continued pulling and tearing at her clothes until she stood naked before him. He smacked her hard on the face, then again.

After the shock of the assault, she screamed loudly. He pushed her down on to the wooden deck and threw himself upon her, fumbling drunkenly in his attempt to have his way with her. Moll reached for the discarded brandy bottle and hit him a resounding thwack which stunned him long enough for her to grab her dress and run to her cabin, putting a chair in front of the door to hold it fast. A rapping on the door brought her back to reality and caused her to sob bitterly at the pain in her face. One of her back teeth was broken, and she knew the bruising on her body was extensive. Hannah called softly, 'Mistress, 'tis me. Please open the door. I have some urgent news to impart. My lady,' she called loudly once more, 'please open the door. Is something wrong?'

Moll dragged her weary body, and slowly opened the door to see the shocked white face of Hannah, who cried, 'Who did this? Was it Captain Caleb, m'lady?'

'Yes,' whispered Moll, 'it was.'

Hannah gently helped Moll on to the bunk and soothed her, rocking her back and forth like a child. She brought soothing ointments and soft bandages and laid Moll's poor battered body to rest, not mentioning the news she had heard about the Captain's marriage.

On the ship sailed, due to dock in Spain on the morrow. Moll awoke next morning, aching and miserable, and demanded a mirror.

'Oh, ma'am, please don't look,' said Hannah, not wanting her mistress to see the ugly black marks. And when Moll saw her discoloured swollen face, she said angrily, 'Help me dress, Hannah. I have a task to do this day.'

Moll, helped by her servant, limped to the Captain's cabin which was quiet save for the loud snoring of the Captain. Caleb was still abed, no doubt sleeping off the drunken stupor of the previous night. The servants had cleared the debris, and Moll rang the bell to summon his personal valet.

'Simpson, ma'am, at your service,' grinned the one-eyed little weasel-faced man.

'Simpson, go wake the Captain now,' said Moll. 'Now, I tell you,' her voice dropping ominously.

'Sorry, ma'am, I can't do that. He'll keel haul me if I do.'

'I am the owner of this ship, and I want him sent to me in five minutes in uniform, or I'll have you flogged!'

Simpson touched his forelock, 'Aye Aye, right away, ma'am.' Floggings in the merchant fleets were commonplace, in fact Simpson had administered quite a few himself, and well he knew the battle-scarred men on board would only be too anxious to reciprocate in kind.

Soon Caleb stood before her, wincing from a pounding headache, and angry that his sleep had been disturbed. He was certainly not prepared for what came next.

'Captain Caleb,' said Moll, 'this will be the last time anyone will address you with this title that you have so abjectly disgraced. You are henceforth relieved of your command, and will be put ashore in Spain. Had we been in England, I would have had you thrown into Newgate Prison. Now, leave my ship! Your personal belongings will be left on the quay within the hour. Good day, Jacob Caleb.'

With this, she leaned heavily on Hannah and returned to her cabin, leaving Jacob standing in shocked disbelief.

'Hannah, send for the second-in-command immediately.'

Soon Mr Rogers, an elderly seaman, reported for orders, and Moll informed him of her decision. 'You will take command of my ship, stores and cargoes, and we will return to England next week. Your cooperation will be greatly appreciated.'

'I shall do my utmost, ma'am. Do the crew get shore-leave?'

'Yes,' said Moll, 'four days should give us time to take care of our business in Spain. Then we sail on the tide.'

Moll needed rest badly, and a small inn was found close to the sea where a motherly Spanish lady spoiled her in every way possible. Her bruised body healed, and only then did Hannah tell her the news about Captain Caleb's wife and children. By then, it didn't really matter to Moll at all.

Chapter 29

Moll Looks Back

The episode with Captain Caleb had affected Moll more than she cared to show or say. Her sleep was disturbed by dreams of violence, and she often awoke screaming in the night.

Hannah had left her service, and had gone to join her handsome new husband in the pretty cottage he had refurbished in Tiverton. Moll and her son spent many happy hours with Hannah and Thomas, where they were always treated as honoured guests, and they were loath to return to the big impersonal residence in London, where the child's schoolwork demanded most of his waking hours.

Moll's son was growing up all too quickly, and the times they could spend together were a delight to both of them, for the private tutor Charles had arranged for the boy was diligent and strict, and demanded great things from such a small child. Besides his studies, riding and fencing lessons left little time for mother and son to spend more than a few stolen hours in happy idleness.

Once more, Moll was alone, as her son had returned to his tutor. Moll felt a deep depression coming over her. 'I'll go into the city and buy myself a new bonnet,' she said to herself. 'That will brighten up my day.'

With this thought in mind, she rang for the servants to bring her coach to the door. Dressing quickly, she was soon bouncing along the cobblestones and heading through the streets of London for East Chepe. The streets were crammed with people, and Moll ordered the coach to wait for an hour or so. The coachman tipped his hat politely and said, 'One hour, ma'am, I'll be waiting.'

'Get yourself some marchpane and gingerbread,' laughed Moll, pressing a silver coin into his hand.

'Oh, thank you very much,' was the reply.

Moll browsed through piles of ribbons and books and odds and ends, and purchased a few things that she didn't really need, and soon retraced her steps to a tiny bakeshop where they sold the most delicious strawberry tartlets. Seating herself at the long trestle table, she bit into one of the succulent morsels, murmuring with pleasure as the fresh cream and fruit filled her mouth. From behind her a soft voice surprised her, saying, 'Good morning, my dear.'

With her 'kerchief placed daintily over her overstuffed mouth, she gazed into the brown kindly eyes of Sir James.

'May I sit with you a little while? I have news about Captain Caleb which should be great interest to you. He is one of your captains, I believe, Moll?'

She nodded assent and cursed herself for putting so much food into her mouth, wincing as it went down her throat in a lump.

'Here, sip this,' he said, handing Moll his glass of wine.

'Thank you, James, do sit down.'

He seated himself next to her and smiled at her obvious discomfort. 'As I said before, Moll, I have something most unsavoury to tell you about your Captain Caleb.'

Moll attempted to interrupt him, but he patted her hand gently and said, 'Nay, Moll, let me finish. It is difficult enough for a man to disparage another, but for the safety of your crew and ship I feel I must speak. The man is a drunk, unfit to command. The Spanish authorities are even now searching him out for an assault upon a young girl.'

'Oh, James, please don't go on, my dear. I know enough from first-hand experience to know your words ring true,' Moll said. 'He no longer commands my ship, is no longer a captain, and I do not class him among my friends or employees.'

'Let us not discuss the man further, then, as it obviously distresses you. But there is another matter that I need to speak to you about, that is of great importance to me. I so want to speak to you about our last parting, and the selfish conditions of marriage I placed before you. Please forgive me, insensitive jealous brute that I am. Please, Moll, please forgive me.'

Moll looked at the slim earnest figure, the kindly face that she had always loved, and smiled gently. 'There is nothing to forgive, James. It's all forgotten.'

'I'm damned if I'll propose to you in a bake house!' he said. 'Come to the house for dinner this evening, and I shall rehearse my proposal for the rest of the day.'

'Of course I will, darling James,' laughed Moll. 'I'll be there at half past seven of the clock.'

He took her arm and escorted her back to the coach where Ben, the coachman, was biting into the biggest piece of gingerbread they had ever seen. They laughed heartily as James helped her into the coach, and off Moll went, back to her home to bathe and prepare herself for what promised to be the most important evening of her life.

Chapter 30

The Wedding

James's very romantic proposal was accepted gracefully, and he placed a beautiful sapphire ring on Moll's finger. He decreed that they would be married in his personal chapel.

He arrived promptly at seven, and Moll was seated beside him in his beautiful carriage. They settled back comfortably as they drove through the city to Richmond. The scenery was lovely, and soon the most charming white house she had ever seen came into view. The carriage swung into the drive which was an avenue of flowers, the perfume drifting into the coach, and Moll felt she had experienced nothing quite so heady before. It took her breath away.

James smiled and held her hand for he was nervous as to whether his prospective bride would like her new home. The house was certainly not as large as the Gables, but was much more comfortable looking and tastefully appointed. It was called Whitfields, and Moll found it absolutely enchanting.

She racked her brain trying to decide who to put on the guest list at such short notice. Another problem was her gown, and she did not want to consult James on this matter, for according to tradition it was to remain a secret, and white was now unfashionable for weddings. Most of the other details were left in the capable hands of the household staff, but James and Moll were both kept extremely busy tending to their own lists of things to do.

Moll was awakened in the morning from a heavy sleep by loud laughter and giggling outside her bedroom door. She needed no-one to tell her that Mistress Gwynne had arrived. Delightedly, she raced out of her chamber and joined Nell and Stuart in a romp until, breathlessly, they handed the boy over to his nursemaid whom he adored, and walked together into the gardens to have a heart-to-heart chat.

'I wouldn't miss this wedding for the world!' replied Nell. 'Eleven in the morning at Richmond, ye Gods! I'll be awakened at cock-crow and asleep in church, I'll be bound.'

Since Moll was so busy with wedding details, Nell cut her visit short, and with a parting kiss and a wave, bade her coachman drive to the city, for she had decided to buy some rich brown velvet to have a gown made to wear to the wedding.

Later that afternoon a messenger called at the Gables with a casket, chained and sealed. He would not release it to the household staff, insisting that his instructions were to give it to nobody but M'lady. The messenger was conveyed to Moll, who was busy arranging flowers for the house. The messenger produced keys and soon the chest was opened. A note from James read, 'For your wedding day, darling.' A delighted cry escaped from her throat, for lying in the folds of cream lace was a beautifully fashioned diamond tiara, light and elegant, the perfect foil for a bride. She pressed a coin into the messenger's hand, and ran upstairs to admire her reflection in the mirror.

'Oh, how perfectly exquisite,' she breathed, clasping her hands in delight.

Friday was upon her before she realized it, and a summons came from the head seamstress for a final fitting of her wedding gown. Patiently standing while pins and tacking were removed and a pin realigned here and there, the dress was finally pronounced finished. A final pressing was required and then it would be ready to wear in the morning.

A horrible thought suddenly occurred to Moll. Charles had not been invited or even informed of the coming marriage, so she hurriedly scrawled an invitation and sent her footmen to deliver it.

Next morning, the wedding day, she was gently awakened at cock-crow by the bustling of her personal maid, who plumped her pillows and gave her a delicious drink of ice-cold milk. Gratefully she sipped it, enjoying the sweet coolness and watching as her bath was strewn with flower petals. After a refreshing and relaxing bath, she put on a robe and took a leisurely stroll through her garden, trying to ease her mind of all thoughts and plans for the day, so she would be in a relaxed frame of mind.

'M'lady, m'lady,' cried a little scullery maid who had run a very long way around the grounds searching for her mistress. 'M'lady, you must tarry no longer, for the dressers await you.'

With a start, Moll realized how quickly time had passed in the garden, and gathering up her robe hurried after the girl into the house. An army of ladies awaited her, and she patiently stood for an hour as they adjusted her hair, her make-up, her gown, her jewellery, and transformed her into a beautiful bride.

At last, Moll turned slowly for the ladies to admire, for her gown was stiff and heavy with pearls. She looked magnificent! The lilac pearl-encrusted dress flowed back into a long train which swept the floor. Her hair was brushed over one shoulder in a profusion of black ringlets and crowned by the finely wrought diamond tiara. Her gloves awaited her on the table in the reception room, and assisted by her ladies, she solemnly descended the great staircase and collected her bouquet. The gardener had taken great pains over her posy, which was edged with lavender, with tiny pink rosebuds nestled in the foliage, which blended perfectly with her gown.

She rode in the carriage with her attendants and the two little flower girls who were the daughters of the nursemaid, looking adorable in their sprigged muslin. Her heart pounded as they drove through the city and into the green vistas of the countryside. As the house came into view, Moll's hands felt hot and sticky, and she tried to calm herself before reaching the doors.

As she alighted from the carriage on to a long red carpet, she was greeted by a line of servants and friends who were all smiling and strewing rose petals in her path, as she made her way to the chapel doors. A peal of bells started and gave her a fright, and soon the great doors swung open to allow her to enter. Two more steps and she would be inside. A tall gentlemen proffered his arm, and to her astonishment, she saw it was King Charles himself! He smiled and said, 'Come, my precious one, I shall give you away,' and he escorted her down the aisle to where James was waiting.

Before she knew it, the marriage ceremony was over, they were pronounced man and wife. To a joyous peal of bells and much merriment from the guests, they walked into Moll's new home. A very long table was laden with every kind of food imaginable, to the accompaniment of fools, music, dancing, puppetry; indeed, it was the merriest gathering this house had ever seen.

Nell left the church breathlessly on the arm of the King who was flattering her outrageously, much to her delight, but as the music became slower, he politely walked Nell over the dance floor to where Moll and Sir James stood, and requested the first dance with the bride. Moll found the dress heavy and awkward, but nevertheless they made a gracious picture as the guests watched admiringly from the edge of the ballroom. Nell found little difficulty in breaking the ice with Sir James, and he soon realized she was a fascinating woman, like a diamond cut with many facets. He could understand why Moll had befriended her, and realized how unfair his first opinion of her had been.

As midnight arrived, Moll realized she was dreadfully exhausted, and James whispered to her, 'Bid our guests goodnight, darling, this merry making will continue till dawn.'

They slipped away to the beautiful large bedroom overlooking the twinkling river, which was bathed in myriads of lights, and the soft sound of the music from the party drifted in through the open window. James left her whilst the maid servant helped her prepare for bed. As the maid left, James entered and kissed her fingers, eyes, hair and breasts, and quietly held her in his arms, whispering how much he loved her, and that for as long as he lived his only prayer would be for her well being.

'My wife, he murmured, 'my adorably beautiful wife, how I love thee.'